In the Dead of Night

Alex Crowe

ISIS
LARGE PRINT
Oxford

First published in Great Britain 2010
by
Sphere
An imprint of Little, Brown Book Group

Published in Large Print 2011 by ISIS Publishing Ltd.,
7 Centremead, Osney Mead, Oxford OX2 0ES
by arrangement with
Little, Brown Book Group
An Hachette UK Company

British Library Cataloguing in Publication Data
Crowe, Alex.
    In the dead of night.
    1. Lake District (England) - - Fiction.
    2. Abandoned houses - - Fiction.
    3. Suspense fiction.
    4. Large type books.
    I. Title
    823.9'2–dc22

ISBN 978–0–7531–8780–7 (hb)
ISBN 978–0–7531–8781–4 (pb)

Printed and bound in Great Britain by
T. J. International Ltd., Padstow, Cornwall

IN THE DEAD OF NIGHT

CHAPTER
ONE

The sun was rising over Scafell Pike when the first signs for Keswick appeared. Amanda had been on the road for five hours; it was not yet eight in the morning. She had left in panic, too terrified to consider rationally what she should do. The image of that falling body was etched irrevocably into her brain. But now she had other priorities: the conference was scheduled to start at nine and she still had to find the hotel and check herself in. Seventy delegates from the Pru were gathering here, as they did each year, for their end of October morale-boosting bash. Amanda Page, from London head office, had quite a significant role to play. She had risen fast and had now been lumbered with being the bearer of very bad news. The world recession was going to mean major cutbacks. She did not relish what she had to do but it should, at least, help keep her mind off last night and the terrible fight with Max that had ended so badly.

She had called his number repeatedly once her anger abated and fear set in but not even now, when he should be driving to work, was he picking up. Either he was exacting revenge or things were as bad as Amanda feared. She would try him again once she reached the hotel; she prayed he was simply playing one of his mind-games.

The conference centre was close to the lake, a vast traditional stately home with turrets and battlements built from local granite, all very imposing. When Amanda gave them her credit card, nobody flickered or said a word. The receptionist smilingly checked her in and called for the porter to show her to her room. She tried ringing Max's number again, this time using the hotel phone so he would not know it was she who was trying to reach him. Still nobody answered.

But she had no time for panicking now. It was nearing nine; there were things she must do. She swapped her jeans for a business suit, touched up her hair and went smilingly into the fray.

The conference room contained seventy chairs, arranged in regimented rows; the delegates were already filing in. All were dressed in conservative clothes, the men with ties, the women in skirts, most of them wearing white shirts, as recommended. Amanda was seated in the front row, waiting to take her place on the platform after the area manager had given the initial address. She checked the time: only ten past nine. She faced a gruelling few hours before they broke for lunch.

This morning, the start of the four-day event, was dedicated to positive thinking. A valiant cry exhorted the troops to do even better than in the past year, to increase their targets and show their sterling worth. They had come from all over the British Isles, representative of the faceless mass of workers devoting their lives to their alma mater, the Prudential. Accolades were bestowed; there was much applause. They broke for lunch at a quarter to one and all trooped into the private bar for a restorative pre-prandial sherry.

Amanda, still burdened by what she must do, made fast excuses and fled to her room. The next three days' proceedings would be less festive. Twenty per cent of the workforce must go, cutbacks to be effective from January the first. She flicked through her folder and found the list. The names were all grouped according to grade. A few, she was startled to see, were here in person, attending the conference. Mismanagement at its most inept; she decided to alter the programme sequence and hold that announcement back till the final day. And even then, she figured grimly, she'd be lucky to get out alive.

She brushed her hair and perfected her makeup. At thirty-eight, she still looked good. As she recalled the happenings of last night, her mouth instinctively tightened. He had taunted her with his faithlessness, reminding her he was not yet free, implying that she had ground to make up before he would even consider a firm commitment. The final straw; she closed her eyes and tried to control her rapid breathing. This would not do. She still had a turbulent afternoon to face. She spritzed her mouth with a freshening spray and, cautiously, picked up the phone again. Still no answer. Amanda felt a cold chill.

★   ★   ★

Things went better than she had hoped. There were delegates here with good news to share. Pension contributions were even booming because of the crisis. One by one they came on to the stage, the bright and hopefuls from out of town in their ill-fitting suits, their faces alight with hope and determination. Amanda, contrary to her expectations, slightly relaxed. The one she liked best was from the Midlands, small and perky with curly fair hair and a smile that lit up the room. *Jilly Sutton*, the name-card read; she worked in a high street branch in a Birmingham suburb. Amanda mentally checked her list but could not be totally certain.

Later she sought Jilly out in the bar and congratulated her on her stirring address. "I love your enthusiasm," she said. "You must be a favourite with the punters."

"I do what I can to make their lives a little less dismal, poor dears," Jilly said.

"Please allow me to buy you a drink," said Amanda.

Jilly was single and twenty-eight with a boyfriend called Derek she hoped to marry the following year if they could afford a mortgage. "I am lucky to work where I do," she beamed. "The current climate in the housing world is certainly pretty dire." And steadily worsening.

Amanda agreed but her heart went cold. There were thousands in Jilly's position, she knew, who — come the New Year — would be looking for jobs in a highly competitive market. She could not warn her. What good would that do except to blight this social weekend? Even without her intervention, Jilly would

4

find out soon enough. Amanda intended not to be there when she did.

So instead she chatted about social things and discovered that Jilly, like her, was a keen hill-walker. "Great," she said. "Did you bring your boots? I was planning a Sunday hike up Scafell Pike."

The peak, over three thousand feet and acknowledged to be the highest point in England, was exactly the sort of challenge Amanda enjoyed. She needed to work some adrenalin off; the past few days had been overly stressful, what with her role at the conference plus her current worry about Max. She asked around for more volunteers but most preferred to relax in the spa. On Monday they would be returning to work, some, though they did not yet know it, to clear their desks. Amanda made a coward's decision. She would post her list on the noticeboard last thing on Sunday before she turned in, then make an early departure. At least all these machinations helped to take her mind off Max.

Who still hadn't called. He knew where she was and that she'd be staying the whole four days. He must be aware she'd be out of her mind with concern. She switched on the news when she got to her room and sat through the regional bulletin too. There was nothing of any outstanding note beyond finance and terrorists in Mumbai. Even the new US presidential candidate was already off the front pages.

No news was good news she told herself as she took off her clothes and prepared for bed. He was simply playing his heartless trick of keeping her endlessly dangling. Why did she love him? She wiped off her makeup and turned on the shower, trying to find an answer. After six years of these ups and downs he was now little more than an irritating habit. She was nearing forty; it was more than time she sorted her life and made a fresh start before she was over the edge and her clock slowed down.

She could not prevent herself worrying though. She was up at seven and hurried downstairs to check the morning papers in case there was news. There was nothing of very much interest today, and no mention of anyone being found dead or even failing to turn up for work as expected. She rang Max's landline and also his mobile but all she got on either was the answering machine. Hearing his voice made her nervous again. He sounded so normal and relaxed. Perhaps if she prayed it would all turn out to have been just a ghastly dream.

Jilly came over, carrying her tray. Amanda invited her to join her. They whiled away twenty minutes or so discussing the weather conditions. The sky was clear and the sun rode high. Apart from a sharpish nip in the air, it looked as if the weekend would turn out fine.

"I hope we'll be lucky," Amanda said. "You can never be sure in the Lakes at this time of year."

What she needed most was to get away and disappear up that mountain.

By Sunday morning there was still no news. Amanda didn't know what to think. Her colleagues were tucking into the breakfast buffet.

"I guess we had better stoke up," Jilly said, piling bacon and eggs on her plate and adding two pieces of buttered toast for good measure.

"You are lucky you don't have to watch your weight," said Amanda, who fretted about such things. Max was always getting at her. She wondered what he was up to now, whether he might have reported her to the police. She would not put it past him. His charm concealed an inherent coldness, which was why they had come to be fighting that night. He knew precisely how to get under her skin and twist the knife.

Their point of dissension was usually women who emailed him and kept turning up. One had the gall to phone Amanda to tell her she was in love with Max.

"How can that be?" Amanda asked. "When you know how often he plays the field. The man is a jerk as well as an absolute liar." She felt nothing but scorn for the deluded creature. Yet, in her own way, she was as bad. She put up with stuff that a person with pride never should. She worried that if she pushed him too hard he might dump her. Truly pathetic.

It was almost ten. The sky was still bright though ominous clouds were now rolling up. A wreath of mist encircled the top of the mountain. They ought to be off.

"I'll meet you outside in the car park," she said. She just had to make one last call.

CHAPTER
TWO

They drove the few miles to Seathwaite Farm and left the car in the car park there, first exchanging their shoes for climbing boots. Amanda peered anxiously at the sky. The cloud formations seemed denser now. They had both brought weatherproof jackets and thick woolly scarves. Jilly had a compass.

"You never know," she said cheerfully. "We might need it if we happen to stray off the path."

This expedition was a bit of a lark; she had never climbed anything quite this steep. Most of her walking till now had been confined to the lower slopes. It went to show how ambitious she was, out to impress a head office nob. She was slightly in awe of Amanda Page, who was sleek and well groomed and unnervingly bright, but she was not going to let her trepidation show. Much might depend, in any number of ways, on how she acquitted herself today. She had heard rumours since being here of possible job cuts across the board, but right now she was feeling on top of it all. It was she, after all, Amanda had picked for this walk. Jilly looked up at the mountain peak, bright when sunlit though wreathed now with mist. She needed a challenge like that — and to stretch her legs. Derek had laughed at her for bringing the compass but it did not hurt to be over-prepared. You never know what might be needed was one of her sayings.

"All right?" asked Amanda, locking the car.

"Lead on," said Jilly. "I'll race you to the top."

To start with, the walk was an easy stroll, and despite the steadily gathering clouds the sun remained visible, on and off, and the temperature was quite pleasant.

"How many miles?" Jilly studied her map.

"Ten," said Amanda, "though mainly uphill. With a couple of places where we may have to scramble. I trust you can cope with that."

Jilly just smiled. Bloody nerve, she was thinking. She has to be ten years older at least and, from the look of her, not remotely as fit. But the air was as crisp as a mountain stream and Jilly felt great just being outside. The conference seemed to have been a success; she felt she had acquitted herself quite well. She was certain Derek would have approved. A lot depended, right now, on the security of her future. It was time they made things official and thought about having children.

There was one small worry where that was concerned though there was no need to think about it now. The nurse had been very reassuring; she should have the test results by the end of the week. Jilly squared her shoulders and brightened her smile. She would let this Londoner see what she was made of.

After a mile they reached Stockley Bridge and stopped to admire the magnificent views. A straggle of other walkers were out though too few to impinge on their sense of isolation.

"This, most certainly, is the life." Already Amanda felt far less stressed. There was bound to be news by the time they got back, some plausible explanation.

Beyond the bridge, the path grew suddenly steeper. The terrain was grassy and strewn with rocks and occasionally there were patches of scree, shifting rock fragments that made for uncertain footing.

"Be very careful," Jilly warned. "It's easy to fall."

She produced two chocolate bars and they paused in the sun to remove their jackets. "I'm jolly glad of that breakfast," she said. "We'll not be back much before dark."

Amanda laughed. "It's only ten miles."

All of it, though, from this point on, uphill.

The sky was gradually darkening and a sudden chill wind blew down from the fells. They stopped again to replace their jackets and wind their scarves tightly round their throats. The weather could change amazingly fast in these parts.

"I'm jolly glad I brought gloves," said Jilly, undaunted.

"Do you want to turn back?"

"We can't quit now." She would not have Amanda thinking her weak. Her whole career might hang in the balance depending on how today worked out. They were very tough in head office, Jilly had heard.

Amanda was glad. She really enjoyed a challenge.

"Concentrate on your feet," she said. It was what the professionals always said. They claimed this was the biggest climb in England. The summit could not be seen from here because of the undulating fells but every now and again they caught glimpses of Keswick below them. They carefully skirted their way round the rocks, in places almost having to crawl; then the path grew narrow and even steeper as they turned a corner and found themselves staring down into a ravine.

"Blimey," said Jilly, alarmed and startled. "It didn't look quite so horrendous on the map."

Again they debated: should they go on? Again they refused to be thwarted now.

"After this rocky bit," said Amanda, "we reach a tarn on the edge of a plateau." Sprinkling Tarn; it was on the map. They would stop there for a breather, she promised Jilly.

They slowly progressed in single file, gingerly clinging to outcrops of rock while the wind from the fells screamed round them and tried to dislodge them.

"Whoops!" said Amanda, suddenly losing her footing.

For one agonised moment they hung in space as Jilly valiantly grabbed her sleeve and clung to her for dear life until Amanda regained her balance.

"That was a close one." Her lips were white and she dared not look down at the steep ravine. Now she wished she had stayed in the spa with the others.

They edged along till they reached a ledge and perched for a moment to study the map. Jilly produced more chocolate bars from her jacket's voluminous pocket. Amanda, though shaken, made light of it.

"You'd have made a great Girl Guide," she said, having once been leader of the Cheltenham troop. The mist was closing in; it was growing quite chilly.

"It feels as if there's snow in the air."

Amanda shivered. "Don't even think that," she said.

It was almost four. It was hard to believe so much time could have passed. Maybe they ought to think about turning back.

"Without even reaching the summit?" moaned Jilly, though secretly she was vastly relieved.

"You can go on," said Amanda, "but I quit."

So back they went to the scrambling part, only now they weren't certain which path to take. The wind was bitingly cold and the mist had closed in. Which was when Amanda stumbled and fell and slithered some feet down an unseen slope. She must have hit her head on a rock for the next thing she knew it was dark and she was alone. She peered at her watch but the fall had shattered the glass.

"Jilly," she called but could not hear a sound. Terror gripped her. She had no idea where she was. She touched her forehead and found a lump. It was lucky she hadn't gone all the way down. Carefully, she crawled to her feet in the shifting scree. She hadn't the faintest idea what to do: go on or just stay here and wait to be found. She was terrified Jilly had fallen right over the edge.

She reached for her cellphone; at least she had it with her though who she would call she was not quite sure. She would start with the number she knew, the emergency service. Thank God for modern technology; then she discovered she could not get a signal. She decided she would rather not stay here and freeze. At least now the path was levelling out. She concentrated again on her feet and fervently prayed to be rescued. And then something moved in the swirling mist: a sheep, maybe, or a mountain goat.

"Amanda?" a voice said faintly.

It was Jilly.

They clung together with fervent joy, overwhelmed by the fact they had both survived. Jilly had slipped and then lost her bearings, but she appeared to be quite unharmed. Amanda's head was hurting a bit; though the lump was growing, she hadn't broken the skin. The most important thing now was survival.

Jilly's phone also would not work.

"I don't suppose you remembered a torch?"

The compass was one thing. Jilly laughed. "You were the Girl Guide," was all she said.

They trudged on in silence for fifty more yards, having to grope their way in the mist, holding hands now for fear of losing contact. Jilly tried shouting but knew she would never be heard.

Then all of a sudden it came into a view, a bright white light on a far-off crag, high in the distance like a guiding star. They hugged each other, faint with relief; just when they'd feared their luck had run out.

"Shall I lead the way," asked Amanda, "or will you?"

It was quite a lot further than they had thought. Whenever they reached the top of a ridge, the light was still far ahead of them, leading them on.

"You are sure it's not a mirage?" Jilly said. A light-house or something set high on a rock. Her teeth were chattering now with cold and exhaustion.

"No," said Amanda firmly, "it's definitely there." She could see some sort of building now, outlined against the sky in a break in the mist. "We ought to make it in less than an hour. Please don't give up on me now."

And they did. They climbed a steep slope and after a while further lights appeared and the outline of a huge edifice loomed in front of them. For a moment Amanda was gripped by fear. There seemed something forbidding about the place, though as they drew closer she saw it was simply a heavily fortified pele tower. Still, any shelter was better than none. With luck it might even have a working phone.

CHAPTER
THREE

A pele tower it was but a glorious one, what they could make out of it in the darkness, four storeys high and constructed of stone, with battlemented towers at each corner. The windows, through which came pinpricks of light, had originally been arrow slits, though those on the lower floors had been opened up at some later date. It had been built to last, had already survived at least six hundred years. They followed the walls till they found the imposing entrance.

"It doesn't exactly look welcoming," whispered Jilly.

Indeed it did not. It looked more like a prison, but they'd come so far they could not turn back now. The massive door was of solid oak, strengthened by diamond-shaped iron studs, with a lighted lantern and a thunderously heavy knocker. Boldly Amanda crashed it down; echoes reverberated throughout the building. Too late she realised the occupants might be sleeping. Yet lights could be seen on different floors, discernible through the narrow slits, and one window right at the top was ablaze with a brilliant white light. Someone was obviously still awake; Amanda hammered again. Now she realised how cold she was. Exhausted, too . . . if only they'd open up. If they had been asleep, they surely could not be now. She stamped her feet to restore the circulation.

Jilly went off on her own to explore, returning after a rapid circuit. "This is the only entrance," she confirmed.

They waited a while for someone to come then Amanda cautiously knocked again. There was no other option; the mist had closed in. They would never be able to find their way back in the dark.

"Imagine being this isolated," said Jilly, "and lugging the groceries up." Away from the biting wind, she was feeling much better.

"They probably do it by helicopter. And spend their winters elsewhere in the sun. Dubai or Monaco would be my guess. That's what I would do." Amanda continued to stamp her feet and blow on her fingers to keep them warm. "Come on," she muttered impatiently. "There are people freezing out here."

Slowly the truth was beginning to dawn. Though the lights were on, perhaps no one was home. "Check the garage," she suggested to Jilly. "See if the car has gone."

While she waited Amanda tried knocking again, then cautiously twisted the great iron knob. To her amazement, it easily gave; it wasn't even locked. She pushed and the door swung smoothly open as if inviting her in.

No car, said Jilly, returning, nor even a garage. When she saw Amanda had opened the door she reacted with alarm.

"You're not suggesting we go inside?"

"I'm not staying here and freezing to death." The weather conditions were still worsening, and the wind had now reached gale force.

"Maybe they just popped out," Jilly said. "In the circumstances do you think they'll mind?"

"Popped right down to the valley, you mean? To pick up the papers and a pint of milk?" Amanda, who always made fast decisions, was already inside.

The first thing she noticed were the walls, which were massive, as much as seven feet thick, and the spiral staircase cut into one of them. The vast main hall, where the animals had lived, was tunnel-vaulted and windowless. The space, now stone-flagged, was softly lit by copper-based lamps with parchment shades, arranged at different levels to make it more homelike. All this floor contained as furniture was a massive sofa and several carved chairs. In the centre of the facing wall stood a mahogany grandfather clock with a powerful tick that underlined the silence.

Jilly lowered her voice as if in church. "What do we do now?" she asked. The sofa looked plenty large enough for them to doss down for the night.

Amanda pointed to the narrow stairs. "The living quarters must be up there." Efficiently she unlaced her boots. There was no backing off on a night like this so they might as well finish what they had started and trespass even further. With Jilly timidly following behind, she led the way up to the floor above and found herself facing a second fortified door with an iron grille.

"They certainly knew how to build in those days." She rapped with her fist on the polished oak, waited a second then twisted the handle. Again the door swung open.

This floor had a totally different feel, an attractive open plan living room with whitewashed walls and a separate kitchen, accessible through an arched doorway. It was warm; the embers of a dying log fire still smouldered in the grate. On the table were the remains of a meal with a loaf of bread and a slab of cheese, olives and a bowl of wilting salad. Next to them, neatly folded, lay that morning's daily paper.

"Hello!" called Amanda tentatively, but she sensed the place was unoccupied.

"Well," said Jilly. "They may not be here but they can't have been gone very long."

Amanda, emboldened, strode into the kitchen. The first thing she saw was a telephone. "Thank God." She tried it but the line was dead, probably because of the weather.

There were dishes drying on the draining board but no sign at all of the washer-up. Crude crayon drawings were taped to the wood-panelled walls.

"Cosy," said Jilly, looking around. The Aga was on, a tea towel draped on the rail. Whoever lived here appeared to have left in a hurry.

"We shouldn't stay. They may soon be back." Jilly was feeling like Goldilocks.

Amanda was in the living room now, checking out family photographs. There were several dotted around, all showing a smiling family group. Good-looking parents with wide healthy smiles; a small boy and girl and a dog.

"So what do you suggest we do now? Go back outside and freeze in the dark? We are in so we might as well stay," said Amanda. Subject closed.

Next to the food was a bottle of wine, two-thirds full with the cork still out. Amanda looked on the dresser and found clean glasses. Ignoring Jilly's protesting cry, she carefully poured them each a glass, then raised hers in a toast. "We've certainly earned it."

They warmed their hands in front of the fire. Their casual Sunday stroll was turning into a mini-adventure.

"Did you ever read *Swallows and Amazons?*" asked Amanda.

Jilly had not so she outlined the plot, Lake District children learning to sail and spending idyllic summers in the open. "I would bet there's probably a copy here," she said. They looked like the sort of kids to read Arthur Ransome.

The wind was rattling the windows still. They had found this haven in the nick of time. The place had a sense of timelessness that made them feel safe and secure. Amanda was ravenous. She sliced the loaf and chopped them both hunks of cheese. Her toes were starting to thaw; she felt much better. It must be late, though she did not know the time having smashed her watch when she fell. Jilly's, too, had stopped, which seemed odd, but the grandfather clock downstairs was audibly ticking. When Jilly popped down to check it was ten past eleven.

"We can kip up here in front of the fire." It was more inviting than that massive hall. They threw on another log and shed their top layers.

"What do you think they will say?" asked Jilly, a model of bourgeois propriety.

"With luck they won't even know," said Amanda. "Unless they come back while we're here."

Before they settled down for the night they decided to check out the rest of the tower. There were at least two more floors plus the battlements. The spiral staircase went right to the top with iron sconces sunk, here and there, into the stonework. Someone had done a superb job of renovation. On the floor above the main living space were several bedrooms, all in use. They peered into each before switching on lights; this clearly was the family home, with interconnecting doors between all the rooms.

First a playroom, then two children's rooms containing double bunk beds that led, in turn, to a nanny's suite, after which was the master bedroom. The playroom contained a rocking horse as well as a large assortment of toys, a shiny train set, obviously new, and a shelf of elegant dolls. It seemed these children lacked very little.

"They're not very good at tidying up." Amanda pushed open another door and found the children's bathroom, the floor strewn with clothes. Then she stopped in her tracks with an intake of breath. On the edge of the bath was a sopping wet towel while the mirror held unmistakable traces of steam.

"What happened?" she whispered, suddenly spooked. "Why did they leave in a rush like that?" From high on a crag in a howling gale, without turning off the lights or locking the door.

The lights were on, too, in the master bedroom, where the door to the wardrobe stood open wide and a pile of neatly pressed clothes lay beside a suitcase.

"We ought not be here." Something was wrong. They had stumbled into a mystery. Jilly instinctively made for the door. "It's like the *Marie Celeste*."

They were too tired now to explore the floor above so decided to give that a miss. From the absolute silence they sensed there was nobody there. Maybe tomorrow, after they'd slept, though they'd have to be out of here pretty sharpish to reach the hotel before the conference ended. In a linen cupboard they found spare blankets and pillows, which they carried downstairs

Cocooned in their blankets they felt toasty warm in front of the fire, and thanked their stars that they weren't still outside in that weather. Amanda wondered when they would be missed, then recalled the notice she had meant to post to announce to some of the delegates that they'd soon be out of a job. She would not be able to avoid them now, but that would keep until morning. As her eyelids drooped, she thought about Max and wondered if he was all right.

Suddenly Amanda stiffened, certain she had heard voices outside, faintly discernible through the sounds of the wind and the creaking shutters. It wasn't a dream, she was sure. She found herself suddenly fully awake.

"Jilly," she whispered urgently.

"What?" Jilly murmured, almost asleep. The clock downstairs was striking the hour.

At which point somebody banged on the main front door.

CHAPTER
FOUR

The two men standing outside on the step, with chattering teeth and dusted with snow, wore furlined leather jackets and flying boots. Amanda, draped in a blanket, simply stared.

"Thank God," said one when she opened the door. "We were starting to think there was nobody home." He was tanned and handsome, with a friendly smile, and several years younger than her. "Mark Hanson," he said, extending his hand. "And this is my business colleague, Richard Brookes." His other arm hung at an awkward angle and was tightly bound in a blood-soaked rag, too bulky to fit inside his sleeve so he looked a little lopsided.

Amanda made one of her fast decisions. They seemed harmless enough and it wasn't her house. "Come in," she said. "There's loads of room." She moved to allow them to pass. Her first reaction was relief that they weren't the owners suddenly back. The last thing she needed right now were explanations.

"Sorry to disturb you this late," said Richard, also extending his hand. All three looked at the blood dripping on to the flagstones from Mark's damaged arm.

"You're hurt," said Amanda, taking control and closing the door behind them.

Mark Hanson flashed her the sweetest smile. "It's not quite as bad as it looks," he said. "I buggered it up in the dark scrambling over the rocks."

Amanda shuddered; she sympathised and showed him her own huge bump on the head. Now that she was safe inside, the memories of her fall were slowly fading.

Jilly now joined them, more or less dressed, assuming the owners had come back. She was hugely relieved to discover it was strangers.

"We were just settling in for the night," she explained. "Come on up."

The two men followed them up the stairs and Jilly threw another log on the fire. She folded the blankets neatly and straightened the cushions. "Your arm," she said to Mark, concerned. "First we must see to that."

Amanda, quietly impressed, looked on. It would seem this Brummie counter clerk was possessed of hidden resources.

The arm was not broken, just badly sprained, with a deep jagged cut from elbow to wrist. Wincing, Mark struggled out of his jacket and Jilly staunched the fresh bleeding with a towel. Amanda, as acting hostess, offered them drinks.

"Not wine for me. Have you nothing stronger?" In the lamplight Mark's face shone a luminous white. "I hate to be a nuisance, but . . ." He was looking decidedly ropy. Amanda rapidly steadied him and helped him across to a chair by the fire. She really came

24

into her own at times of crisis. She opened a carved mahogany chest on which stood a crystal decanter. Her hunch had been right: it revealed a selection of spirits.

"Macallans do you?" She flourished the bottle.

"Perfect," said Mark, and promptly passed out.

They rushed to revive him and Jilly brought ice to bathe his face though he waved her away when, in a matter of seconds, he came round.

"Sorry to be such a big girl's blouse." The poor chap seemed in a terrible state. Beneath the tan, his skin was now faintly greenish.

"Perhaps you should lie on the sofa," suggested Amanda.

Jilly was doing a first-rate job, plumping up cushions behind his head. Perhaps she'd do better as a nurse than selling insurance. The four of them settled close to the fire, Mark slightly revived by the excellent malt. Both of the men wore expensive watches; their accents were posh and their hair impeccably cut.

City boys, Amanda guessed; she'd put money on it.

Now was the time for explanations; none of them seemed in a hurry to sleep. Jilly gave the newcomers the rest of the cheese and offered to knock up a meal, should they want one. She had found off the kitchen an old-fashioned larder containing a well-stocked freezer, as well as a store cupboard with the basic essentials. At least, if they had to be stranded here, it seemed unlikely they'd starve. Nor would they be missed for twenty-four hours, also reassuring.

Amanda explained how they came to be there, that they'd found the tower unoccupied and that the owners appeared to have left at precipitate speed.

"The door wasn't locked and the lights were still on. It was almost as if they expected us. A fire was lit. There was food and wine on the table."

There was plenty of room, and now they were four Amanda felt, for decorum's sake, that they should spread out and not just camp on the sofa as she had intended. She suggested they sleep in the children's rooms since each was equipped with a couple of bunks. It seemed too intrusive to use the master bedroom.

Mark and Richard seemed happy with that; Mark was in no sort of state to move on and Jilly felt reassured at having them there. It turned out Amanda's guess had been right. Mark managed a hedge fund and Richard was a tax lawyer. They'd been shifting money to Reykjavik by private jet when the mist closed in and they'd had to make an emergency landing a hundred feet up on the crag.

"So how on earth did you get down here?"

"We slithered," Mark said. "In the dark on our bums."

Now that the whisky was doing its work, he slowly revealed a quite dazzling charm. The men had met at prep school and been close chums ever since. The plane was not his but borrowed from a Russian acquaintance who would not be best pleased if Mark failed to get it back to him in one piece.

"But to hell with all that for tonight," he said, flashing his megawatt smile.

★ ★ ★

The children's rooms were quite adequate so they bade each other goodnight and withdrew, all of them hankering after a good night's sleep. The fire would slowly burn itself out; they would deal with the glasses in the morning. Jilly climbed on to the upper bunk and was testing it for length when she heard a noise. Definite voices floating up from outside.

"Cripes," she said, horrified. "Can that be them?" There would be some awkward explaining to do, though they now had allies to back up their story. They listened intently, then pulled on their clothes when someone started hammering at the door.

"Leave it to me," Amanda said, assuming her corporate voice. Jilly was grateful to do just that; they were in it up to their necks. Though it seemed unlikely it was the owners because they were having to knock.

Slowly Amanda descended the stairs, steadying herself with a hand on each wall. The stairs, like the doors, were designed to repel invaders. The grandfather clock was ticking away and the whole vast hall was still dimly lit. Whoever it was had been probably drawn by the light. A second knock. She took a deep breath and carefully drew the bolts on the massive door.

"Yes?" she said to the couple on the doorstep.

Despite their thick coats, they looked frozen with cold and were totally inappropriately dressed. How they came to be wandering on the fells at this time of night, dressed in evening clothes, Amanda could not imagine. He was fiftyish and well built and wore an expensive

27

cashmere coat with a white silk scarf wrapped tightly round his throat. The girl, only half his age, was skinny and stylish. She wore silver fox, with the collar turned up, and her breath was visible on the night air. Her face was so pale it resembled a Halloween mask. She was standing there in her stocking feet, one reason perhaps why she looked so cold. From one hand dangled ridiculous shoes with six-inch heels and delicate silver straps. Over her arm was slung a huge Gucci handbag.

"Come in," said Amanda, appalled. "You look frozen to death."

"We lost our way in the mist," said the man. "And later had to abandon the car. We saw this light in the distance. It was our lodestar."

Amanda led the way upstairs. She empathised with the way they must feel. Since it wasn't her house she did not have the right to be turning lost travellers away. She called to Jilly, who quickly came down and immediately offered to feed the new arrivals.

"No thanks," said the man. They were on their way south from a dinner.

He was Angus McArthur (he produced his card), proprietor of a clothing firm, and she was Dawn, his office PA, though from the way Dawn was looking at her Amanda guessed her to be a good deal more than that. Keep your hands off my man, said the dark hostile eyes.

Jilly fetched logs from the stack in the porch, and built up the fire till they'd thawed enough to be able to take off their coats. She was wearing backless silk and he a dark suit with a Savile Row cut. They were lucky not to have perished out there on the fells in such clothes in this weather.

"We have been on the road for hours," he said. They had been in Carlisle for a business function and had taken the wrong turn off the motorway. Now the mist was too thick to risk moving on.

Amanda insisted it was no problem. "Two rooms?" she asked. Well, you couldn't assume.

"One," said Dawn firmly, stressing proprietorship.

Amanda suggested the nanny's suite, not stylish but warm and self-contained. And right next door to the children's rooms the rest of the bunch were using. She explained about Richard and Mark and how they had also got lost and just followed the light.

Full house, she decided, bolting the door. They could do without any more interruptions. Though she felt relieved, as she went back upstairs, not to be entirely alone in this place.

CHAPTER
FIVE

The sunlight was hazy because of the lingering mist that partially eclipsed the magnificent views. Despite the disturbances of the night, Amanda, from habit, awoke at seven. The little girl's room, with its two narrow bunks and heaps of teddies and other soft toys, was cosy in the pearly dawn light though the view through the arrow-slit window was very restricted. Without getting up it was hard to assess the exact state of the weather.

Jilly, still out of it, sprawled on her side, one arm dangling, dead to the world, so Amanda stayed put and ran through her mind the events of the previous day. Then, remembering Max, she jerked fully awake with a palpitating heartbeat. She had to get back to the hotel in case there was a message from him. She had missed her chance of a fast getaway once she'd posted the list of redundancies. But, with luck, she'd be out of there by the time Jilly saw it. She badly needed to know about Max, whose fate was now dominant in her mind. Yesterday's happenings had slightly eclipsed the aftermath of their row. She tried her mobile but there was still no signal.

She slid from the bunk and under the shower; the children's bathroom was littered with toys but she found clean towels and the water was blessedly hot. What a heaven-sent place they had chanced on here, high on this desolate mountain top. The owners, whoever they were, had enviable taste. Once clean, she slipped back into yesterday's clothes; since they'd brought no luggage, she had no choice. She opened the bedroom door but could not hear a sound. Nobody else in the house, it seemed, was yet stirring.

Downstairs, while waiting for the kettle to boil, Amanda peered out through a dense bank of mist which, from this angle looked, if possible, thicker. There were no more logs; they would have to sort out a rota for lugging them up from the porch. If they were going to co-exist, it must be on a strictly democratic basis. Amanda was a staunch feminist, the basic cause of her altercations with Max. She heard soft footsteps and Richard came wandering in.

"Sleep well?" she asked as she made the tea.

"Like the dead," he said, "though poor Mark did not. He moaned and groaned for much of the night. I think his arm is hurting him more than he says."

They stood at the window, checking the weather. "I doubt we'll be able to leave today. Did you happen to catch the weather forecast?"

"No," said Amanda. She had been far too busy trying to get her cellphone to work. It was really frustrating the landline here was dead.

There was a television in the living room. Richard tested it but could not make it work. He tried all the buttons without any success and fiddled around with the aerial. Only then did he see that the cable was cut.

Amanda was slightly disturbed by this. Who in their right mind would do such a thing? They were surely quite remote enough here without also having to do without television.

"Perhaps the kids were watching too much," Richard suggested. "A diet of *Neighbours* could have that effect." Still, the reaction seemed over the top. He looked through the family photographs and studied their bright and innocent smiles. "Cute dog," he remarked. "I've always liked Jack Russells."

Amanda was no longer listening. She was messing about again with that blasted phone.

Jilly was the next one down, rumpled but smiling, her natural curls damp from the shower. "Mmm," she said with a languorous stretch. "I haven't slept so soundly in months. It must be the rarefied atmosphere — plus the silence."

She rummaged around and found cornflakes and milk and the rest of the bread, which she toasted. It amazed her how well provided for they were here. She was still concerned, though, about the owners and why they had suddenly disappeared. She felt nervous that they might come back at any time.

"What will they say?" she asked Richard, the lawyer.

"I'm sure they'll be pleased to have been of some help. Living up here they'll be used to itinerant walkers lost in the storm."

He agreed, however, that it might be nice if they had a whip-round before they left to compensate for the food they were consuming.

The light was growing progressively stronger. By ten they could actually see the sun, like a fiery orange ball in the sky, though still through a fine veil of mist. Amanda pressed her nose to the glass. "Soon," she said, "we should take a walk and check the weather conditions from outside."

Angus was the next to come down, barelegged beneath his expensive coat. Dawn was having a soak, he reported, and had sent him in search of fresh orange juice. It seemed she regarded this place as a five star hotel.

"As soon as she's dressed, we'll be off," he said and pulled out his state of the art mobile phone. Amanda held her breath as he punched in a number.

Angus frowned. "There's no signal," he said. He had tried last night but put it down then to the weather.

"No," said Amanda. "Nor does the landline here work."

"So what do we do?"

She shrugged. She'd been hoping he'd tell her.

Dawn, when she finally did appear, had shed any vestige she might have had of charm. Her tight little face with its huge panda eyes seemed fixed in a permanent scowl. She blamed their predicament solely on Angus, who should never have made that vital turn. It was highly inconvenient, she said, to be stuck in the middle of nowhere. Not a word of thanks for being taken in on a night so cold she could not have survived. Amanda marked her down as a waste of space.

Dawn, being small, was incongruously dressed in a child-sized nightdress sporting rabbits and lambs, with a pair of pink woolly socks on her skeletal feet. At least she looked warm, which was more than she had last night.

Amanda and Jilly made for the door. "We're popping out for a stroll," they explained. "To get some air and check out the weather conditions."

Outside Amanda apologised. "She's starting to get on my wick," she explained. "That brainless bimbo fixated on catching her man."

Jilly agreed in principle, though it must be said that it seemed she'd already succeeded.

The air was milder and the wind had dropped, though visibility still remained poor. They walked till they found the path by which they'd arrived here.

"Perhaps there is a less direct route." Jilly quailed at the thought of facing that scree again, though at least downhill should be slightly less strenuous going.

That was true. Very soon the path flattened out and walking became a lot easier. Occasionally, through the vapour, they glimpsed blue sky. For a treacherous second Amanda was tempted to leave the others and just keep on walking. They owed them nothing, had come together by chance. If they kept up this pace and the mist fully cleared, they could make the conference hotel in record time. Which reminded her; she pulled out her phone and tried the emergency number again. No result. She still was not getting a signal.

They glimpsed movement ahead through the thickening mist. It might be a sheep, but with luck it would be fell-walkers to show them the way. Jilly clutched hold of Amanda's arm, determined not to lose her again. The memory of the day before still filled her with total panic. A man appeared out of the mist, walking briskly towards them.

He greeted them cheerily. "Out for a stroll?"

"We're trying to find our bearings. I think we're lost."

"Surely not. I very much doubt that," he said.

He looked fit and lean and was wirily built, with eyes so deepset the women could not tell the colour, his hair an anonymous mixture of silver and grey. His voice was cultured, with mellow tones and the faintest hint of an accent there. Huguenot, thought Amanda, though she wasn't sure why. He seemed surprisingly lightly dressed for walking outside in weather like this, especially here near the peak of England's highest mountain. His jacket was tweed and his shoes were suede. That was the detail Amanda never forgot.

Without discussion, he quickly took charge and ushered them briskly along the path, not even bothering to ask where they were headed. On the way, he introduced himself.

"Lucian Demort, at your service," he said. "A longtime resident of these parts, here to show you the way back to where you are staying."

Amanda attempted to argue with him; they were set on going the opposite way so if he would kindly show them the path they need not waste more of his time. Lucian, however, just smiled and continued walking.

CHAPTER
SIX

He seemed to know the territory well and led them sure-footedly back up the slope, negotiating the scree with ease despite being so inadequately shod, and showing them useful short cuts. In a matter of minutes, it seemed, they were back at the pele tower. Amanda explained how they came to be there: they'd been lost in the mist and had stumbled upon it. Lucian agreed it was easily done, especially in this weather. They'd been fortunate to have found any shelter at all.

The sun had retreated behind the mist and the tower looked unwelcoming and neglected. Not a single light could now be seen through its windows. Without even a knock, Lucian opened the door and ushered them both inside. They stopped in the hall to remove their boots but he didn't bother.

"You know the owners?" Amanda said, confused as to how he fitted in.

"I do," he said with a casual smile, leading the way up the stairs.

"Then perhaps you also know where they've gone," she said. "We're starting to be alarmed. It looks as though they vanished in quite a hurry."

Lucian shrugged. "Don't worry," he said. "They'll be back, I'm sure, once they've done whatever it was." Beyond that, it seemed, he would not be drawn; nor did he seem in the least concerned. Amanda, since it wasn't her business, resolved to stay out of it.

Angus had vanished upstairs again, and they heard the sound of a running shower. But Mark was down, looking not at all well, having his breakfast with Richard. By daylight Mark's face was a mass of abrasions, acquired, no doubt, on the scramble downhill. He was quick to reassure them they were superficial. Lucian introduced himself and Richard explained about the plane, skipping, for whatever reason, the Reykjavik bit.

It was clear Lucian knew his way around. If they used all the logs that were stacked in the porch, there should be plenty more in the woodshed, he said. He took Richard outside and pointed out where it was, round the back of the tower.

Angus came down, impeccably groomed, in a different shirt from the previous night's which he must, they could only assume, have had in his briefcase. Dawn, still wearing the same flimsy dress, had covered it up with some kind of shawl and had her fur coat draped round her narrow shoulders. She was clearly still in a very black mood though brightened slightly when Lucian appeared, an automatic response from a natural flirt.

Amanda introduced them all and Angus pumped Lucian for information. He had to get back to London, he said, as fast as he possibly could. Lucian smiled and stroked his chin. It would not be easy to do that, he said. Not until the weather cleared and planes were flying again.

"Where did you leave your car?" he asked but Angus was vague; he had no real idea. Somewhere down there on the mountainside where the rural farm track he'd followed had petered out.

"And you walked from there?"

"I guess so," he said. They had simply seen the light and followed it here.

Lucian beamed. "That's its purpose," he said. "To rescue travellers lost on the fells and show them the way up here to safety and warmth."

Which was all very well, but Angus was keen to leave. "There has to be some sort of transport," he said. "How do the farming folk get about?"

Lucian explained that there weren't farms as high up the mountain as this.

"What about the people who live round here?" Angus persevered.

"They drive tractors and four by fours," Lucian explained.

"Which this lot have naturally taken with them," said Angus, increasingly frustrated.

Lucian tried an alternative tack. It was clear to them all he was trying to help. "The scenery is spectacular," he said. "If you'll only wait for the mist to lift."

But now the sky was darkening fast; they were clearly in for a thunderstorm. The mist had been bad enough but a storm would be worse.

★ ★ ★

Lightning flashes dissected the sky and heavy clouds descended so fast the tower was very quickly plunged into virtual darkness. They went around switching on all the lamps as rain poured down in a steady flow. It was madness even to think about leaving now.

"Bugger," Angus cursed under his breath, a sentiment generally shared by them all. Amanda was still very much on edge about Max.

All they could do now was hang around, hoping for news from the world outside and for the visibility to clear.

"If I may make a suggestion," said Mark, who was now showing signs of perking up. "What we are all in need of is a drink."

It was not yet noon but what the hell. He pulled the cork of a fine Chablis while Jilly plundered the freezer for makeshift lunch. She came up with gull's eggs, Pacific prawns and a carton of home-made mayonnaise. Whoever they were, their absentee hosts appeared to enjoy good living. Angus and Richard lugged in more logs and built up a truly magnificent fire while Dawn took possession of the best chair and sulked. She was not so miserable, Jilly observed, that she wasn't aware of Mark's good looks; was sending him covert flirtatious glances which he appeared not to see. He must be twenty years younger than Angus and very possibly richer too, though what he might see in Dawn was anyone's guess.

Lucian, meanwhile, had slipped away though no one actually saw him leave. He seemed to have vanished into thin air without so much as bothering to say goodbye.

"Odd sort of cove."

"You bet," said Amanda. What puzzled her most about him were those shoes.

By four the rain was still pelting down and the urgency to depart had gone. Angus and Dawn were back upstairs, preferring to spend their time alone though Amanda strongly suspected that they were fighting. The others were into a hot game of Scrabble which Richard had found on the playroom shelf. It was growing very competitive so she thought she would take the opportunity to do a little private exploration.

The third floor, above the bedrooms, was also reached by the spiral stairs but was oppressively dark as well as much colder. She searched for a light switch but couldn't find one so she quickly returned to the floor beneath and, instead, traversed the long corridor that ran the full length of the tower, past the family quarters. Right at the end a short flight of stairs led downwards into the entrance of one of the corner towers. This time the massive door was ajar. Amanda pushed it open and stepped inside. Then, stupefied, stopped dead in her tracks, just staring.

She was in a library of vast proportions, stacked from floor to ceiling with ancient books and lit by a stained glass window that took up the whole of one wall. It was like a chapel though lacked an altar. Brass oil lamps, like censers, hung from the vaulted beams. Amanda stood there, transfixed with awe, inhaling the ages-old musty smell of leather-bound books infused with archaic beeswax. This was a room that cried out to her; the lamps and leather-topped tables were burnished with care.

What a wonderful place. She'd find solace here away from the sound of bickering strangers, a sanctuary where, perhaps, she could sort out her head. But she wasn't alone; she sensed a presence that made her instinctively freeze on the spot. She caught the discernible sound of somebody breathing.

"Enter," said Lucian's mellow voice, "and do, please, close the door behind you. Draughts and all that. You understand, I know."

He was comfortably settled in front of the fire, wearing monogrammed slippers and reading a book. It was in some strange language, she wasn't sure what, and printed on very thin paper. He peered at her over gold-rimmed lenses, a benevolent smile on his face.

"Wow," said Amanda, looking round. "You certainly seem to belong in this place."

Lucian nodded. "I have known it most of my life."

"Does it belong to your family?"

"In a way. Although an extended one."

"Then why on earth did they leave it unlocked and just go?"

"They had their reasons, I have no doubt," he said benignly, returning to his book.

Despite the stained glass, the room felt tomb-like. The walls were so thick she could not hear the wind though she guessed it was probably still raging outside.

42

"Do you mind if I take a proper look round?" Since he seemed to be in charge, she deferred to him.

"By all means," he said. "But do me a favour and keep your friends away."

"We are hardly friends," Amanda said. Ships that passed in the night, more like. She understood, though, what Lucian meant. Their presence here would be sacrilege. She imagined Dawn's little greedy fingers defacing the precious books. She drifted round, inspecting them all, a thousand years' reading or even more. She gently caressed their polished spines and inhaled the essence of learning.

"I would like to get to know you better." She found herself quite unusually shy. "I am sure you know all the answers though I really don't want to disturb you now." Her expectation hung in the air. She waited for him to ask her to sit.

He paused and looked at her thoughtfully, as if on the brink of divulging something.

"Later," he finally said, and returned to his book.

CHAPTER
SEVEN

She was greeted by sounds of merriment. The Scrabble game seemed to have cheered them all up. Also, in the little girl's bedroom, Jilly had unearthed a transistor radio. It was pink and plastic but did the job, despite the fact that reception was poor. The weather reports were increasingly grim. Flights in and out of Carlisle had been cancelled and a hundred competitors in a fell race had just been reported missing.

"Not in these parts, I hope," said Amanda. Supposing they all turned up at the tower?

"Honister Pass," said Richard. "Not very far."

They were keen to know where Amanda had been.

"Just poking about upstairs," she said. Her odd encounter with Lucian Demort lingered disturbingly in her mind. There was something unnerving about the tower and not just the way it was built. In some weird way she could not explain, she felt they had entered a time-warp.

"What was up there?" they wanted to know.

"Not a lot," Amanda replied. Honouring Lucian's request, she said nothing about him.

They had banked up the fire and were gathered around it; Jilly was talking again about food. It was, unbelievably, almost six. Though mainly time stood still it could also race.

"The cocktail hour at last," said Mark, who was starting to look more human now. His recent pallor was almost gone, his colour returning to normal, along with his looks.

Dawn and Angus had reappeared, she now wearing his other shirt which one of them must have washed and let drip in the bathroom. It looked rather good with her boyish looks and trendy androgynous urchin cut. The problem with Dawn, though, was she was awfully silly.

Mark did the honours with the drinks and they raised a toast to their absent hosts. They had booze enough as well as food to last them weeks.

"I certainly hope it won't come to that." Jilly was fretting again about Derek as well as her clinic appointment, scheduled for Friday. So much had gone on in the past few days she had pushed it to the back of her mind, mainly by becoming the kitchen drudge.

Angus was anxiously pacing the room and popping outside for weather checks. The mist was even thicker, he glumly reported. The rain had ceased but more was due, so the radio said, within twenty-four hours. He needed to get away from here soon since he had important meetings. Dawn, now ignoring him altogether, was rather too obviously cosying up to Mark.

Amanda, keen to avoid the tension, withdrew to the kitchen and offered Jilly a hand. Jilly had dug out a leg of lamb and left it to defrost for the following day, though she sincerely hoped they would all be gone by then. For tonight she thawed out some readymade pizzas and concocted a salad with the last of the greens. "We will soon be in need of fresh vegetables," she remarked. As they ate she told the others about her plan to compensate their absentee hosts for what they had consumed while under this roof.

"Good thought," said financial expert Mark, as if he was likely to give a damn. A chunk of his fortune, Amanda guessed, was stuck up there on that plane. The reason, perhaps, that he didn't seem anxious to leave.

He looked healthier now and his wit had returned though he winced whenever he moved his arm. Jilly had made him a makeshift sling. At heart she was very domestic, and Amanda feared she was being landed with more than her fair share of the household chores. It wasn't right that Jilly should cook while Dawn sat painting her nails and idly flirting.

Amanda suggested they draw up a rota; management, after all, was the field she was in.

"I don't mind cooking," protested Jilly. It helped take her mind off the other thing.

"It's mainly a question of principle," said Amanda.

Lucian was still very much on her mind, cocooned in his comfortable sanctuary upstairs. She'd have liked to go back and talk to him but hesitated to interrupt without express invitation.

One of them mentioned hide-and-seek, which wasn't at all a good idea, but Amanda couldn't say no or they would ask questions. The place was ideal for a game like that, especially since they could not go out. It was later that night; they had eaten well and perhaps had a couple of glasses too much. They were all growing tired of playing infantile board games.

"How about ghost stories?" somebody said but Jilly vehemently ruled them out. Not in a place like this, she said; you never quite knew what might come. Everyone laughed but nobody pressed the issue. Amanda regarded her speculatively. Jilly had far more depth than she showed. She felt a sharp pang, remembering Jilly's redundancy as well as her own role of messenger. Which brought them back to hide-and-seek. Amanda fell in with the plan.

Dawn had a speculative look in her eye; she might manoeuvre herself closer to Mark. But Mark said he still wasn't up to racing around. He would stay where he was.

"Shall I be It?" Jilly, as usual, was ready to throw herself into the game. She'd have made a superb Brown Owl, Amanda reflected. That was why she was so effective at work, not that it had protected her in the long run. Twenty per cent of them had to go; it was as if they had picked the names out of a hat. Which perhaps they had; you never quite knew how things were decided at boardroom level. It gave Amanda a very bad taste in her mouth.

"You can indeed." None of them cared, though Dawn looked as though she might change her mind. She was clearly torn by the prospect of staying here, by the fire, with Mark.

"We will take it in turns," said Amanda firmly. "Just be sure to count up to ten."

"One," Jilly started obediently.

"Wait," said Amanda. "Before we begin perhaps we ought to set a few basic ground rules."

"Such as what?" There she went again, thought Richard, Miss Bossy Boots laying down the law. He was suddenly keen to start, felt increasingly restless. They had been in this house a whole twenty-four hours and nothing, including the weather, had changed. They needed to rescue the plane, if they could, before it froze in until spring. He was worrying, too, about Mark. He was putting on a very brave front but Richard had seen the way he flinched when he wasn't aware he was watched. His injuries looked far worse than he said; he should see a doctor soon.

They could, however, do nothing right now so a game to pass the time seemed innocuous, provided Mark didn't exert himself. Staying here by the fire couldn't do him much harm, as long as the bimbo, still painting her claws, had the nous to leave him alone. Her predatory glances were bothering Richard. Plus the sergeant major was barking again. Who the hell did she think she was? A tiny speck in the firmament of investment.

"I think we should stick to the areas we know and not intrude any more than we need."

The others looked at her in surprise. The point of the game was the size of the place. All they intended was harmless fun. Besides, the owners weren't here.

Amanda, however, stuck to her guns, accustomed to having the final word. She didn't want them invading Lucian's privacy, though she did not say that.

"What are you scared of? The dark?" Richard mocked.

"Perhaps," said Amanda obliquely.

Off they went, even Mark. She had done all she could. Jilly started counting again. Amanda found herself scared of the consequences.

"Shift yourself," said Jilly, "or else I'll catch you."

They'd agreed that the kitchen should be their base where, conveniently, the booze was set out. Amanda stood in front of the fire, hearing their laughter and footsteps fade as they ran up the spiral staircase into the darkness. She felt uneasy about the game, though could not quite put her finger on why. She was feeling suddenly spooked and wanted to leave.

"Ready or not, here I come!" yelled Jilly, leaving Amanda alone with her doom-ridden thoughts.

CHAPTER
EIGHT

After some time they straggled back, each one alone and in some way subdued, all of them claiming not to have found the others. Jilly had managed to catch just the one, Amanda, who'd never actually left and was now peacefully settled in front of the fire, gin and tonic in hand.

"You lousy cheat. That's not playing fair." She was the one who had set the rules. Richard, taking his lead from her, helped himself from the fridge.

"What was it like up there?" Amanda asked him.

"Dark," he replied. And unnervingly quiet. Due to the solidness of the walls there had been no sound at all from the outside world. The wind, still gale force, could not be heard; nor had he been aware of the other players. It had felt a little like being entombed, though Richard was far too laid back to say that. There was something about this ancient place that was starting to have an effect on him too. The sooner they got away, so much the better.

"Why didn't you light the lamps?" asked Amanda, who wouldn't have fancied it either in the dark.

Richard shrugged. It had not occurred. He had simply followed where others had led but managed to lose them up the twisting staircase. Besides, that was surely the point of the game. Hide-and-seek you played on your own, not like sardines, which was far more fun, when everyone squashed together into tight places. He had chosen the playroom, warm and safe, where he must have nodded off for a while, only emerging eventually when Jilly failed to appear.

"What happened to you?" Jilly sounded peeved when she tumbled into the firelit room, slightly flushed. She had run the whole length of the corridor, opening doors and flicking on lights, looking in cupboards and under beds, alert for the sound of breathing. Finally she had admitted defeat and groped her way back to the safe place by the fire. The thing that had scared her most was the deathly silence.

Richard laughed. "That's for us to say. You weren't a very effective It." He suspected she couldn't have looked very hard, though he didn't entirely blame her. No one, it seemed, was anxious to play again.

Mark's apparent improvement was over, and he looked unusually pale and strained when he came back. He flopped in his chair and closed his eyes. He looked worse tonight than he had the previous day.

Next down was Angus, who had gone up two floors and encountered another massive oak door which led outside to the battlements, wreathed in mist.

"What was it like?" Amanda asked, not mentioning that he had broken her rules. He was quite a lot older and knew his own mind. She would hate him to think her a shrew.

"Like Elsinore," he said. "Icy cold. Only without Hamlet's father's ghost. Enough to freeze off your balls. I don't recommend it. I fancy there might have been snow in the air, though in that moonless darkness I couldn't be certain."

"So it still hasn't cleared?" Amanda was deeply despondent.

"If anything," Angus said, "it's worse." In addition to which, his bloody phone still wouldn't work.

He looked for Dawn; not a sign of her. "What have you done with my girl?" he asked. It wasn't clear whether or not he was being ironic.

"I haven't seen her," said Mark, not that he'd looked.

Pathetic Dawn, with those puppy dog eyes, was rapidly starting to piss him off. He had started to feel she was shadowing him and so had managed to lose her. There were loads of places here to hide; he'd been playing the game since his infant days in the family mansion in Hampshire, which had several wings. It could be fun if you had the right crowd and sufficient players to jolly things up. Six was too few, especially if one was Dawn who was tediously drippy.

"Where has she gone, then?" Angus asked, though he showed no real sign of being concerned. Amanda sensed he was losing interest since they had first arrived here.

"She will turn up when she is hungry," she said, though in actual fact she couldn't care less. The game had turned out to be a really damp squib.

52

"Does anyone want to play again? Though bags I not be It this time." Jilly, too, was reluctant to leave the friendliness of the firelight.

They all stared wordlessly into the flames. Dawn would be back once she realised the chase was off.

Amanda, half dozing, thought about Max and the shocking events of that terrible night. When she closed her eyes, she could still see his slow-motion fall. She should not have left without checking out first if and how badly hurt he had been. It might just have been one of his mindless stunts, but she could not be totally certain. By now he was surely regretting it, might even be trying to track her down. He knew more or less where she was, had booked the hotel himself. If only somebody here had a working phone.

Jilly jerked awake with a sudden snore, glancing around in embarrassment. No one took any notice, though. They were all in a similar state of sluggish torpor. As soon as Dawn appeared they should all go to bed.

Amanda wondered about Jilly's life which, from the little she knew, seemed enviably normal. She had mentioned a boyfriend and also a forthcoming wedding. But then she remembered the cold hard fact that Jilly, for all her bubbling charm, in just a few weeks would be out of a job and possibly also homeless. Stricken with sudden guilt, she snapped into action.

"This is ridiculous," she said. Not even Angus appeared concerned but was comfortably settled, his eyes half closed, a glass of Scotch in his hand. Dawn was probably hiding, stupid girl, attention-seeking as always, spoilt brat. "Maybe we ought to look for her," she said.

Angus checked the time but his watch had stopped. "I guess you're probably right," he said with reluctance.

It was, if possible, even darker when Angus slowly retraced his steps up the narrow spiral stairs, Amanda following closely. Here, on the family floor where they slept, not a chink of light was showing. They'd extinguished the lamps because of the game and the slit-like windows let in almost nothing, especially this late on a moonless night. Amanda groped for Angus's hand, surprising them both with her nervousness. It was not like her to show any sign of weakness.

"Please don't leave me," she hissed in his ear, gripped by an inexplicable fear. This tower had stood for six hundred years, repelling invaders with battering rams. She sensed malevolent presences all around her.

Angus, more pleased than he cared to let on, did as she asked and held on to her hand. She was far less tough than she usually showed and he, though he'd never admit it, was similarly spooked. Damn that girl; the sooner they found her, the better.

"Dawn!" He spoke with authority though all that came back was resounding silence. It was almost as if the walls had absorbed her existence.

All the doors on this floor were closed. One by one Angus opened them, switched on the lights and rapidly checked out the rooms. It was only a very cursory search. He was thoroughly sick of the childish game and badly needed his bed and a proper night's kip. Tomorrow, with luck, they would manage to leave. The weather would clear and he'd find some way to contact a local garage to fix his car, providing he found it. After which he would have the long drive south, late for his meetings, with Molly to face. In a moment of mindless weakness, he had mentioned commitment to Dawn. And now she was messing about in the dark. He hadn't the patience for nursery games. There were just a few more rooms to check and then he was packing it in.

Amanda tensed. They were almost there, at the steps leading down to the library door. Lucian had asked her to be discreet so she still had not breathed a word.

"I wonder what's through that door," Angus said, with no expectation that she would know.

She held her breath as he tried the door but, much to her relief, he found it locked. Good, thought Amanda. Now she could go to bed.

CHAPTER
NINE

It wasn't possible Dawn had gone far, not without making a great song and dance. She hadn't set foot outside since she first arrived here. Besides, she wasn't equipped for the cold with her cocktail frock and ridiculous shoes. It was far more her style to have thrown some kind of wobbly. She craved the limelight and always had, by nature resenting all other women. Having transferred her attention to Mark she had been trailing after him like a pathetic poodle. The likeliest reason for her absence now was that she was trying to make a point. Angus was growing bored with her — it did not take Einstein to figure that out — and Mark was simply not rising to her bait. Wherever she'd gone, she was bound to have some agenda.

There was plenty of room in the tower to hide, including a whole top floor they had not yet explored. The place was a fortress with walls at least seven foot thick. It was possible she had just nodded off and could not hear them calling her, or else she was simply enacting a juvenile prank. Amanda, bored, had gone off to bed. Now the others should too.

Angus, however, was slightly concerned. He was growing used to Dawn's antics now but still remained responsible for her safety. It was his fault that they had lost their way and landed up in this spooky place and he had let his irritation show. One thing at least was now clear to him. His declaration had been a mistake, based on a mixture of lust and too much whisky. Had they not been detained, he might well have spilled the sordid details out to his wife which could have proved the biggest mistake of his life. Nevertheless, he owed it to Dawn to make an effort to keep her safe. She was starting to get on his nerves but that was hardly the poor child's fault. She was only eighteen months older than his daughter.

Jilly, slumped in a chair by the fire, resisted the impulse to turn in too. She might appear comatose but was fully awake. If they weren't out of here by the end of the week she would miss her appointment at the clinic and thus delay the diagnosis she dreaded. She could handle the pain, which wasn't too bad, just mild discomfort that came and went, and might still be nothing more serious than indigestion. What was scaring her were her family genes and the premature deaths of two of her aunts, both at around the age that she had reached now.

Not even Derek knew about that as she hadn't wanted to worry him too. Her mother said it wasn't quite nice to discuss such things with a man. Even saying the words aloud might help to make it real. More than anything else in the world, Jilly had always wanted to have children.

She had thought of discussing it with Amanda, with whom she was rapidly starting to bond and whose heart, despite the occasional brusqueness, seemed in the right place. She could be bossy and overbearing, with her Oxford degree and cut-glass vowels, but their shared experience on the fells had drawn them irrevocably closer. Amanda was warmer than she showed but also knew what she wanted from life. She had not reached her position in head office without superlative management skills. Sorting out people's problems was one of her strengths.

There seemed to be something troubling her too, another reason Jilly felt she could trust her. Sometimes Amanda whimpered in her sleep. Jilly suspected there was a man from whom, for some reason, she was running. Throughout that fairly horrendous climb, with its terrifying aftermath, she had noticed her more than once looking over her shoulder. It might be extreme but she'd take a chance and trust her older colleague's compassionate side.

Amanda, however, had gone to bed whereas Dawn was still missing and had to be found. It was likely that she was just acting up, but none of them would sleep till they knew she was safe. Jilly herself had left school at sixteen and worked ever since in a mundane job, regularly putting money aside for a mortgage and future marriage. Dawn was no more than a petulant child, greedy, spoilt and self-absorbed, who was leeching off somebody else's man and not even faithful to him. She had now fixed her sights on the hedge-fund boy who was doing his best to shrug her off. It seemed she cared nothing for others' feelings. Jilly disapproved.

Mark was visibly fading fast; his eyelids drooped, and he could barely stand. Richard ordered him and Jilly off to bed and said he would stay and help Angus. Dawn must be somewhere in the tower. It should not take long to find her.

The obvious place to start their search was through the door in the downstairs hall which none of them yet had even attempted to open. Richard assumed it led to a cellar or even, considering the building's age, a fortified mediaeval dungeon, the thought of which made him shudder. The tower was creepy enough as it was without that extra embellishment. His mind flashed to skeletons chained to the wall or, even worse, rotting corpses. He doubted that Dawn would have dared go down there but they should, at least, take a look.

On the other hand, they might get a surprise and find an underground swimming pool or even a bar with a disco floor; you never knew till you looked. The owners had obviously spared no expense on modernising the rest of the tower. It would take two minutes to check it out before having to climb all those stairs.

Angus was losing his patience fast. "Wait till I get my hands on her," he growled.

As they'd half expected, the door was locked. Which meant they were able to rule it out. Richard privately breathed a sigh of relief. Now they had only the top floor left to explore.

The temperature dropped by several degrees as they wended their way up the spiral stairs, bypassing the floors they already knew, the living quarters and the bedrooms. The iron sconce at the very top threw a limited pool of light into solid darkness. Richard shivered and stopped in his tracks. This was more daunting than any cellar, as well as abnormally cold, which he didn't quite understand. A draught that must come from the battlements hurled itself with force down the narrow passage. As his eyes adjusted, he could just make out that the windows up here were unglazed. They must have run out of cash, he thought, but that had nothing to do with him. He could not believe that Dawn would stay up here long.

Angus went on out of Richard's sight, but came back a minute later. "There is no way she's here. She's scared of the dark." He was even more grumpy now. He wanted to go to bed and forget all about her.

Richard agreed. It was far too cold. They went back down the stairs, calling her name. Richard told Angus to check his own room in case she had simply slipped off to bed. Knowing Dawn and her selfish ways he'd by no means put that past her.

Angus agreed that he had a point. He apologised for keeping Richard up and they parted on the landing. They were just going into their separate rooms when a half-heard something halted them both in their tracks.

"Dawn?" called Angus, listening hard. From above he could hear a familiar sound, the tippety-tap of expensive heels coming cautiously down the staircase. Both men moved forward and watched as she slowly appeared.

She had always been pale, it was part of her look, but now what they saw was a bloodless wreck, just a handful of skin and bones with unfocused eyes. She looked, Richard thought, like the living dead and he hesitated to touch her corpselike skin.

Angus, however, was more of a man and stepped forward to catch her before she fell. "What happened to you?" he cried but Dawn didn't answer.

Her eyes rolled backwards into her head as she took one last step and fell into his arms, collapsing against his chest like a broken doll.

CHAPTER
TEN

The light was filtering through her eyelids. Morning already; Amanda sat up. She swung out of bed and peered through the slit to be confronted again by just rolling mist.

"Damn," she said. "If this continues, it's going to drive me bonkers."

Jilly was up already and fretting. She had calculated it was Tuesday. She tried the radio for the news but all she could get was a flurried crackle. She ought to be back at work today so they would soon know she had not returned. Would anyone bother to check her out or might they assume she was simply bunking off? Though the hotel would know she had not yet vacated her room. Derek would worry. It was not like her not to turn up when she'd said she would. No one, of course, was to know that her phone didn't work.

All the others were in the kitchen, apart from Dawn who was still asleep. Angus was wearing a towelling robe, filched, no doubt, from the master bathroom, his hair sleeked back from the shower. He looked rather dashing.

"Where do you think she was hiding last night?" Amanda still thought it had just been a prank, but then she had not seen Dawn when she reappeared.

Angus, who had and had hardly slept, simply shook his head and made no comment. Deep inside he was now profoundly disturbed. It wasn't like Dawn to behave like that. To start with, she lacked the artifice. She hadn't the basic intelligence to have pulled off quite such a show. Since she'd been out like a light ever since he hadn't been able to ask her.

"Did she hide in a cupboard?"

"Perhaps," he said. He wished Amanda would leave it alone. He sensed how much she disliked the younger woman. And until he could talk to Dawn rationally, he simply didn't have answers. All he was sure of was that she hadn't been faking.

"There is something seriously wrong with this place," said Jilly, shuddering despite herself. As her nan might say, she could feel it in her water. She had managed to find a radio station that confirmed what she'd thought: it was Tuesday today. She could only hope the Prudential would try to find her.

"Try to catch the weather report," called Angus, making himself some toast. He mainly seemed to fend for himself even when Dawn was around. Which wasn't right, not in Jilly's eyes; she'd been raised to believe that men deserved to be spoiled.

She twirled the dial and fiddled the knobs. The static was dreadful; she almost gave up. But at last she found a weather report which said that conditions in the Lakes were erratic. The cloud base was low and exceedingly dense. The airport in Carlisle had cancelled all flights for a second day.

Angus cursed beneath his breath. He really hated to be out of touch. A self-made man, he involved himself in every minor detail of his business.

Amanda was also seething inside. She rinsed her mug and left it to dry then stepped outside the door for a weather check. Not that it made much difference; she still couldn't see.

She was sick of wearing the same old clothes and having to rinse out her underwear every night. Her hair felt gritty, her skin was dry, there was soap in the bathroom but no shampoo. She hated to be at less than her elegant best. She restlessly paced the living room; it was after eight but the light was like thick pea soup. She wanted to go for a proper walk but knew she'd be taking a terrible risk. If she wandered off in the mist they might never find her. And her head still ached from the tumble she'd taken on Sunday.

She wondered idly where Lucian was, whether or not he was somewhere near. He seemed to have the run of the place; he was the one who should sort things out and devise some method for them to leave. She couldn't believe they were so much in thrall to the weather. She shot up the stairs to the library, determined to have it out with him. But when she tried the door she found it was locked.

Her thoughts once more returned to Max. She badly wanted to hear the news on the off chance that there might be a mention of him. Though it seemed an age it was only six nights since the fatal row on his balcony. She was so steamed up, she had driven away determined never to see the bastard again. So much, though, had occurred since then that it felt as though they had been in this tower for months. This horrible tower which now she totally loathed.

She slipped back into the living room where no one seemed to have missed her. Angus and Mark were at the table and Jilly was making them scrambled eggs while Richard was busily mixing Bloody Marys. He was starting early, at breakfast time; even for him that was pushing things although, truthfully, there wasn't much else to do.

"The hair of the dog," he said with a grin, liberally spicing it with Tabasco. He handed the glasses round and everyone took one. He asked what the schedule was for today. They ought to be out there, doing something. He, for one, was starting to stiffen up.

"Logs," said Amanda, producing a list. They had. already been through two basketfuls. "If some of you guys could bring up some more I will keep a tally of what we use. And if we run low, perhaps you would chop a few more."

"Count me out, I'm afraid," said Mark, "since I only have the use of one hand." He seemed to be using it more, though, and looked slightly better.

Amanda, displaying her leadership skills, took another look at her list. "You could try cleaning bathrooms or sweeping the stairs," she suggested.

"The devil makes work for idle hands," quipped Richard.

"Then since I can't help with the logs," said Mark, "I hereby appoint myself weather clerk." Soon he would need to get back to the plane so would do what it took to expedite the process.

The morning sped by. It was now almost one. The mist still hung like a curtain of gauze, obliterating all but the Scafell summit. Amanda, still anxious to catch the news, dropped her damp cloth on the shelf she was cleaning and turned the radio on. Jilly was basting the leg of lamb; what they didn't eat now she would keep for a shepherd's pie. She seemed to be quite enjoying herself, was nothing if not resourceful.

"That smells really good," Amanda said, having never been bothered to cook herself.

"If I didn't keep busy, I'd go bananas," said Jilly.

The radio crackled and then went dead.

"Damn," said Amanda, shaking it hard.

"Don't!" shouted Angus. "You're only making things worse."

They glowered at each other, prepared for a fight. Tempers all round had begun to fray. A few more days of confinement here and they'd be at each other's throats. Lunch was ready, Jilly announced. She summoned them all to the table.

"What about Dawn? Should we let her lie in?"

"I think so," said Angus, who had just been to check and found her still out for the count.

He had sat beside her and stroked her cheek. She slept flat on her face and was snoring slightly, reminding him of his kids in their infant years. There was nothing about her that was intrinsically bad; the fault had only

66

ever been his. She had thrown herself at him for long enough but a stronger man would have resisted. She was cute in a slightly vapid way and available, which had been the main thing. She had crossed his path at a time when he needed diversion.

His marriage was stable, and he had few regrets. He and Molly remained good friends and the kids were both turning out well. His business empire was thriving, too, despite the high street's general demise. Angus was rich and daring enough to have learnt to diversify.

Bringing Dawn up here had been a mistake and given her hopes she had not had before. No way had he ever intended to risk his marriage. He stroked her hair, which was feathery and soft, and wondered again what had happened last night. Whatever it was appeared to have traumatised her. He would leave her alone to sleep it off and then perhaps she'd be able to tell him more.

There was definitely something about this place that was gradually starting to get to them all. Just now, in the kitchen, he'd wanted to thump Amanda. He had no idea where he'd left the car or he'd be legging it down there now. He would sooner face the weather than endless confinement. He needed a phone and a local map or, better yet, a taxi cab. A city man, he was disempowered when he couldn't control his own life.

CHAPTER
ELEVEN

Dawn woke suddenly to distant laughter and no comprehension of where she was. She could recall nothing of what had occurred or why she was lying alone in this bed in a small cramped room with a sewing machine on the table. It was totally dark because the curtains were closed. She fumbled for the watch on her wrist but could not make out what the figures said, though she sensed it must be later than she had expected. Laughter again; there were people downstairs. She forced her mind to concentrate hard until some of the recent past started filtering back, though still only obliquely.

This horrible place. They'd been lost in the mist and had somehow managed to end up here, in the middle of nowhere high on the side of a mountain. When the mist came down on the motorway and traffic had been reduced to a crawl, it was she who'd had the bright idea to switch to a minor road. It was important they get back to London that night. The news was great; they must celebrate, but the rate things were moving up here they'd never get there.

So instead they'd swung off at the Penrith exit, where the mist had been worse but the traffic less dense, and meandered for hours down those small country roads, all the time squabbling between themselves, until a rutted cart track had petered out at a total dead end. They had left the car and scrambled uphill, on a path so steep that she'd had to remove her shoes, blindly following the only light they could see, near the top of the mountain. All the way she had thought they would never make it but Angus had said that they couldn't turn back. Lost, as they were, in a thick dense mist, that light was their only beacon. Luckily Dawn had healthy feet plus the coat he had squandered so much upon, which she could not wait to flaunt in front of her colleagues.

No one would miss her. She lived on her own, and since she had been away with the boss not even her absence from work would be remarked on. Except, of course, in a scurrilous way. In any office, especially theirs, it was nigh impossible to maintain any secret. Angus, on whom she had long set her sights, had finally mentioned the word divorce and undertaken to tell his wife the moment they got back. He was fifty-two, more than twice her age, but she relished the lifestyle he could provide. Since rising out of the typing pool Dawn had had her greedy eyes focused on rapid advancement.

She was pretty enough, with ivory skin and a moody pout which, from studying the mags, she fancied made her look hot. Angus was in the cheap fashion trade, selling in mega amounts to the high street stores. It was not a model Dawn wanted to be, which was just as well since she lacked the height, but first a buyer and then, in due course, the chief executive's wife. So far, in just a couple of years, she'd advanced to being his number two PA.

The reason for the excursion north had been a trade fair in Carlisle at which they had shared a room in a classy hotel. It was just the chance she'd been waiting for (number one PA was down with the flu) to chip away at Angus's inbuilt resistance. His children were grown and his wife was a bore. Dawn had seen her a couple of times and didn't consider her any serious threat. She was frumpy in that middle-class way, in twinset and pearls and sensible shoes, was active in the WI and worked as a volunteer at the local Oxfam. She seemed immune to their fashion lines, had little interest in her husband's career. Not so Dawn, who wanted it all but was not prepared to wait for it very much longer.

They were laughing again. Even in this place, with its solid walls, she could hear them downstairs and imagined she also heard the clink of glasses. All this group seemed to do was drink; they couldn't care less that she hadn't come down. They would miss her when she was gone . . . which triggered off something. Last night . . . the light. At last things were filtering back.

She had shot up the stairs in her Jimmy Choos, hoping Mark might come after her, and, when he didn't, had gone up that extra flight. It was very cold; she remembered that because she was wearing just Angus's shirt over her knickers, tied with a sash she had found in the nanny's drawer. It was also dark and certainly far from inviting. Yet something intangible drew her on,

70

beckoning her in a curious way just as the beacon light had lured them up here.

She looked down the long dark passageway and saw at the end a brilliant light that seemed to be issuing through a three-quarters-closed door. She fancied there might have been music too, that or a voice singing somewhere far off. Dawn, unable to stop herself, had found herself wafting towards that door as lightly as if her feet were not touching the floor. She had felt really great, she remembered that, and less cold the closer she got to the light.

But then she'd heard sounds of voices calling and was suddenly able to stop and turn back. Everything else remained a blur. All she remembered after that was waking to find herself tucked up in bed. She had thought at first that it must have been just a dream. Now, however, she was less sure. As soon as she could she was going back up to discover what lay behind the enticing door.

She could now read her watch; it was almost three. She checked that it had not stopped in the night. She crawled from the bed and peered through the window to be faced by the same wall of mist. Somebody tapped. It was Jilly to see how she was feeling and if she wanted to eat.

"We thought it best to let you sleep on." Jilly had always been nice to Dawn. "I nearly brought up a tray but thought I'd check first."

Dawn still wasn't certain how she was. She looked small and fragile tucked in that bed and, without the slap and expensive clothes, like a waif from an orphanage, all skin and bones.

Jilly's warm heart went out to her. "Come down and sit by the fire," she said. "It is not the same without you there. We miss you."

Dawn considered, then stayed in bed. Her feet were cold though she didn't know why. She was wearing Angus's cashmere socks which he must have slipped on to her feet last night before he tucked her in. The thought of the fire almost tempted her, though going downstairs would mean seeing Mark.

"No thanks," she said. "I'll wait till later." Once she'd had time to reassemble herself.

Amanda and Jilly were having fun, surprising in the circumstances. They had felt like an afternoon off doing girly things. It all started with Amanda's hair. Her scalp felt itchy, could do with a wash. Soap would not do: too alkaline. She needed a branded shampoo. Which was when inspiration had struck. They had left the master bedroom untouched — and also its en suite bathroom. A squeeze of shampoo would not be missed and while she was up there she'd have a long soak in the bath.

Jilly was certainly up for it too. She was tired of being the resident drudge. Leaving the men to the clearing up, the two of them skipped away for a beauty session. Amanda's guess had been spot on. The master en suite was a miniature spa, all pale blue marble and crystal lights and equipped with every possible human need. Shampoos, conditioners, fancy oils. A dryer with a circulating hood and a neon-lit mirror, just like a Hollywood star's. It was paradise.

Amanda hooted and clapped her hands. "Forgive me," she said, "while I tend to my ablutions."

Jilly, left to her own devices, inspected the master bedroom for clues. They had not been in here again since the night they arrived. The lights had been on and the wardrobe door wide, a suitcase waiting and clothes on the bed. Why leave without their luggage? It didn't add up. Whatever had happened had happened fast. They had left the lights on and the door unlocked, a fire in the grate and a meal only partly consumed. There was something missing, although she wasn't sure what. But she would not be able to sleep till she'd figured it out.

CHAPTER
TWELVE

Dawn eventually made an appearance, though not before she was good and ready. Amanda and Jilly dropped by to check and found her engrossed in putting on her slap. So that's what the huge Gucci handbag was for; Amanda made an effort to stifle her mirth. Since her own hair was still wrapped in a towel and Dawn had spent most of the day in bed, all this fuss seemed excessive, to say the least. But something had happened to traumatise Dawn; they hadn't yet got to the bottom of that so Amanda buttoned her lip till they had more details.

Dawn, as usual, was ghostly pale and carefully applying her panda eyes before painting three layers of gloss on her lips. She was wearing her backless dress again which showed how undernourished she was. Anorexic was the word that came to mind.

"Won't you be awfully cold?" said Jilly. "If I were you I would keep on the socks."

Dawn ignored her, as well she might, just sprayed herself in a cloud of Chanel, checked that her hair looked its unkempt best then slipped into her skyscraper shoes and stood up. She's like a rebellious teenager, thought Amanda.

They both followed humbly in her tracks, impressed how she managed the stairs in those heels. They tried to imagine how she'd climbed the mountain, then remembered she had arrived with them in her hand. They both held back to allow her to make her grand entrance.

"Dawn," said Richard, rising to greet her while Mark simply flapped one hand from his chair. "How lovely to see you. How pretty you look." He was pulling out all the stops.

Angus was reading and seemed surprised. "Should you really be down here?" he asked. Something chilly about his tone made Amanda mentally flinch. He is off her already, she registered, which didn't entirely surprise her. She had never been able to comprehend how a man like that could fancy a moron like Dawn. Ruled by his penis; they were all much the same, which brought Max back to the surface again. Dawn was a child dressing up as a vamp with no true sexuality there. Amanda was pleased that Angus had come to his senses.

"We are dying to know what happened last night," she purred with a smile that was falsely bright. Beneath the pantomime makeup Dawn still looked shaken.

Angus was wanting answers too. He closed the book that he'd casually picked up, which was probably something the children had left behind them. Not *Swallows and Amazons*, though; Amanda checked. Without his financial forecasts to hand he seemed at a loss for casual chat. But Dawn was hardly saying a thing, was subdued and slightly less abrasive than usual.

Mark did the honours with the drinks, mixing for Dawn a weak rum and coke though, since she was not going out tonight, surely its strength did not matter. Like it or not, they were stuck up here so the least they could do was enjoy themselves and try to reduce the tedium of confinement.

"Now please enlighten us," he implored as soon as they all had their bevvies of choice. "We are all of us dying to know what happened last night."

There weren't any answers, or easy ones. Just something about a bright white light. It was clear the poor girl was still somewhat confused. She had wandered up to the floor above and found herself plunged into darkness. There had been no other lights, none she could find, though she'd stayed there a while before turning back. When they asked her why, she became even less coherent. She delivered her story in a flat, toneless voice. Now she had their attention, she couldn't deliver the goods. She only remembered the darkness and cold, and the light that had seemed to be beckoning her on.

"Where did it come from?"

"The room at the end," she said.

"Next to the battlements?" Angus asked. He had opened that door when he was looking for her and had almost been blown off the roof by the roaring gale.

"Leave her alone," said Jilly quietly. "I think she's already been through enough."

They might possibly never discover the truth but would not achieve much by bullying her. Jilly went over and gave her a hug. "Come and help me in the kitchen," she said.

Amanda went off to dry her hair and returned still wearing her hostess's robe. Her standards were slipping but she didn't care. It was strange how rapidly one could adapt. She had been in this place for less than three days yet no longer much cared how she looked. In London she'd never be caught slobbing round like this.

Jilly had asked if they wanted to eat but none of them had any appetite left. They'd been stuffing themselves since they first arrived and now were pretty much sated. Also they'd had no exercise which was something they really would have to correct. If they didn't take themselves in hand, how would they ever escape from here? They needed to be super fit to get down that mountain.

Angus and Richard had drawn to one side and were talking quietly between themselves. When Amanda reappeared, they beckoned her over to join them.

"We were talking about Dawn's escapade, which somehow doesn't add up," Angus said. "She cannot account for the length of time she was missing."

"We thought we might go on a recce," said Richard, "and check out the room where she saw the light."

Amanda, who was equally curious, said she would tag along.

Mark was now entertaining the girls with lurid tales of his misspent youth. In his thirty-four years he had certainly been around. Dawn was clearly obsessed with him so wasn't aware when the other three slipped away.

They instantly noticed the temperature drop which hit them as they went up the stairs. As Dawn had said, it was totally dark with only one iron sconce throwing limited light. Amanda drew her towelling robe tighter. She would not have fancied being here on her own.

Angus remembered Dawn's stricken face, her eyes rolling back, when she came down. Something had happened to her up here though she still had not explained what. Somehow it seemed she had managed to blank it out. All they could see, now they were here, was an empty passage that stretched, long and dark, right across the tower to the other turret. The windows at this level were slits that let in minimum light.

"That's the door." Angus pointed it out, the one at the end where the battlements were, which now appeared to be firmly closed with nothing distinctive about it.

"Let me," said Richard, bouncing ahead, keen to get this mystery solved and return downstairs to his comfortable seat by the fire. Amanda clutched Angus's arm as they watched, a sudden tremor running down her spine. Richard tested the handle; the door was locked.

Angus was keen to find his car and get on the road back to London again. In theory, he should be able to go straight down the side of the mountain to where he had left it. In the Lakes, however, paths twisted and turned and were never quite as straightforward as that. Still, with luck, in daylight he might find that rutted cart track.

"Well, how did you get here?"

"We followed the light." The light that no longer appeared to be on, though all six of them could bear witness to its existence.

"Maybe it's something to do with the mist." Nothing appeared to make sense any more.

Richard suggested they go back downstairs and think again in the morning.

CHAPTER
THIRTEEN

Dawn seemed now to be back on form, holding court in front of the fire with Mark as her captive audience while, in the kitchen, Jilly ransacked the freezer. Both were playing subconscious roles. Amanda, watching, could not suppress sudden laughter.

"What?" said Dawn, preternaturally thin-skinned. She could dish it out, and frequently did, but could not handle jokes at her own expense

"Nothing. Ignore me," Amanda said. It amused her how stereotyped people could be. Nubile Dawn, on the hunt for a mate, unswervingly went for the healthiest genes which, in the case of Mark, meant also the richest. Angus and Richard, protecting the herd, were circling the territory, leaving their mark, while Jilly, the nurturer, fussed about food in the kitchen. Though unsure of her own hierarchical place, Amanda considered herself a born leader. They had known each other a matter of days yet, as a working unit, could not be improved on. Life did that sometimes, created its own natural order.

Another day had been frittered away. They were still no nearer to quitting this place. Angus's car was lost somewhere on the fells. They would soon be needing more logs and fresh vegetables too. Logs were easy; vegetables less so. They should concentrate first on getting one cellphone working. The transistor batteries were fading too and must be conserved at whatever cost. Amanda had not liked to listen in to the news.

Which meant she still had heard nothing about Max who might, conceivably, be on her trail. Part of her longed to see him again though she quaked at the thought of his anger. Her feelings about him were so undecided, she no longer knew what she wanted from him. Max, the philanderer, back in her life or herself in court on a possible manslaughter charge.

She decided to visit the library again on the off chance Lucian might be there. She knew no other way to contact him but felt sure he would have the answers to their problems. They needed a car and a phone that worked as well as an updated weather report. They'd been hanging around quite long enough; what they needed most was action.

Whenever Amanda looked outside the weather was still unremittingly grim but they couldn't stay here indefinitely; they all had lives to get on with. Lucian seemed to exist on a quite other timescale. But he had been charming and, furthermore, had promised her a longer talk. The problem now was trying to pin him down.

Jilly was making a shepherd's pie. It would be at least an hour until it was ready. Amanda had no appetite left but eating at least gave them something to do. If she went to bed early she knew she would not sleep.

"If you need any help, I shall be upstairs." Now was as good a time as any to find the elusive Lucian.

Jilly, distracted, nodded her head and went on silently mashing potatoes. It seemed she had problems of her own she was not yet ready to talk about. "In about an hour," she said, "would you set the table?"

This time Amanda's luck was in. The lights were on and the door ajar, and when she stuck her head inside Lucian hailed her heartily from the fireplace. He was dressed as before, in a smoking jacket with a matching tasselled cap on his head, looking like something out of a Tenniel woodcut.

"Greetings," he said, apparently pleased, using one finger to mark his place. "I had a feeling I might see you today."

"I've been looking for you," Amanda said. "But whenever I do you're never here."

"I'm here when you really need me," said Lucian, smiling.

Amanda bluntly came to the point. "We have been here quite long enough," she said, "and need to be leaving right away if only we can find transport. Or, at the least, a phone that works so that we can summon help from Keswick."

Lucian laughed. He was very laid back. He placed a silk ribbon inside the book and shifted it on to the table. "You'll not get far on a night like this, so draw up a chair and just sit," he said. "There's another storm on its way and more heavy snow. You'll simply have to wait it out."

82

"We haven't got time," Amanda cried. "We have lives of our own in the outside world. Two of us need to get back to the lake. Two others are headed for London." As for the two who'd arrived by plane, it wasn't her business to say any more. It was up to them if they needed anyone's help, which she slightly doubted.

Lucian smiled and stared into the flames. "That's the problem with modern living," he said. "No one ever has time any more so they overlook what really matters."

"Such as what?" asked Amanda tartly. Her job was waiting and so was her life. She had to find out what had happened to Max and whether or not the police were on her trail. With neither telephone signal nor radio, they had no contact with the world outside. It might suit some to be trapped up here but Amanda would never be one of them. She was growing increasingly frantic.

"What I always find," said Lucian calmly, "is that things you think really important quite often are not."

She stared at him, could not quite make him out. Was he laughing at her or being profound? His deep-set eyes showed no merriment despite the fact that he was smiling.

"I don't understand you," she said, on the brink of despair.

"Look at it this way." He steepled his fingers and held her gaze with hypnotic force. "Nothing is ever as urgent as it may appear."

It was time to go. She must set that table. "How will I find you again?" she asked.

Lucian smiled enigmatically. "I am always here when I'm needed," he repeated.

Lucian no longer seemed to be on their side. Feeling that there was now no reason to keep his presence a secret, Amanda slipped back to the living room where the others were gathering round the table, ably set by Richard in her absence. Loyalty was a two-sided thing. It might help if they added their voices to hers and insisted that Lucian come to their aid by facilitating their departure. He had no right to detain them here. As far as Amanda knew, it wasn't his home.

Dawn, now glowing, still fawned over Mark while Jilly, flushed from the stove, was serving the pie. Angus was manfully pulling corks and Richard was passing round the peas. A wave of affection swept through Amanda; they felt like a genuine family. She took a deep breath and tapped her glass for attention.

"There is something I think you should know," she said. She briefly summarised Lucian's position that, although he knew they were keen to leave, he seemed in no hurry to help them. He must, at least, have a working phone or some form of transport that they could use. He could not possibly live up here in permanent isolation. The very least he could offer to do was help Angus find his car.

Angus agreed. "That's preposterous." He swelled with rage at the very thought.

"Why is he here at all," Richard asked, "if he doesn't understand our predicament?"

"And how can he manage to come and go without us being aware of it?" Even Mark showed signs of indignation.

Amanda had answers to none of that except that he seemed to be well installed. And was usually wearing indoor shoes as well as a smoking cap.

"What's a smoking cap?" queried Dawn.

"Nothing of any importance," Amanda snapped.

What could be his reasons for wanting them there unless he were lonely, which seemed not the case? If he sought company, he would join them for meals.

"I think we should all go and talk to him," said Angus, accustomed to getting things done. "He may not understand how serious we are."

"Who is he anyhow?" Richard asked. What right did he have to interfere? Though he could prove useful in leading them back to the plane.

"He is some sort of local. His name is Demort. He's known this house for the whole of his life so he must be based somewhere close at hand since he seems to come and go whenever he pleases."

"That settles it." Angus laid down the law. "We will go up there as a deputation, as soon as we've finished the meal, and demand our rights."

They were all agreed. Richard raised his glass.

"To liberty!" They clinked in unison.

The grandfather clock was striking twelve. At which point the lights all went out.

CHAPTER
FOURTEEN

"Bloody hell . . .?"

Mark's glass went flying as absolute darkness enveloped them all. The only light left was from the dying fire.

"Damn," said Richard. The power had failed. That or, perhaps, a busted fuse. None of them had the remotest idea where the fuse box might be. Especially not in the dark at this time of night.

Lucian was their immediate thought. Angus groped his way up the stairs but, again, he found the library locked. What was it with the man, that he was so elusive? He knew from Amanda about their plight and how keen they were to be out of this place. The least he might have done was come down and take over. Instead of which he had slipped away to wherever it was he went at night without a thought for them or their discomfort. There were things going on that just didn't add up, but at the moment Angus was too tired to care. It had been a very long day; all he needed was sleep.

At least they were all sharing rooms in pairs, which made things easier in the dark. It was really quite cosy. Jilly had found a whole drawer of candles and handed them out when they all trooped upstairs. There were also Victorian candle holders, as illustrated in nursery rhyme books, made of plain white china, with handles for safe transportation.

"They are obviously used to power cuts here," said Amanda.

Up they went like a row of kids, with muffled laughter and childish jokes. Somehow this latest happening had raised their spirits.

"Whooo!" said Richard, who lacked any tact. "I wonder if there are ghosts about."

"Shush!" said Jilly, slapping his thigh. If he wasn't careful, he'd get the lot of them spooked. Which wasn't what they needed right now, faced with a night on the fells in total darkness.

"Would you like to crawl in with me?" asked Amanda.

"No thanks," said Jilly. "Just as long as I know you're there."

And, in the event, both slept very well, having blown out their candles by mutual consent, each reassured by the sound of the other's breathing. The rest of the house was quiet as a tomb, without so much as a creak, which was oddly unnerving.

Jilly woke on the dot of seven. She peeked through the window to check things out but all she saw was the same dense mist, the light as opaque and murky as pond water.

"I am starting to understand," she said, "the effects of light deprivation." She had pronounced circles beneath her eyes and her skin had developed a pallid hue. A few more days confined in this place and they'd all be reduced to spectral shades. Perhaps they were stuck here for ever, which wasn't a joke.

Amanda stirred then sprang into life. "How did Lucian do that?" she asked. "Vanish into thin air when we were all present?"

Jilly had also had that thought. It seemed he had supernatural powers. There had to be some sort of rational explanation.

"Maybe he never left," said Amanda, "but spent the night on his own up there." He certainly seemed well settled in with his books, his cigars and the fire. There was bags of space in the tower to hide, including the whole of the empty third floor. It would explain how he changed his clothes, including his monogrammed slippers. But it wasn't their business. She kept remembering that.

They dressed without even bothering to wash since the unheated water was now stone cold. Jilly boiled the kettle on the Aga.

"How does the Aga retain its heat?"

"Wood," said Amanda. "At least, I assume." She opened the top and peered inside. Her theory was correct. They must find the fuse box and chop more wood. It was Wednesday already, she believed. The transistor batteries were now quite dead so they had no contact at all with the outside world. Things were getting serious now. They must sort something out.

"First," said Amanda, "let's take a walk." A breath of fresh air might help get their thinking straight.

One by one the others appeared, yawning and scratching and out of sorts. The miasma of dark despondency seemed to be catching. Angus, for one, had not bothered to shave; Dawn looked mutinous and withdrawn. Mark seemed under the weather again. Only Richard retained his Tigger-like bounce.

"Who's for a spot of country air?" Amanda had her waterproof on, while Jilly triumphantly flourished the compass she'd brought.

"You can certainly count me in," said Richard, glad of a chance to stretch his legs and escape the depressing atmosphere of the tower. He was starting to feel like a battery hen in this place.

"What do you hope to achieve?" Angus asked, confined to quarters by having no suitable clothes. Not for the first time, he cursed himself for leaving the luggage in the car. Though he could not have managed to bring it up here on his own.

"Well I, for one, am not giving in. If I have to crawl down to the valley, I will." Fighting talk; Amanda had not made head office by being a wimp. "We will check out how things are lower down and, with luck, may manage to summon some help."

"Try to pick up some fresh milk," said Mark. "And send back a stretcher for me."

Having idled over a leisurely breakfast even though deprived of their resident cook, Angus, Dawn and Mark dispersed to sort themselves out for the day. Angus and Dawn seemed on fragile terms, possibly due to last night's display when she'd practically licked Mark's hand, she had come on so strong. He found her repulsive.

Angus, though, seemed a nice enough guy; Mark looked forward to knowing him better. He always admired a keen business brain though habitually took far greater risks, which was why he was not in too much of a hurry to extricate himself now. The longer he waited, the better the chances were that the markets might improve. He hauled himself painfully back up the stairs and made the effort to shower and shave. His arm was still giving him hell though he didn't let on. If they'd made the journey to Reykjavik his money might, in any case, have been lost. It was better off where it was for now, stuck on that frozen fell.

One of the outside drains was blocked and the overflow was beginning to freeze. As winter drew in and the temperature dropped, conditions could only deteriorate and possibly end up affecting the inside plumbing. Mark, one-handed, was prodding away, clearing debris with a long-handled rake but finding it hard to extricate the rubbish. He needed help.

"Here!" he shouted when Dawn appeared, sulky still but in dungarees which she'd found, she said, hanging on a hook in the cloakroom. They made her look cute.

"Grab a bucket," he said, "and start bailing fast."

She looked affronted, then suddenly smiled, which instantly changed her entire demeanour. The rebellious Goth was revealed in a different light. She faffed around and then popped inside and came out brandishing rubber gloves.

"Great," said Mark with his luminous smile. "If we work as a team, we should very soon get this sorted."

Richard led and the others followed. Always allow a man to take charge had long been Amanda's maxim, mainly in jest. Especially if it did not involve his having to over-tax his brain. Why do something a man can do was another of her ironic mantras. One reason, Max often pointed out, she was thirty-eight and still single.

Richard made an excellent guide, keen, sure-footed and chivalrous too. If either of his companions lagged, he was back there, helping them like a reliable sheepdog. He took possession of Jilly's compass though had little need of Amanda's map. Down was down. That didn't seem much of a problem.

If anything, the mist had thinned and now and again the sun peeped through. Amanda's spirits soared and she felt like singing. She removed her jacket and rolled up her sleeves, raising her face to the unseen rays. An aroma of greenery, pine perhaps, came wafting into her nostrils. Despite the steady approach of winter, she imagined she detected an echo of spring.

Jilly's spirits were soaring too. Leaving the tower had been all it took. She felt like a prisoner on day release, paroled for good behaviour. Ahead of them Richard had suddenly stopped, was concentratedly studying the compass. Amanda tried her phone; there was still no signal.

Richard was pointing into the mist. "Down there," he said, "we should find the tarn."

All three narrowed their eyes and peered, but could not make out any details.

"We ought to have brought a picnic," said Jilly, who never went far without thinking of food.

"I do have my hip flask," said Richard, patting his pocket.

Laughing, they scrambled down fifty more yards while Jilly made jokes about having a swim. But when they arrived on the level ground, they could see no trace of water. Also, to their joint dismay, the mist was perceptibly starting to thicken again.

CHAPTER
FIFTEEN

It was growing colder and Dawn was tired. Mark was making her work too hard. She was plunged to the elbow in the rotting mass; the more she scooped, the deeper it seemed to be.

"What is this anyhow?" she asked with revulsion.

"A storm drain, I think," said Mark, who had now stopped work and was watching her idly while having a smoke. He offered her one but Dawn fiercely shook her head.

"Why do we need to clear it at all?" It didn't make sense since it wasn't their place. Why not just go back inside and relax by the fire?

Good question. "I'm not really sure," he said. The sun would be over the yardarm soon. It was, in any case, time to give it a rest. At least they'd be able to tell Amanda they had done something useful while she was gone. Mark's arm ached badly; he was feeling slightly light-headed.

"Hang on," said Dawn, reaching down with both hands to wrestle with something unseen at her feet. "This could be the basic cause of the blockage."

She twisted and turned, then took several steps back as a sudden plop caused her to stagger and lose her footing.

"Look what I've found!" she shouted with glee, handing Mark something disfigured with mud. A white toy rabbit with what had once been pink ears.

"I recognise that face," Mark exclaimed. "From the photos."

"I hate to say this," Richard proclaimed after they'd wandered around for a while, "but I think we may somehow have missed our path and be moving in circles."

"So what do you suggest we do now?" asked Amanda, pleased to have made her point.

"We don't have a whole lot of choices left," said Richard, still clutching the compass. "That way, I think."

Jilly was drooping. She wanted her lunch, either down here or back at the tower. Here would be preferable, though, in the circumstances. They had come so far and tried so hard she would hate to be forced to admit defeat. She kept on hoping the mist would clear and open up proper vistas. It was rapidly growing colder again. Amanda replaced her jacket and turned up the collar. The fragrance of greenery had dispersed, leaving just the smell of acrid mud.

"I don't suppose you brought chocolate," she asked.

"Sorry," said Jilly. "We ate it all last time."

Richard offered a swig from his flask which, after a pause, Amanda declined. This was certainly not the time nor the place to get tipsy.

"One swallow can't hurt." Richard demonstrated, then wiped the flask on his sleeve and passed it across.

"No," said Jilly. "I really daren't. Not stuck up here in this weather."

The mist was now rolling in again and the upward scramble would be that much harder to manage. The scree, in particular, seemed more treacherous than ever. Richard and Mark, on their previous descent, had encountered terrain far more dangerous than this; in total darkness, too. Small wonder that Mark had damaged his arm; it seemed incredible now that they'd made it at all. It would have taken just one false step for either of them to have plunged to his death.

"How did you know where we were?" Jilly asked, remembering that they'd not heard a thing till the two men banged on the door. She also remembered how scared she had been, assuming the owners had returned.

"We followed a distant light," Richard said. "It seemed like a friendly welcoming star, a beacon which led us eventually to the pele tower."

Amanda stared. That had been their experience, too.

They had ditched the plane on a snow-covered plateau. "I can't tell you how lucky we were," Richard said. In truth, as a lawyer, he had from the start been doubtful about the whole expedition. Apart from being illicit, it had put both their lives at risk. "It's amazing we didn't crash," he went on. "It was sheer bloody luck that a break in the cloud occurred when we'd lost our bearings and needed fuel."

"Who was the pilot?" Amanda asked.

Richard smiled. He was not that dumb. And this woman had more intelligence than was healthy. "You know I can't tell you that," he said with a grin.

So the odds were it had been Mark, Amanda supposed. He was the one with the daredevil eyes. In an earlier generation he would have been a fighter pilot. It all fitted nicely, wartime heroes being re-incarnated as hedge-fund boys. Life was repeating itself again. She remembered the constantly striking clock. The odds were, Lucian would show up at any moment.

As it grew darker it also grew cold. Jilly regretted not bringing her gloves which somehow she had managed to leave on the table.

"Are you sure we are on the right path?" she asked Richard.

"So it would appear," he said, now reduced to studying Amanda's map. "Though we do seem to have managed to miss the tarn." He looked around. "But," he added on a brighter note. "According to this there's a farm somewhere near." They both crowded round while he pointed it out on the map.

"Goody," said Jilly. She liked that idea. They had missed their lunch but high tea would do. She envisaged a rosy-cheeked farmer's wife who would sit them down by a blazing fire and serve up home-baked scones with lashings of cream.

The woman would have a working phone and a husband with an SUV who would whisk them down to the lakeside hotel they had left three days before. The hotel would then send transport to pick up the others.

They all speeded up with the same renewed hope as, in the distance, they spotted a light below them.

"Hurrah," shouted Richard. "We're almost there." Jilly's unspoken fantasy was obviously proving infectious.

They were so overjoyed that they started to sing as they scrambled down, using their hands to maintain their balance. Amanda was thinking again about Max and how, with luck, she might see him soon, while Jilly would get on to Derek to change her appointment.

"There's somebody coming," Richard said. He could see the faint gleam of a pocket torch, and footsteps were audible moving steadily towards them. Somebody from the farm, perhaps, with a tractor handily parked nearby. Jilly was in the mood to give him a hug, she was so relieved.

The footsteps grew closer. They all three relaxed. Amanda desperately needed to pee.

"Greetings," called Lucian's voice from the mist. "I thought perhaps it was you."

CHAPTER
SIXTEEN

Mark had been right: it was there in the photos, a white toy rabbit with a large pink bow, staring out of its black bead eyes from under the little girl's arm. Dawn washed it carefully and left it to soak; with luck, once it dried it would soon fluff up. The child need never know it had ever been lost. So what was it doing rammed down a drain? She appealed to Mark and Angus, who shrugged.

"Stuff gets lost," said Mark. "It is no big deal."

But the child must surely have missed her toy, so special that it appeared in most of the pictures. The playroom upstairs was immaculate, with all the dolls lined up in neat rows. Dawn, who had not had a childhood like that, studied each family group with care. Till now she had given them only a glance. Each one was picture perfect. The four of them had identical smiles, father and mother as well as both kids. Dawn was hazy on children's ages but guessed these two to be something like seven and nine. A girl and a boy, quite clearly siblings. There was also a cute Jack Russell terrier to complete the family group.

So how was it possible they had just gone, leaving behind an unfinished meal and a fire still burning, as well as the lights all on? Their luggage had been half packed on the bed, which made it appear they had been disturbed. They'd been missing now for several days, leaving a freezer loaded with food which indicated they must have meant to come back. But then she remembered that the phone did not work and the TV cable had been severed. No matter what Angus and Mark might say, something pretty unnerving must have gone on.

It wasn't Dawn's normal nature to care. She had always been seriously into herself, but her weird experience the previous night had shaken her more than she showed. She requested Mark to check out the phone and try to find out why it wasn't working. The altitude alone should not affect it.

But Mark was now settled with a book, a paper-back thriller he had found on a shelf, and had poured himself a pre-lunch gin and tonic. He was feeling peckish and checked his watch. It was thoughtless of Jilly to stay out so long. She might, at least, have fixed them lunch before taking off for the day. When it came to it, women were all much the same, fundamentally not to be trusted.

"How are you in the cooking department?" he casually asked when Dawn blew in.

She froze him out with an arctic stare. What did he think she was, a frigging waitress? Dawn had never been near a stove, subsisted largely on cheap fast food with bouts of bulimia in between to ensure she maintained her stick figure. If he wanted lunch, he could get it himself or else ask Angus, who was useless too. She told him sharply to put down his drink and find out what she wanted to know. She wasn't messing about, was truly concerned.

Mark sighed and stretched but did as she bade him. There was clearly no peace for the wicked, he said. He knocked back his drink and went off to check the obvious places where telephones are connected.

"And while you're at it," snapped Dawn, "you can look for the fuse box."

"Yes, ma'am," said Mark with an innocent smile. She was far more fun when he wound her up. Not his type, not in any way, but beneath the vapid exterior a tigress snarled.

At first he just wandered round the house, but then he put on his shoes and went out to do some more serious scouting. Dawn quickly poured herself a gin and tonic and knocked it back.

He found it almost immediately. The line had been cut just before it entered the house. No one had noticed before because of the bushes and the weather conditions. Dawn was right: there was something fairly strange going on in this place.

"Suppose," Angus said, "we have it all wrong and misread the signals right from the start. Perhaps the owners have not been here since the summer. Or even longer."

"A winter tenant?"

"Not even that." Angus had Mark's full attention now. "There might have been burglars, or even worse, who Amanda and Jilly just stumbled upon."

"Causing them to leave in a hurry?" said Mark.

"Exactly," said Angus. It seemed pretty obvious to him.

Mark considered. There had been no car, at least not one visible at the time. Nor had they heard an engine starting up. In any case, no vehicle could have possibly come up the mountain this far since all there was was a very narrow path.

"It would have to have been parked some distance away," said Angus. "And then they slipped away when the girls arrived, forced to abandon their spoils."

"So where are the spoils?"

"Who can say?" said Angus. They had seen no obvious signs of disturbance apart from the fact that the door had been left unlocked. Only the suitcase on the bed and the pile of neatly pressed clothes beside it. Which, come to think of it, could well have been a burglary in progress.

"Without knowing what was here," said Mark, "we can't really check if there's anything gone."

"So what we need to do now," said Angus, "is try to contact the owners."

Dawn reappeared and Mark foraged for lunch, just biscuits and cheese and stuff from the fridge. Since the power had failed, they should eat it all up, he said. The others had now been gone quite a while. He wondered what could be keeping them. The news could surely only be good or else they'd have been back sooner. Dawn seemed quieter today and subdued, no longer endlessly sniping at Angus. As a couple they could not be more mismatched, with nothing obvious between them but sex. Mark knew more about life and love than the two of them put together.

It was, however, no business of his as long as she kept away from him. He briefly filled her in on their latest theory.

"You're saying nothing weird happened at all?" She sat there open-mouthed, which was not attractive. "That Amanda and Jilly arrived just in time to prevent a burglary taking place?"

"Something like that." It fitted the facts and also helped put them all in the clear. If they'd interrupted some felony, the owners could only be grateful.

"Which accounts for the phone and the TV cable." But not for the current failure of power, though that was something that happened a lot in high places.

"I think this calls for another drink," said Mark, well-pleased with himself. Locating the owners should not prove too hard. Though they'd been reluctant to snoop, they should do so now. The possibility of a break-in and the need to inform the owners was reason enough. It ought not be hard to track them down if they had some idea where to look. Lucian, if they could find him, must know who they were. All they had done in their brief stay here was confine themselves to the children's rooms, plunder the freezer and drink their way through some truly excellent wines. Nothing they'd taken could not be replaced and all of them had been meticulous guests. They cleaned the bathrooms and tidied up after themselves, even straightened their bunks.

"We must try to find Lucian," Angus said. "And ask him what to do next."

It was well after dark when the others returned, very subdued, their high spirits crushed. They also seemed slightly evasive about where they'd been. The surprise was that they had Lucian in tow. Angus and Mark exchanged a glance. He had found them lost in the mist, he explained, and led them back by the most direct route. He seemed amused that they kept on losing their way.

As before, he was lightly clad, this time in a fashionable jacket and cords, and was wearing shoes in place of hiking boots. He glanced around at the candlelit room which had a distinctly festive look.

"The fuses went," said Mark. "Do you know where the box is?"

"The cellar, I'd guess," said Lucian without much interest.

"Well, I'm not going down there tonight," said Mark. The thought of it curled his toes.

Lucian offered the use of his torch which Angus was pleased to accept. They had only not interfered till now since they weren't supposed to be here at all. Lucian seemed to understand, though also felt that Mark might be over-reacting.

"Do you know how to reach them?" asked Angus, who seemed to recall having asked that before.

"I am sure they'll be back," said Lucian, "when they're ready."

"Where is it you actually live?" demanded Amanda, thoroughly sick of playing the cat and mouse game. She could not understand what the mystery was. They were only here from necessity and would be gone as soon as the weather started to clear. All they wanted to know was the whereabouts of the owners.

"My home," said Lucian, slightly obscurely, "is where my ancient forebears lie. On Scafell Pike and the Mickledore Col. Their blood was shed on this soil for generations."

"But this place?" The pele tower.

Lucian smiled. "Is shelter for all when they need it," he said. He seemed to prefer to leave it at that, so they let the subject lie.

"So where did you find the rabbit?" asked Jilly, changing the subject as fast as she could. It was balanced now on the Aga to dry, its furry satin-lined ears restored to perfection.

"Stuffed down an outside drain," said Dawn who, for some elusive reason, now seemed angry.

CHAPTER
SEVENTEEN

Last thing that night, before turning in, they had a look round for possible clues as to how they might get in touch with the legal owners. There was no desk, or at least none they could find, though several of the tables had drawers, revealing only the usual household clutter of many years. Pruning scissors, a ball of twine, a child's wax crayons, a bunch of spare keys, plus the business cards of a garage and a butcher in Keswick. They could ring the garage if they had a phone (or the butcher should they run out of meat) but no one was currently in the mood to make any jokes about that. With the onset of darkness their spirits had spiralled downwards.

"I wonder if there's a safe," said Mark. Tomorrow he'd look for the fuse box too, though he doubted it would be located in the cellar. But a safe was different, something you'd want to hide.

"Master bedroom," said smartass Amanda, presuming as always that she was right. Apart from using the en suite bathroom, they had not set foot in there since they first arrived.

Together, they all trooped up the stairs, candles in hand like the previous night. They were getting used to the constant dark though preferred to move around as a pack. You never quite knew what was hovering outside your vision. They positioned their candles round the room then divided the space for a thorough search. There didn't seem to be a safe, so starting with the bedside tables they went through everything very fast. Nothing of any note emerged: Wordsworth's poems, a box of tissues, a miniature torch, the usual bedroom stuff. Richard, who'd hoped for something more (a Rampant Rabbit at the very least) quickly called off the search. They were getting nowhere. He did, however, appropriate the torch for future use.

So where else would one look for a safe? Somewhere, well, *safe*. The cellar perhaps, though none of them felt like going down there tonight. Apart from the fact that they didn't have keys, the one thing all of them yearned for was bed. Three of them had been walking all day while the others cleared out drains and did stuff in the house. Tomorrow was Thursday. They'd have been here five days. The situation was past a joke. They would also make a concerted effort to find that elusive fuse box.

Amanda dreamt about Max that night, a dream so vivid it woke her up. It seemed so real, for a second she thought he had been there. Her heart was pounding; her palms were damp. Jilly, she sensed, was still fast asleep. She longed to be able to talk to her but hesitated to wake her, so instead lay silently in the darkness, fretting.

By now they had to know she was gone. Head office would have called the hotel and found out that she had never checked out, at which point they'd make enquiries. The police would quickly locate her car, left in the car park at Seathwaite Farm, after which they would surely have mounted a proper search. It wasn't just her, it was Jilly as well, who, apart from her colleagues at the Pru, had a steady boyfriend who must be sick with worry. Amanda was single, but Jilly had mentioned a wedding. Her fiancé wouldn't just let her disappear without raising some sort of hue and cry. For all she knew, there were masses of them out there searching even now.

Richard and Mark had abandoned their plane, which must also be known to somebody somewhere. They were both extremely high profile and Reykjavik-bound. Why had no one come looking for them, at the very least the financial squad? People didn't just disappear without an official inquiry. And what about Angus, the clothing tycoon? Dawn might not matter but he was a bit of a big shot. So where were the hordes of rescuers? If they had a working radio they would, at least, know if they were being looked for. And if the weather should clear, they could light a bonfire.

She lay in the darkness and thought about Max and the violent rage he'd provoked in her. This time he had overstepped the mark; she knew she could never forgive him. But she needed to get back home very soon; too much still remained unresolved. The very least she needed to know was if he were still alive.

"Are you awake?" asked a tiny voice: Jilly, sounding too scared to speak.

"I am," said Amanda. "I just didn't want to disturb you."

"May I light a candle?"

"Please do," said Amanda, relieved there was somebody here with whom she could talk.

Jilly was wearing her underwear, minuscule briefs and a thermal vest, and had bunched the duvet up round her like an igloo. She was tired of washing her undies each night; her hygiene standards were starting to slip. The only thing she cared about now was getting out of this place.

"Why aren't they looking for us?" she asked, her voice reduced to a tearful whine. Just like Amanda, she had been reviewing the options.

Now she would miss her doctor's appointment, though Derek still did not know about that. They had so much longed to have children together, she didn't know how she would tell him. It could mean the end of their most cherished dreams, in which case how could she marry him? The darker fear she shoved to the back of her mind.

"Do you have family?" she asked. She still knew very little about Amanda.

"No," said Amanda, an only child who'd been orphaned since her twenties.

Jilly had parents and brothers and sisters as well as Derek, which made it odder that no one so far appeared to be coming to find her. Didn't they care? She had always assumed they did.

"They are probably circling above us right now." The story must surely have hit the news. Even Max, despite his numerous faults, was bound to be some-what concerned.

Amanda, frustrated just lying there, no longer felt in control of her life. She threw back the covers and got out of bed, climbing into yesterday's clothes.

"Come on," she said. "Let's go downstairs and make an early start."

As the dawn slowly broke, at first it appeared that the mist had magically cleared in the night. They stood at the window and studied the sky, which was strewn with a tracery of stars. Jilly was feeling less tearful now, having commandeered one of the owner's shirts which enveloped her tiny frame and looked rather fetching.

"I don't imagine he'll mind," she said. She would launder it carefully before she left and leave a note to thank him for its loan.

"I doubt he will even know," said Amanda grimly.

Since the lights still weren't working, they lit all the candles and built up the fire with the last of the logs. Then Jilly was struck by a terrible thought: what if the freezer was off? But the food was as solidly frozen as when they arrived. "It must be a separate circuit," she said. Whoever had restored the house had done a first-rate job.

"I wonder if they are here all year round." Amanda could think of few things worse.

"It might be all right in the summer," said Jilly. "Providing you had a car somewhere."

"Also a phone and a TV that worked." Monastic living was not for her. "And a bunch of kids and a nanny and gardeners too."

Which was what the current incumbents had. The white toy rabbit was proof of that. Jilly pressed it against her face and found it now soft and sweet-smelling. She longed for a baby, but now no more. She must put that particular dream on hold until she was home and could have a frank talk with the doctor.

Seeing the rabbit reminded Amanda. What was it doing stuffed into a drain? It was hardly a place for a toy to turn up, especially not a cherished one as this rabbit apparently was.

"You would think she'd have taken it with her," she said.

And the dog. "What happened to him?" Amanda was suddenly gripped with alarm. He must have gone too; they would not have left him behind. He was very much part of the family group. His water bowl was in the porch and his lead still hung behind the kitchen door.

Something was nagging in her brain, some minute detail that wasn't quite right. In a minute she'd think what it was. It made her uneasy.

CHAPTER
EIGHTEEN

The door to the cellar turned out to be locked, as so many doors in the tower were, though the keys must surely be kept in an obvious place. They checked the spares they had found in the drawer but none of them fitted the ancient lock which was wrought of iron as old as the studs adorning the massive front door. Depending, of course, what was kept down there, it was likely the key would be in the owner's possession. But, surely, somewhere there should be a spare. Amanda considered it inefficient to have moseyed off without leaving one out. Except, of course, they were not supposed to be here, which she kept forgetting. She wondered what else could be done about fixing the fuses.

"Just leave them," said Richard, who no longer cared. They would all be out of here very soon and, in the meantime, could cope with just candles and firelight.

Yet the situation remained the same. They were stuck here, praying the weather would change. The freezer worked but they had no lights, no car, no radio nor TV, not even a single cellphone with a signal. Thanks to the Aga, they did still have heat and hot water. They had food in the freezer and plenty of wine, though they needed more logs to replace what they'd used. The bunks were okay, if a trifle cramped, but none of these orphans in the storm was complaining. As way stations went, this one still scored very high points.

Best of all, they got on as a group. Amanda and Jilly had now become friends, thrown together by circumstance but also because they shared a mutual employer. At least for now; Amanda kept shtum about the bad news she'd been meant to impart. Which, since she had never made it back, presumably was still unknown by the staff unless, in her absence, she had been overridden. But now it would simply be cruel to upset Jilly further.

Richard and Mark also rubbed along well, having known each other most of their lives and working together now on Canary Wharf. Despite Mark's injury, they laughed a lot and did not appear to mind sharing a room. It was like being back on cricket tour, Richard explained.

Things had changed between Angus and Dawn, though Angus had solved the initial problem by dragging a mattress into the playroom and setting up camp on his own. Dawn wasn't sleeping well, he explained. It was only fair she should have some space. No one was fooled but they managed to keep their mouths shut. It wasn't their business what went on. The thing that mattered was that they all rubbed along. They were six quite different individuals, thrown together by circumstance and making a very good shot at living together.

112

The sky, which had started off clear and bright, was rapidly clouding over again. Jilly was worried. They seemed to be back to square one. If they didn't have access to the cellar, how would they fix the busted fuse? Or find out the whereabouts of the owner? It was altogether too much for her. Derek might well be imagining things, even that she had changed her mind and dropped him. Recently, due to her unspoken dread, she had been a little offhand with him and the poor boy had never had much of an ego to speak of.

Amanda was made of far sterner stuff. She had got where she had through determination and refusal to compromise. There were six of them stuck here, half of them men. If necessary they would wrestle the door off its hinges. She refused to be defeated by minor hiccups.

"You'll be lucky," Richard said. He had limped a little when he came down: yesterday's mammoth hike had taken its toll. Also, he hadn't been sleeping well because of Mark and his damaged arm. When Richard had examined it, he hadn't at all liked how it looked. Instead of healing, the gash was angry and swollen.

"I think he may have a temperature, too," he said, which was even more alarming, but they couldn't find a thermometer to check.

There was no first aid box that they could see, nor even aspirin which might have helped. Neither Amanda nor Jilly had anything with them. Dawn might well; she did not travel light. But Angus, when he appeared, said she was still sleeping, as far as he knew. "I haven't heard a sound, and it's not like her to get up till she has to." Which was how they found out he had altered his sleeping arrangements. Looks were exchanged and eyebrows raised, though none of them was very surprised. Dawn had been on Angus's case since the moment they first arrived.

Amanda explained her plan to the men, that they pick the lock of the cellar door or, failing that, batter it down. It should not be too hard.

Richard whistled. "Have you looked at it? It's made of solid oak, like the other doors."

"Built to last, as these places were. I would guess it's around six hundred years old." Angus knew what he was talking about; his hobby was architecture.

"Then how are we going to fix the fuse?" asked Amanda, slightly nonplussed.

"I doubt we can," said Richard calmly, slicing stale bread to make himself toast. He rather preferred things as they were, found candlelight very restful. He wasn't a reader so did not need bright light, and the flicker of flames took the edge off the place, making the prison-like rooms more user-friendly.

"What are the plans for today?" he asked. Nothing would get him back on that trail and Mark was not remotely up to it either. He studied the sky, which was now overcast. "I hate to be the one to say it," he said, "but it looks like snow."

"How can you tell through the mist?" Jilly asked, having lived in the Midlands the whole of her life.

Richard told her he was an expert skier.

"So," said Amanda, "if we had skis we could send you down to the valley for help?"

"Indeed," said Richard, "though you'd have to come too to stop me scarpering off."

He found this amusing; Amanda did not. Her positive mood was deteriorating. Thwarted of her plan, she became very restless. There had to be something constructive to do, if only to stop herself falling apart. "Maybe we should look again and see what else we can find."

Lucian seemed to have slipped away. He was never there when they needed him. Amanda felt he was toying with their emotions. The least they could do was look for him. She felt no obligation any more. All he had ever done for them was lead them back to this prison.

Richard's forecast turned out to be right and now fat snowflakes were fluttering down.

"Damn," said Angus. "The very last thing we needed."

He was desperate to get out of here. The Dawn affair had been ill-conceived and now he was heartily sick of her petulant whining. She saw herself as a femme fatale when all she was was a scrawny kid with an eye to the main chance, which in her case meant seducing the boss. He couldn't now think what he'd seen in her. Devoid of the slap she was nothing at all, though deluded herself that she looked like Victoria Beckham. Her conversation was pitiful. She soaked herself in celeb magazines and was mainly concerned with the private lives of pop stars. At least they were safely holed up now, the one good thing to have come out of this. Had the weather not worsened and they'd made it back, the odds were he might have been saddled with her for life.

If they'd reached his house on the scheduled night and confronted Molly with what had occurred, he might well have found there was no going back, that his marriage was scuppered for ever. Not just his marriage, the business too, for Molly's input was more than was known. Faced with divorce, he would not be as rich as Dawn now perceived him to be.

As it was, it seemed that someone up there was keeping a friendly eye on his life, for which Angus knew he would be eternally grateful. "Thanks, mate," he said, with a nod to the sky. Although he didn't believe in such things, he had a sudden feeling of being protected.

"Come on," said Amanda, "let's stretch our legs." It was snowing hard but she just couldn't rest and badly needed to get away from this claustrophobic interior.

Jilly, however, had settled in. The fire was seductive and what was the point? Her life was falling apart around her though she wasn't about to face up to that now. The least she could do was stay here in the warm.

CHAPTER
NINETEEN

There was no sign of Dawn who had stayed in bed, still shaken, no doubt, by her recent trauma. Also, perhaps, by the fact that Angus had dumped her. Morale all round was at a low ebb; Mark had also stayed upstairs in his room. Conditions were going from bad to worse; this was day five of their forced incarceration. Amanda paced the living room. Jilly and Angus were slumped by the fire while Richard was out in the woodshed, chopping more logs. He had volunteered as he needed the exercise, or so he had said. For all they knew he might be whittling skis for a rapid getaway. Not that Amanda would blame him for that. She'd be off like a shot herself if she had the means.

The light was poor, but anyway there was little to read apart from children's books. Wordsworth's poems were not to her taste and even Jilly, for once, seemed out of sorts. The food supplies were diminishing fast and soon even the booze would be running out. There were big decisions to be made though she still wasn't sure of the answers. Except that their top priority had to be getting away from this place.

Amanda took a grip on herself. Though reluctant now to take the lead, somebody had to do it and no one was offering. The men surprised her with their lethargy. Mark was accustomed to taking risks while Angus ran his own company and Richard was an extremely high-flying lawyer. Even Jilly was no kind of slouch when it came to selling insurance on the high street. And yet they seemed to be caving in under pressure. Her thoughts, inevitably, turned to Max. He, without question, would know how to galvanise them.

She had been with Max, on and off, for years though had never actually formalised things, mainly because he was not legally free; there was a wife. It was due entirely to his default. Whenever things seemed to be starting to gel, he always rocked the boat with his bad behaviour. Mostly it was other women. They swarmed round him like rapacious flies and he was too intrinsically vain to swat them. Like many men, as Amanda well knew, he loved to play the role of sexual magnet. If she ever objected and made a scene, he taunted her with her jealousy. He saw nothing wrong in playing the field, especially since they had no binding commitment.

Amanda writhed but gritted her teeth, refusing to show him how much she cared. Two could play at the flirting game so then she would have a fling of her own, word of which would get back to him, as she intended. Mainly they worked out their anger in bed, one of the reasons Max still fooled around. It gave him the upper hand which he found a great turn-on. But Amanda was losing her stamina, was sick of the juvenile games he played. She'd be forty in a couple of years and her chances of settling down were fast decreasing. Max could go on for as long as he liked, dallying to his heart's content without the relentless ticking of a biological clock.

In the office, though, they worked well as a team, their competitiveness bringing out the best in each other. He had sent her to do his dirty work and she had not flinched at taking it on, though the final row on the night she left had literally pushed him over the edge. That was why now she was so keyed up and anxious to find out what had happened. He must be all right or else she would know; some inner instinct would notify her. Max was a habit Amanda could never give up. Though she did know one thing; if he were here he would rapidly get this group on its feet and sorted.

She looked at Jilly, warming her toes, and envied her unambitious lifestyle. She knew what she wanted, had found the right man and was planning to marry before her thirtieth birthday. She had not said what the boyfriend did but Amanda imagined him as quite a jock. Something, perhaps, in the building trade, dependable and steady. Which might be all very well for some though not for Amanda who wanted more. Happy endings, despite her angst, made her feel claustrophobic. It was something to do with the end of the chase, with no longer having the run of the field. Her attention flickered across to Angus, idly doing a crossword puzzle he must have picked up somewhere in the tower.

He was a man who was more her type, strong, successful and self-made, with a clothing empire internationally known. She had asked him how he could stand it here without any contact with his team.

He had shrugged and said he was rather enjoying the break. In fact, he was glad to be off the scene until he had sorted the Dawn thing out. She had been an aberration he now regretted. It was symptomatic of this stage in his life; he was early fifties, prosperous and fulfilled. Perhaps not as wealthy as Dawn assumed but enough to be able to slack off a bit, with his kids off his hands and a wife with her own pursuits. They were very well matched and got on well but Angus had craved something more.

Watching Amanda pace the room, intelligent, bossy and highly strung, Angus wondered what she would be like in bed. Like a sergeant major would be his guess but none the less exciting for that. He handed it to her, she still looked good despite the fact that she couldn't be far off forty. Jilly was sweet, with an innocent charm, but not remotely in Angus's league. Give her a couple of years and some kids and she'd lose what allure she still had. Rather like Molly, in fact.

Dawn appeared, looking pale and wan. He couldn't think now what he'd seen in her. She had not even bothered to comb her hair and looked the urchin she was. He had rapidly tired of her coltish cuteness, the more so when the nagging set in. He was glad to have pulled out when he had before things got complicated. Now she had turned her attention to Mark. Good luck to them both; Angus could not have cared less.

The thing that was occupying him now was finding a way to get out of this mess. Not having a workable phone was extremely frustrating. He had no idea where he'd left the car, somewhere down there on the mist-bound fells, in front of a padlocked gate at the end of a cart track. It would almost be funny if it weren't so damned annoying.

Amanda joined the two by the fire since there wasn't anything else she could do. Outside the weather was taking a turn for the worse. The snow was now blowing as thick as the mist and the fire would very soon need more logs. That, however, was Richard's preserve since he had adopted the woodcutter role. Amanda was about to speak when the door burst open.

Richard, wild-eyed, was standing there, clutching his sharpened axe to his chest, his face as white as the snow in his hair, his eyes almost bolting out of his head in sheer horror.

"What?" asked Amanda, back on her feet, alarmed by his obviously frenzied state.

Richard laid down the axe and frantically beckoned.

CHAPTER
TWENTY

"Not you," said Richard. "Just Angus, please." He was inarticulate. All of them froze. The heavy oak door crashed shut in a volley of wind. It was obvious it was no kind of joke; Richard was visibly palpitating with shock.

"What is it?" Amanda cried in alarm, appalled by his haunted expression.

Richard ignored her. "Just Angus," he said again. "I have something to show you."

He led the way wordlessly back down the path to the rear of the tower where the woodshed was. Till now they had only used logs from the porch so none of them, other than Richard, had ever been here. The shed stood alone in a cluster of trees. It was stoutly constructed of hand-cut wood with a shingled roof and a wide low-raftered ceiling. The interior had an attractive smell of fresh pine. An ideal place, Angus immediately thought, for the man of the house to escape from family chaos. He glanced around in appreciation. There were wicker baskets containing logs plus, pegged to the wall, an array of tools, some of them lethal-looking. Honeycomb shelves across one wall contained all manner of useful things, screws and bolts and hinges and gardening tools. A handyman's paradise, somewhere to go when you needed space for serious contemplation.

Richard, however, ignored all this. He swiftly crossed to the furthermost corner where a jumble of old cardboard boxes was loosely stacked. Without another word he simply pointed.

Angus had thought to bring the torch and now focused it upon the spot, momentarily uncomprehending. Then he looked more closely and drew in a breath of horrified disbelief.

The box contained a triangular head, tan and white with intelligent eyes, now glazed over and staring into nothing. There were V-shaped ears and a shortish black snout. It was the pampered face of a much-loved pet, the Jack Russell that appeared in the family photos. Gorge rising, Angus stared into the box, shifting the beam to examine every angle. The neck ended cleanly beneath the throat in a collar of thick dried blood.

"Jesus Christ," he exclaimed in horror. No wonder Richard seemed so distraught. "Who in the world would do something like this? Only a bloodthirsty lunatic." And what, he wondered, had happened to the rest of the sad carcass?

Richard, speechless, tried hard not to gag. He could now detect the aroma of rancid blood. The fur, when Angus gingerly touched it, was matted and cold which was no surprise. It must have been here since before they arrived though the eyes still held a dull gleam that seemed almost reproachful.

The two men stood there stupefied. It had to be more than an accident. The head had been removed with a surgeon's sure touch.

"What do we tell the others?" asked Richard.

Angus pondered. Certainly not the truth.

They passed it off as a rodent's nest that Richard had happened to stumble upon. Typical townie, Angus said. Mark, who along with Dawn was now down, laughed and called Richard a sissy. Jilly and Dawn both accepted this though Amanda paused just a fraction too long. She wasn't a fool. There was something up. She would check it out with them later.

"We need to get out of here right away," said Richard once they were on their own. Mark still felt the need to lie down and Richard was keen to talk. This morning's incident with the dog had upset him more than he cared to show. Something intrinsically evil had happened here and not long ago. It was useless expecting the weather to change. In the time they'd been here it had only grown worse. It was now November and might not improve until spring.

"What master plan do you have in mind?" asked Mark, his voice now reduced to a virtual whisper. He knew he was unlikely to leave without help. Half his body was racked with pain; his injuries must have been worse than he realised. He was playing it down for fear of alarming the women. The crucial thing was to move the plane before it became too frozen in. The future of both their careers lay up on that plateau.

124

But the mist was as thick as a blanket now and swirling like a malevolent cloud. Mark could swear it was growing worse and showed little sign of abating. Even if they manoeuvred the slope, they would stand little chance of taking off. They were stuck here, like it or not, till a break in the weather. He refused to be parted from the plane, though the way he felt now he feared the worst. If Richard had only brought his skis, he might very well have slalomed down to the valley.

Having been close friends since their earliest years, Richard and Mark had a special bond. Their mutual trust was based on shared education. They trusted each other, as Englishmen do, especially those of a certain class. Their word was their honour was what they had always been taught. The collapse of the City affected them both, Mark with his hedge-fund and Richard with his tax expertise. Both had been earning colossal sums and flying as close to the wind as they dared but Mark was a chancer and Richard integrally honest. He had to be; it was what he did, keeping his eye on his clients' affairs and ensuring they stayed on the right side of the law as far as they could. He knew which loopholes were okay to plug and which tax havens it paid to avoid. He had earned his reputation by playing safe.

On the other hand, Mark could not be controlled, was far too reckless for his own good, still the wild schoolboy at heart who had risked expulsion. He gambled hard, with his life and his luck, but always succeeded in staying on top, or had done until this latest turn in events. Things were very precarious now, with fortunes being lost overnight, and Mark was risking his whole career with this daredevil trip to Iceland. If he pulled it off and secured the deal he would more than quadruple his current assets. If, however, he misplayed his hand, he was likely to lose the lot.

He had given Richard the chance to withdraw, to save his good name by pulling out now, but schoolboy loyalty remains second to none. He was sworn to counsel, not undermine, his friend. Fiscal timing was crucial here. They were in it already up to their necks and there now wasn't very much space left for manoeuvre. They could still withdraw, as he thought they should, but the chances of convincing Mark were nil. If they meant to act, they must do so now, but Richard wasn't convinced Mark still had the strength.

The three women huddled around the fire were shaken by what they had just observed.

"Richard looks dreadful," Jilly said, "as if he has had a bad shock."

"And Mark is declining," Amanda said, more worried than she cared to show. It was obvious now that he needed medical help.

Even Angus was not up to scratch. Something appeared to be bothering him too. It just would not do to have all the men fall apart.

"We need a plan," said Amanda firmly, ready as always to take command. It was how she had reached head office in record time. There was no need for her to go out to the shed. Rodents were all part of country life and, unless they invaded indoors, of no relevance. Her own father, a doctor, had been petrified of spiders.

The only thing that mattered now was finding a way to get out of this place. They must pool their brains and come up with a workable plan. The mist was still dense and growing worse so that, even at three, it was almost dark. Tomorrow was Friday, the end of the week. Amanda could not believe they had still not been missed. In the absence of a Verey light, though, she could think of no way to signal their presence here. Even a bonfire would scarcely be seen in this weather.

Jilly, resigned to her missed appointment, decided to put the whole matter on hold to worry about at a future date when life had returned to normal. A minor gynaecological blip was nothing to what they were going through now. The situation was grave indeed with all three men showing signs of cracking up. Two had even gone to lie down; just how feeble was that?

"Who's for tea?" asked Amanda briskly in a valiant effort to rally the troops. They must not lose heart at this stage or they would not survive.

CHAPTER
TWENTY-ONE

Amanda's first thought was Lucian Demort. He knew the terrain and how everything worked though, for whatever reason, remained elusive. She now determined to seek him out and insist he abandon his stupid mind-games. Philosophy was all very well but not in such circumstances. What they needed was a workable plan and top of her list was the stranded plane which must, it had just occurred to her, have a wireless connection on board. She cursed herself for this oversight but Richard and Mark should have thought of it at the start. It underlined Amanda's belief that men, on the whole, were inept. Lucian might help them navigate the dangerous climb between here and the top. He seemed to be conversant with many short cuts.

Mark was in no state to climb but Amanda was willing to give it a go as long as she had backup from Richard and Angus.

"You can't go risking your life on those rocks." Jilly was adamant about that, recalling how treacherous it had been negotiating the lower scree and how very close they both had come to sliding into the ravine. Luck alone had saved them then. "To start with, you don't have appropriate gear." Fell-walking boots would not be sturdy enough. Both Richard and Mark wore flying jackets and heavy duty aviator boots. Amanda had only jeans and a weatherproof jacket.

Perhaps there was suitable gear in the house. Unlikely; from the photographs all they were was an average family with youngish kids and a dog. Why they would want to live here at all was something Jilly did not understand, but they showed little sign, from the stuff in their rooms, of leading an outdoor life. There were rainproof jackets and wellington boots arrayed in the cloakroom off the main hall as well as the dungarees Dawn had found already. Nothing beyond that but regular clothes, cotton and denim, just holiday stuff. Children that young were not strong enough to do any serious climbing.

"Let the men risk their lives, if they want, but don't even think about going with them," said Jilly, who was resolute when she put down her foot.

But Mark was undoubtedly out of it while Angus had only his Savile Row suit; not even walking shoes since he'd not meant to be here. He had only shot up to Carlisle for a working weekend.

"So let Richard do the climb on his own." He'd already established himself as an all-round sportsman.

Too dangerous, though, Amanda felt. He might be handy at wielding an axe but had flipped when having to deal with a simple rat's nest. Besides, it was not up to her to suggest that he even consider risking his life. Only a madman would, in this mist, attempt such a foolhardy mission. It was up to Richard to volunteer without any undue pressure from her. In the meantime she'd try to come up with some other solution.

"We could light a huge bonfire on the hill." Which did make sense although not in this mist. Apart from anything else, all planes had been grounded.

"Or else," said Amanda, who would not give up, "we could have another shot at reaching the farm."

Tomorrow perhaps; it was too late now. And maybe by then the mist might have thinned.

"You can definitely count me out," said Dawn who, apart from anything else, had no suitable footwear.

"So if we girls go," said Amanda drily, "you won't mind being alone with those spineless men?" Stupid question; of course she would not. They all knew she had the hots for Mark and would leap at the chance of being his angel of mercy. Mark might not see it in quite that light, though, even unwell, he could fend for himself. Amanda suppressed a grin. Thank goodness for Angus.

Angus had lately come into his own having shed his initial slight stuffiness. Being a business tycoon must have that effect. He was quite attractive for an older man though Amanda disapproved of his choice of girlfriend. But, since he now appeared bored with her, he had opened himself to the rest of the group and was showing his other side as a man of action. He lacked the requisite outdoor clothes but was more than up for a rugged hike. His motivational drive, like Amanda's, was to get back to London.

"Count me in," he said and went off to look for appropriate gear.

★ ★ ★

130

Amanda had still not quite worked out precisely what about Lucian scared her. He seemed such a mellow and charming man, yet faced with straight questions was inclined to fob her off. She felt he was not being honest with her but had not yet figured his motivation. She had tried, more than once, to confront him again but not found him easy to corner. The library, with its fine stained glass, was just a room she had chanced upon. On subsequent visits the door had always been locked.

Tonight, however, she would seek him out and request assistance in getting away. They all had essential business that must be resumed. She was not convinced by his monk-like life. He must surely have access to a phone. No one could live in a place this remote and be entirely cut off. People out there must be looking for them; her mind automatically flew back to Max. She regretted now having thrown her drink but did not intend to apologise. After the way he'd behaved, he'd had it coming. Nevertheless, she was keen to find out how he was.

Angus, accustomed to being obeyed, was also floundering without a phone and was back outside in a vain attempt to pick up a mobile signal. He was worrying, too, about his car, a brand new Daimler which somehow he'd managed to lose. He would pay whatever it took for alternative transport. A helicopter or a pony and trap, or even a glider would do, provided it got him back to civilisation. Amanda and Jilly were lively and fun and coping tremendously well with their plight. While Dawn seemed in a perpetual sulk, the others were trying to fix things. He had heard them planning another attempt to leave on foot the following day. Equipped with the right footwear he would join them.

He switched off his mobile, which still would not work, and went disconsolately into the house. Jilly was back in the kitchen, cooking. Amanda was not around.

It was worth one more try. She would button her lip and try all her feminine charms upon Lucian. He was their only possible chance of escaping from this damn tower. She had brushed her hair and put lipstick on, tactics that normally she despised, and now was climbing the stairs again in the hope of catching him in his inner sanctum. This time her luck was in. The lights were on.

"Enter," he said when she tapped on the door. He was back ensconced in his place by the fire with a thin cheroot in his hand and a glass of fine port. "Greetings," he said with a genuine smile, motioning her to the opposite chair. The fading light shot jewelled arrows through the resplendent stained glass.

"I have found you," she said with unfeigned delight. She'd been starting to wonder if he was a myth, a figment of her fevered imagination. Yet here he sat in his favourite spot, a weighty volume upon his knee as if he rarely strayed from this fulcrum of learning.

"How are you all getting on?" he asked, regarding her benevolently from over his reading glasses.

"We need you downstairs," Amanda said. "To talk to us all about what we should do. We have been here too long as it is. Almost a week."

"A week is nothing," Lucian replied. "You are still in thrall to your careers. It will take far longer than that to unscramble your heads."

"But we have to get back," Amanda pleaded, hating herself but determined to win. "We were not supposed to be here at all. It was only because of the weather."

"But you are here," he said. "Why not make the most of it?"

Amanda repeated her heartfelt plea. They needed to pick his brains, she said. Tomorrow would be too late. They must do it now.

Lucian carefully closed the book, marking his place as he had before. He took one final draw on his thin cheroot and emptied his glass.

"Lead and I will follow," he told Amanda.

CHAPTER
TWENTY-TWO

They banked up the fire in Lucian's honour and opened a couple of bottles of wine, filched from their absent host's wide-ranging selection. Richard stood them near the hearth to breathe and Amanda dug out some elegant crystal glasses. If you want to make any kind of statement, then do it in style was the code by which she'd been raised. And Lucian's goodwill was vital to them. They needed his cooperation now to escape the endless incarceration and return to their regular lives as soon as they could.

Mark and Richard had surfaced at five, rested and groomed having showered and shaved and taken advantage of the en suite bathroom. Since they'd been stuck here almost a week, they had circumvented Amanda's rules. The owners, as yet, had shown no sign of returning. And when they did, they were bound to understand.

Mark seemed more human after his rest and was almost back to his usual dazzling form. Dawn, in his honour, had slipped upstairs and returned, an hour later, fully made up and wearing her inappropriate cocktail frock. It was early evening; the clock was just striking six as their guest walked in.

Lucian, dressed with consummate care in velvet jacket and slippers to match, extended his hands to the blaze with a beaming smile. On his left little finger, Amanda saw, he wore an elaborate signet ring which bore an imposing coat of arms she had not been aware of before. It would seem to bear a Latin inscription which, from where she stood, she could not decipher.

"So," said Lucian. "Have you settled in? Is there anything more you need?" He sounded like the proprietor of a boutique hotel.

"Everything's lovely," Jilly said before Amanda took over the spokeswoman's role.

"We have to get out of here fast," she said. "We have more than outstayed our welcome." She'd assumed they'd be there for a single night but then the weather had intervened. When were the owners due back, she wanted to know. No more evasions, please, was implied in her tone.

Lucian continued to stare at the flames. "That depends," he said, "on several things." Weather conditions, the time of year; he ticked them off on one elegant hand. And the owners of the tower concluding whatever it was they had set out to do.

"Which was what?" asked Amanda. He never provided answers.

"More to the point," interrupted Angus, "when is this bloody mist likely to clear? Have you heard an up to date weather forecast?"

Lucian smiled. "All in good time. I had rather hoped you might stick around and consider this an unscheduled break, ideal for spiritual reflection."

"Bugger that!" said Angus rudely. "I have to get back to London as fast as I can."

Lucian's eyes were alert and deep and, accordingly, not easy to read. He might have been almost any age, the bones of his handsome face were so finely formed. His teeth, however, were white and strong, as flawless as any public figure's. He looked at Angus reflectively and laughed.

Amanda was sick of his playing games and making light of their situation. He was their only lifeline and well he knew it.

"Tomorrow we plan to walk to the farm." It was time that she laid it on the line. "We need supplies, and to let people know where we are. Will you come with us and show us the way?"

Lucian gave a theatrical bow. "I am ever at your service," he said, "my lady."

Next morning, when she opened her eyes, Amanda was shocked; she could see the sun. She leapt across to the window to check things out. The sky was a hazy greyish-blue, the sun as pale as a butter pat. The mist had all gone; the grass was sparkling with frost.

She couldn't believe it. "Wake up!" she cried, vigorously shaking Jilly's shoulder. Their moment had come. All the mist had gone. They must move with the utmost speed.

She donned her clothes without pausing for thought, which was easily done, she had only one set. Her hair was dirty again but it did not matter. The vital thing was to leave this place before the mist cut them off again. They might not get another chance for weeks.

"Hurry!" she screamed at Jilly then flew down the stairs.

There was no time for breakfast: they had to be off. They could stop somewhere on the road, she said. The worst scenario was that they might go hungry.

She popped outside for a sniff at the air. The clouds were already thickening a bit but the blessed sun still hung high in the sky, fully illuminating the mountain peak.

"I'll go upstairs and wake the boys," she said.

She knocked and entered; no time for finesse. "Wake up!" she yelled. "We have got to leave." The room, with its matching bunks, was extremely untidy. They had dropped their clothes where they stood, it seemed, and simply thrown themselves under the sheets. The children's bathroom, glimpsed through the door, was similarly chaotic.

Richard stirred then leapt out of bed, holding a pillow strategically placed out of deference to Amanda since he slept naked.

Amanda grinned. "Don't worry," she said. It was nothing she had not seen before. He was fit, though; that she had to admit, and in other circumstances, perhaps . . . There was no time for speculation, though. They had to get out of here fast.

Mark was still burrowing his face in the sheets, his breathing uneven, which worried her.

"Is he all right?"

"Don't know," Richard said. "He had another bad night."

Amanda left Richard to sort out Mark and went to waken the other two. They were, as she knew, now in separate rooms and so she started with Angus. He was up already, having heard her shout, and rapidly pulling on his clothes; not his own but serviceable jeans and a khaki sweater, filched from the master bedroom.

"Conveniently he's about my size," he said, well into the spirit of things. He had not shaved, which suited him. Amanda thought he looked rugged and attractive. He undertook to wake Dawn though doubted whether she'd be much use. "She is totally rubbish before noon," he said with a grimace.

In any case, she had nothing to wear apart from the evening frippery she had arrived in. He decided to leave her sleeping and pick her up later. It seemed a bit hard, but Amanda agreed. Dawn would only serve to slow them all down. They could leave her with Mark, which she'd certainly like. They could learn to look after each other. Amanda would leave a note for them on the table.

When Lucian failed to materialise, the four of them set off on their own, Richard in the lead, as before, the other three following closely. Angus was wearing wellington boots, stuffed with thick socks to make them fit. Richard had lent him Mark's leather flying jacket. Amanda decided she liked the dressed down look, which made him seem younger.

"Which way?" they asked.

138

"Straight on," Richard said so off they went in neat single file, trying to ignore the slowly returning mist.

Please let us make it this time, prayed Amanda, who knew that her nerves would not stand any more delays.

CHAPTER
TWENTY-THREE

When, eventually, Dawn came down the place seemed deserted, the dishes all cleared and the kettle now almost stone cold. For a moment she was petrified, assuming the others had left without letting her know, but then she looked in the fridge for milk and saw how supplies had shrunk. They must have gone off on a foraging spree; she seemed to remember that being discussed, and she fervently hoped it was the case. She was starving. She called out for Angus but it seemed that he had gone too. And then she found Amanda's note and realised that Mark had also stayed behind, which instantly cheered her. Something had happened, she wasn't sure what, to put Angus into a really foul mood. He had even changed rooms, which Dawn rather regretted. The lesson she'd tried to teach him had fallen flat. He seemed to have lost all interest in her unless, of course, he was faking.

She finished the orange juice in the fridge and checked the freezer in case there was more. There was still enough frozen stuff, she assessed, to last at least for a couple more days by which time she felt fairly confident they'd have been rescued. She didn't know how to light the fire but the room was still warm from the previous night. There must be some other heating, too, as the temperature never varied. Then she remembered the Aga and understood. She shuffled around, drinking her tea, feeling unloved and rejected by all. They might have let her decide if she wanted to join them.

There was sudden movement then feet on the stairs and immediately she was revitalised. She smoothed back her hair and held her breath as Mark shuffled into the kitchen. Even though his arm was now out of the sling, he still looked decidedly woozy.

"Come and sit down and I'll get you some food. The others appear to have left us," she said. Her radiant smile was a dead giveaway as to how delighted she felt.

Mark, unshaven and scarily pale, was slightly unsteady on his feet. He looked romantic, like the dying Keats or even Rupert Brooke. Not that Dawn had a clue about that. All she saw was a handsome toff who, right from the start, she had fancied rotten. Now, perhaps, was her chance to score. Angus deserved to be put in his place after the shabby way he'd been treating her lately.

Mark smiled vaguely and scratched his head. He had draped a blanket over his vest, having washed his shirt and left it to drip in the bathroom. All their luggage was still in the plane, not that he really cared any more except for that one slim attaché case he should not have let out of his sight.

"Do you know how to light a fire?" Dawn was clueless about most things and sucking up to him now for ulterior reasons. She did, however, make passable tea, though basically Mark was a coffee man.

"It's easy," he said. "Just take two or three logs, screw up some paper and set it alight. I'm assuming you do have matches."

Dawn followed instructions and Mark struck the match then collapsed, exhausted, into a chair. Today he was looking horribly grim; Dawn felt slightly uneasy. Supposing the others got lost again and she was stuck here with a dying man. This was not the romantic scenario she had imagined.

"Would you like some toast?" she asked. It was all she could make.

"No thanks," said Mark to her secret relief. He closed his eyes and drifted off into a stupor.

Damn, Mark was thinking, just his luck to be here on his own with this really dumb cluck. At the best of times she was not his type; and all he wanted now was to sleep in peace. He seemed to be running a temperature and his arm was throbbing and hurt like hell. He slipped in and out of consciousness and had a series of frenzied dreams in which he was trying to land a plane upon a sea of marshmallow. In his more lucid moments he worried a bit about what would happen to all that dosh if somebody else should get to the plane before he did.

These last few years he'd lived high on the hog, sailing as close to the wind as he could and leading all those investors a merry dance. He had loved every second. It had all been huge fun; he was good at his job as well as a social hit. He had never, throughout his hectic career, been short of attractive squeezes. He was thirty-five and earning a bomb. He had no desire to change anything in his life.

Lately, though, things had wobbled a bit. He was moving the hedge-fund to Reykjavik to invest in high interest Icelandic bonds till the markets steadied again. He was doing it with great sleight of hand, because the City must never get wind of it. He had to be back on Canary Wharf before his absence was noticed. He had said he was off to Val d'Isère for an extended weekend's skiing. He had lost track of what day it was but must have exceeded that limit. Richard, his lawyer, would back him up. They were in this together and sharing an alibi. But Richard appeared to have disappeared, though Mark had a feeling he'd told him where he'd gone. He would trust Richard with anything, even his life, should it ever come to that.

He called Richard's name but nobody came, only that tedious little girl. She was moping by the fire but raised her head when she heard his voice.

"He's gone down the mountain with the others," she said.

"Why would he want to do that?" croaked Mark. Richard was always the sporty one although Mark was the one who had borrowed the plane from the Russian. He ought to be here now, as moral support, instead of skiving off on a jolly day's outing.

"They've gone to try to get help," said Dawn, still miffed because they had not asked her. The least she would have liked was the chance to say no.

She stood at the window and looked at the mist which was back like a forest of cottonwool. Though not yet noon, the sun was eclipsed and the sky had become an angry shade of purple. It was growing colder; more snow must be on the way. Dawn was beset with a terrible fear. Mark had lapsed into a coma-like drowse. Suppose they never came back and he died and she had to cope on her own. She quickly changed into the dungarees, just in case.

Her thoughts returned to her night-time scare and the bright white light that had beckoned to her. When the men had gone up to check, they had found the door locked. There were things in this place she did not understand, that frightened but also slightly intrigued her. A powerful presence they could not see had assumed control of their lives. Lucian knew more than he let on but that didn't much help since they never knew where to find him.

She went to the foot of the stairs and peered up but the power was still off and the candles unlit. Nothing would ever induce her up there again. If it weren't for Mark, she'd be out of her mind, alone in this place with forces unknown. She moved from her seat by the fire to sit beside him.

What if the winter had now set in so that no one could reach them until the spring? Food was short and she didn't know how to cook. Nor did she have any nursing skills. Mark's skin was almost translucent now and all the colour had drained from his lips as well. He was breathing very irregularly, almost as though he were starting to drown. Gingerly she touched his hand and he opened his eyes and smiled.

"Sorry," he said in his classy way. "This can't be very much fun for you." He wished she would just go away and do something useful. He could tell from the way she was staring at him that she thought he was not very long for this world. The way he felt now she might well be right. What wouldn't he give for a drink.

"A glass of something might do the trick."

"Whisky or wine?" She knew his tastes.

"I don't suppose there's any brandy," he said and she scurried across to look in the old carved chest.

"Why not have one yourself," said Mark. So she did.

CHAPTER
TWENTY-FOUR

It felt good to be stretching their legs at last and the walk at first was an easy one till they reached the scree, where they knew to be ultra careful. There was no point in breaking an ankle now. That was one complication they did not need, though Richard went leaping ahead like a mountain goat. He reached out a steadying hand to Jilly, who gratefully clasped it then clung to his arm. She found him hugely appealing today with his foppish fair hair and high spirits. He had the intrepid courage she liked in a sportsman.

Angus offered Amanda his arm but her feminist spirit obliged her to reject it. She slithered unaided down the steep slope, remembering how she had slipped before. What they had been through since then, however, put other things into perspective. Today she managed to stay on her feet without any mishaps at all.

"Hang on," she said on a sudden thought, fumbling to check that she'd brought her phone. This should be the ideal place to try for a signal. Angus and Richard had both brought theirs but Jilly had inadvertently left hers behind. She held her breath as they tapped away but again not one of them had any luck. "We can try again lower down," said Amanda, stifling her disappointment.

Despite the mist, which was rising fast, they could see right down to the valley floor and the track they should have been on before in order to reach the tarn. Today would be easy; they could not fail to make it. Their spirits soared.

After a while Richard pointed ahead. "Look," he cried, having spotted a glint of water through the trees.

"Great," said Amanda. It must be the tarn, and that meant they were also quite close to the farm which promised them all the things they'd been lacking till now. A farmer with a tractor, perhaps, who could take them back to their cars. At the very least, a telephone that worked.

Richard instinctively speeded up, rehearsing in his mind the next manoeuvre. He and Mark could now disengage themselves and find their own way up to the plane and then, belatedly, fly to Reykjavik. True gents would offer the others a lift. It was just as well that the jet was restricted for space. Besides, they were headed in totally different directions.

"Damn this mist." Here it came again in wisps that thickened until the sun was more or less blotted out. The fleeting glimpse they had had of spring had now reverted to antumn again. Amanda found herself increasing her speed.

The others followed and did the same, and soon the sun broke through again. Richard was starting to fantasise about the lunch they might get at the farm; he was peckish through having skipped breakfast. But

147

Amanda's only concern was getting home. Home to London, real life and her job, to the aftermath of the end of year cuts. To face the grim economical truth and settle what unfinished business she still had with Max.

Max was two years older than her and now her immediate superior in the hierarchy of London head office. Both graduates, they had much in common: hard-headedness combined with consuming ambition. They had joined the Pru at much the same time and almost instantly clashed. Amanda considered Max arrogant while he was dismissive of her degree which was only an upper second, compared to his first. His manner was chilly and mainly abrupt, though he could surprise you with dazzling charm. He had very pale eyes and short-cropped hair that, even in his thirties, had started to grey. He kept himself fit with golf and squash and a series of fairly high-profile affairs that had earned him the doubtful sobriquet of office Casanova. At first Amanda had despised him for that. There was little attractive about the man who had the habit of cutting her dead or simply interrupting when she was talking. To start with she kept well clear of him, but then she was drafted into his department.

There wasn't a lot she could do about that, short of quitting which wasn't a smart career move. Amanda had worked long and hard for the job, which still had brilliant prospects. She managed to bite back her rage for a while, then outwitted Max in a series of deals that earned her promotion as well as applause from above. Only then did he recognise her as a possible threat. He attempted to nobble her career by using the means he knew best, seduction. Which had worked, in the end, to Amanda's detriment. Their sexual life was stormy and fraught, rooted more in rivalry than in passion. As with everything else they touched, they were locked in perpetual combat. It shocked Amanda to realise now how deep the attraction went. What had started off as a cynical fling had sucked her into a vortex from which she had not yet escaped.

On that last fatal night before she fled, having lost her cool and bawled him out, he had driven her far beyond all rules of engagement. She regretted now having ever revealed the depths of her growing infatuation but his final taunt had turned out to be one too many. They were standing outside on his balcony, admiring the pageantry of the river and sharing a late night bourbon before she left for her four-day weekend. When he ducked back inside to take the call and she heard him chuckle then turn away, deliberately out of her hearing, she lost her rag. Who in hell's name would ring this late and why did he need to chat for so long? No one important, was all he would say; nothing that need concern her. And when he moved past her to his place, his back against the balcony rail, she lashed out in fury by tossing her drink in his face.

What happened next remained a blur. She could still not be sure she had got it right. It was late. She was overwrought. They had both been drinking. She remembered only the shock on his face and the shattering glass as it slipped from his hand. Then the stupefying slow motion of what came next. The rest was a blank; all she now recalled was leaving in a hurry.

In another two hours they reached the tarn, a mountain lake formed by a glacier. It was stunningly beautiful, deep and still, without a ripple across its glassy surface. They stood in silence along the edge, just staring.

Amanda pulled out her phone again but now the battery had gone flat. Neither Richard nor Angus could get a signal.

"Bloody hell!" She stamped her foot and started looking out for the farm which should, by now, be visible at this level. They could none of them see a sign of it, though; just barren hills with Scafell Pike soaring above them, majestic and remote. Up there in the mist were Mark and Dawn, undoubtedly at each other's throats, trustingly waiting for someone to come and collect them.

They walked along the edge of the tarn, debating which direction to take. The compass was not a lot of help since they didn't know where they were heading. The sun was now sliding down the sky; in less than an hour it would be dark. So far, it seemed, they had not achieved very much.

"I can't face that horrible climb again," moaned Jilly, whose legs were aching now. She was starting to wilt. Inside her gloves her hands were frozen and stiff.

"I'm afraid," said Richard, "if we don't move fast, we aren't going to make it back before dark."

Back to that cell-block in the clouds where claustrophobia would drive them mad, where once again they would be entombed, cut off from the rest of the world. The alternative, though, was equally daunting. The climb was one thing but staying down here, without food or shelter, could well prove equally harsh.

"We should turn back," said Richard firmly, loyal to Mark and remembering the plane. From the house they stood a chance of recovering it.

"I'm not sure I can make it," wailed Jilly, her valiant spirit defeated now.

"Chin up," said Angus, surprisingly calm despite the fact he was so much older. "Hang on to me till you get your second wind." He seemed to be rather enjoying himself, his management worries put on hold. He realised how long it had been since he'd last had a break.

It was then, in the last dying rays of the sun, that they glimpsed a dark object sunk in the tarn, only inches from the edge just below the surface.

"What's that?" said Amanda, squinting hard and moving as close to it as she could. "There seems to be something quite large submerged in the water."

They all had a look. It seemed to be some kind of vehicle, Richard thought. Most probably a jeep or an SUV.

CHAPTER
TWENTY-FIVE

Eventually they made it back, through luck more than navigational skills once the mist rolled in again and eclipsed all landmarks. Steady progress was what it took, rather than chancing the odd short cut as they would have done had Lucian kept his promise. Richard led them, compass in hand, and after what seemed like hours they saw in the distance the bright white beckoning light of the pele tower guiding them home. When they finally got there and thumped on the door the clock in the hall was striking twelve. Amanda glanced at her watch which, of course, she had smashed when she took that tumble.

"What on earth kept you?" demanded Mark, irate and unshaven and draped in a blanket. Unusually, he appeared to have lost his cool.

"I'm glad to know you're feeling better," said Richard, at his driest.

Dawn seemed close to hysteria and hurled herself into Angus's arms, apparently having forgotten their current froideur. Amanda, watching, was curious to know what, in their absence, had been going on. When they left, Dawn and Mark had both still been asleep.

Amanda was silently screaming inside. They had very nearly made it this time, might have succeeded had Lucian not let them down. His unexplained and continuing failure to help them was making her crazy.

The house was almost unbearably hot. Mark and Dawn had piled on the logs, which would mean another foray into the woodshed. The homecoming party did not complain, just sank on the sofa to pull off their boots and wearily remove their outer layers. Jilly seemed hardly able to stand so Richard assisted her to a chair while Angus poured out the dregs of the brandy which it seemed that Mark and Dawn had been consuming. He looked at them both suspiciously but, since he no longer cared, said nothing. Dawn was above the age of consent; he was just relieved to have her off his hands.

Richard was frantically looking for food, having not had a thing to eat all day. It was after midnight; the four of them were famished.

"I'm afraid there isn't a lot of choice," said Jilly, as if it were all her fault. Six of them eating three meals a day had take its toll of supplies. Even the wine was running low; if they didn't get out of here soon they might have a problem.

Amanda offered to knock up pasta which was, more or less, all she knew how to cook. At least they still had parmesan cheese and finest quality olive oil, plus twelve-year-old balsamic vinegar and sun-dried tomatoes. Their absentee hosts had excellent gourmet tastes.

Now Mark piped up, surprising them all. "The least I can do for you guys," he said, "is knock together some supper." He and Dawn, it appeared, had already eaten. Using one hand with amazing skill, he threw the remaining eggs into a bowl, worked his magic with hollandaise sauce and produced, in a matter of minutes, eggs Benedict.

"Where did you learn to cook like that?" asked Dawn, now even more impressed.

"You forget," said Mark, "I have been round the block a few times."

They sat by the fire and ate off their knees, glad to be home and warm and safe, reunited after a long and frustratingly wasted day. They had started to think of this place as home, their refuge from the hostile fells, with its solid walls to resist the harshest of weather. Jilly was too exhausted to talk but the meal had given Richard his energy back. He apologised to Mark and Dawn for having returned empty-handed. Somehow they'd managed to miss the farm but, not to worry, would try again. Which reminded him . . . the vehicle under the water.

Mark shot suddenly wide awake. "Bizarre," he said. "Were there bodies inside?" He looked at them keenly. "Or did no one bother to check?"

Shiftily, they exchanged shocked glances. Until this moment that thought had not occurred. The light had been fading; the water was black and the four of them tired and obsessed with survival. All they had seen was the submerged top just inches below the surface.

"So how do you suppose it got there?" said Mark.

None of them had the vaguest idea. There wasn't a road nor an obvious track nor any sign, come to think of it, of a crash or other disturbance. Most probably, all were agreed, it had simply been dumped. The tarn itself was very remote though supposedly close to the mythical farm. But an SUV sliding into a lake must have made a bit of a splash. Unless it had happened at dead of night, perhaps for nefarious purposes. Mark hadn't been joking. They all turned pale. He was right; there could well be a body or bodies inside.

Amanda and Jilly were shocked to the core. Why had they not thought of that? The least thing they should have done was raise the alarm. But they had no phone and now it was late. They stared at each other with stricken eyes.

"Relax," said Angus callously. "There isn't a chance, in the circumstances, that anyone could have survived."

Which certainly made them concentrate. Something horrific might well have happened, though now was hardly the time to be thinking about it. All four of the walkers were dead on their feet. They would be more lucid once they had slept. They said their goodnights and shuffled off to their bunks.

No one had mentioned the beacon light nor how it could possibly work when the power was shut off. When Angus checked, before going to bed, the whole top part of the tower was, as usual, in darkness.

Next morning he seemed to have taken charge. He was drinking tea when Amanda came down, fully dressed and making notes at the table. It was eight o'clock but quiet as a morgue. The others must still be sleeping it off. Angus had opened the curtains, revealing more mist.

"Do you want breakfast?"

"No thanks," he said. Though still unshaven, he was fully dressed in the jeans and sweater he'd filched from his host and looked disconcertingly sexy. His expression, however, was very grave. "We can't afford to lose time," he said, "in letting the authorities know about that submerged car." Not to mention the fact they were all of them stuck on this mountain.

"How?" asked Amanda, reheating the kettle, relieved to have somebody else, for a change, take command.

First, Angus said, they should recharge their phones then walk as far from the tower in different directions as it took till one of them picked up a signal.

"But failing that?" Amanda said, not believing that it would work. It had to do with the mountainous terrain, she was now pretty certain.

"There has to be some other way," said Angus.

They could easily now retrace their steps but would not be able to raise the car. At the very least, that would need some sort of tractor.

Mark appeared. Angus turned to him. "About your plane," he said. "Could it still take off?"

"Absolutely," said Mark. "Though not in this mist." It was merely a matter of scaling those rocks and getting up there again in these lousy conditions. Mark laughed as Amanda handed him tea. He looked a lot better after his sleep and seemed, like Angus, more alert to the urgency now. "Believe me," he said, "if I thought

156

I could, I would do my damnedest to try to reach it right now."

"We don't want you taking unnecessary risks. But we can't just sit here and twiddle our thumbs."

One by one the others appeared and Angus produced the list he had made. They also needed more logs, he said. They were getting through them exceedingly fast. Richard seemed suddenly less than keen and Mark was unable to wield an axe.

"I don't mind having a go," said valiant Jilly.

Which brought them back to the question of food and what they could possibly do about that. If the weather cleared they would look for the farm unless they could get at least one phone to work. Otherwise Angus proposed they move on to Plan B.

"Which is?"

"We must find that fuse box," he said, "and get the power reconnected."

He was mesmerised by that elusive light, so bright and compelling when viewed from afar yet, now they were back here, invisible. The top of the tower was in darkness. Yet Dawn had seen the light close up, so she claimed.

CHAPTER
TWENTY-SIX

Phones first. That seemed the way to proceed. The mist was clearing, at least a bit. Richard and Mark, in particular, watched the weather. As soon as it showed some sign of improvement they had secret plans for slipping away, plans they did not intend to share with their accidental housemates. It was hugely frustrating not to know the latest happenings in the money markets. This hedge-fund transfer was crucial to their survival. Mark, though still frail, seemed energised and back to his customary cheerful self, a big relief to Richard, his partner in crime.

But first there was the question of phones and how to connect with the outside world. Amanda took Richard's, since hers did not work, then set off with Angus and Jilly to try them out.

"Shout if you get a result," said Angus, "and the rest of us will come running."

Mark posted himself outside the front door, his own phone in hand as he waited to hear the results.

Meanwhile Richard reassumed his duties as resident woodcutter to the tower, taking the axe from the porch where he'd left it the last time. The girls still knew nothing about what he'd found and he was resolved to keep things that way. Some time, when he felt up to it, he would gear himself up to dispose of the head. He blocked his mind to where the body might be.

The phone brigade walked slowly away, each following a designated course mapped out by Angus with the help of the compass. At regular intervals each of them stopped to check if there might be a signal yet but, disappointingly, had no joy. After a while they admitted defeat and trekked back to the tower again. It seemed Amanda was probably right and the bulk of the mountain was blocking the radio waves.

They sat dejectedly at the table, each clicking away at their separate phones. Amanda focused on Jilly and took her picture.

"I don't see the point of these cameras," she said, having never bothered to use one before. "How can it possibly work if it doesn't use film?"

"It's modern technology," Angus said. "The results are quite often surprisingly good." He aimed his own camera at Jilly and caught her off guard.

Amanda smiled. She'd grown fond of them both; of all of them, now that she thought of it. Even Dawn had improved and was not nearly as much of a pain as she had been before. As random groupings went, things could have been worse.

Richard returned, having chopped more logs and lugged them round to the stack in the porch. He seemed revived; it was thirsty work. He grabbed a beer from the fridge. What luck with the phones, he wanted to know. All shook their heads. No result so far. It was inconvenient in the extreme that the landline had been disabled.

Amanda was studying Richard's mobile hard, a frown of perplexity on her face. "Call me stupid," she said, "but you're not in the picture."

The light was on and the shutter had clicked, she could see every detail of the room, but somehow Jilly was not in the place where she should be.

"You must be aiming the camera wrong." Men always thought they knew more about such things. Angus took the phone from her hands and pointed it at Mark.

"Smile," he said and Mark complied, crossing his eyes and pulling a gargoyle face.

"One for the archives," said Jilly. "Bags I a copy."

"Here," said Amanda, reaching across, but Angus was staring transfixed at the phone. There was the table and a coffee mug, with a glimpse behind of the crackling fire. There was the chair in which Mark sat, but as with Jilly there was no sign of Mark. In neither photograph was the room occupied. Angus shook his head then picked up his own phone to check the snap he had taken of Jilly. Another blank; just a room with nobody in it.

It was totally weird. They were all perplexed and stared at each other, bewildered.

"I can't think what," said Angus slowly, "but there's something seriously strange about this place."

"Rubbish," said Richard, though he failed to explain it either.

160

"Come along, chaps." They were all mildly spooked but Angus had chores for them all to do. The phones didn't work but they must still report that sunken car in the tarn.

"I can't get that image out of my head," he confided to Amanda. They should have done something on the spot. He kicked himself now for not thinking of it, but they had been tired and lost and increasingly anxious.

"Should we go back there?"

He shook his head. There was nothing constructive they could do now except inform the police as soon as they could.

"So what do we do?" Amanda asked, relieved not to have to make all the decisions. She trusted Angus to sort things out, was content to play second fiddle.

Angus, however, was equally stumped. "I wish I knew," he said.

Jilly had drifted off on her own. There was so much that needed explaining here, not least of which was where the family were. She worked her way through the photographs, studying each of the family groups that showed a smiling couple with two lovely kids. As someone who longed for a child of her own, her heart went out to all four of them; father, mother, boy and girl, and the cute Jack Russell. They looked like people she'd like to know, whose tastes were reflected in their home. She wondered why then she was gripped by intense foreboding. How could they possibly vanish like that, leaving no clue as to where they had gone, with a lighted fire and the lights still on and the door unlocked so that anyone could walk in?

"What are you up to?" Dawn was bored, the more so since Mark had withdrawn upstairs and no one else was taking notice of her. Amanda and Angus were talking quietly, heads close together in front of the fire, while Richard had disappeared once again to the woodshed.

Jilly explained she was hunting for clues though to what, she was not quite sure. Maybe a telegram if such things still existed. Some explanation of why they had gone in such a great hurry at the dead of night; also some indication of who they were. There was no computer, or not one she could see, and in any case it would be useless without any power. Which reminded her. They still had to fix those fuses.

At least they were treating the place with care, constantly clearing up after themselves, keeping away from the top of the tower and restricting themselves to the family rooms. As trespassers went, they were doing the best they could manage. True, they had eaten a week's worth of food and very nearly emptied the fridge but would hope to restock the freezer before they departed. Also the wine. She had lined up the empty bottles and made a list.

On the subject of food, she must make some bread. It was almost noon. She had mouths to feed. It was starting to be a chore, doing all the cooking.

"You can come and help me," she said to Dawn. "Though if I were you, I would change my clothes." Dawn was sloping around draped in Angus's evening shirt.

The mist was now thicker. Perhaps the sun was eclipsed for ever and this was the end of the world. The way Jilly was starting to feel, she was no longer sure she cared.

CHAPTER
TWENTY-SEVEN

Dawn obediently popped upstairs and came back dressed in T-shirt and dungarees. It was clear the T-shirt was not her own as it hung in folds on her scrawny chest, but the dungarees covered it adequately and made her look cute and appealing.

Jilly laughed. "Well, I'll say this for you, you are certainly full of surprises."

Dawn smiled at that, which transformed her face. Poor little waif, thought compassionate Jilly. It didn't appear she'd had much of a life up till now. Angus had lost all interest in her and Mark was adept at self-protection. She meant no harm yet managed to get on his nerves. Amanda made no secret of the fact that she despised her. Richard seemed not to have feelings either way. Only Jilly was bothered at all and already her efforts were starting to show. She could see distinct potential in her new pupil.

While Dawn was changing, Jilly had found white flour, a baking tin and even yeast. It was lucky that their absent hostess clearly cooked.

"Have you ever made bread before?" Jilly asked.

Dawn said no, had not known you could; only knew it wrapped from the corner shop.

"It's the easiest thing in the world to make," said Jilly, and it would help augment the lunch. Sandwiches it would have to be, made with cheese and the last of the ham. With shop mayonnaise; she would have made fresh only Mark had used up all the eggs. How they'd survive for future meals she had no idea at the moment. They would just have to find that elusive farm or some way to send out an SOS. They had lived pretty well for the past seven days but things would shortly be changing. The least she could do was teach Dawn the basics.

First Jilly showed her how to mix dough, then carefully knead it and stretch it out. When she wasn't throwing herself at Mark or having a tantrum in front of Angus, it seemed the girl had a tactile skill she had not, until now, been aware of. The smell of baking attracted the men. Richard appeared, looking faintly distrait though with no explanation of why that should be, whereas Mark seemed refreshed by his half hour kip in his bedroom.

"Mm," both said, keen as Bisto kids, sniffing the air with appreciation. "When is lunch?" For them the sooner the better.

"Soon," said Jilly, preoccupied with how they would fare for the evening meal since provisions were running out fast and could not be replaced. All they had left in the vegetable line were a handful of carrots, an onion or two and a head of celery, definitely past its best.

"How about these?" Angus appeared, holding a couple of brace of grouse. "Game shouldn't hang

165

around too long. We'll be doing our hosts a favour if we eat them."

Jilly stared at him open-mouthed. A minute ago they had not been there. "Where in the world did you find them?" she demanded.

"Hanging in the larder," said Angus. "I suppose they must have been there all week."

Which was not true, as Jilly well knew; she was in and out of there all the time. Someone had recently put them there, but who? The only possible person was Lucian Demort. How kind of him and thoughtful too. She wondered how he had sneaked them in and why he had not been open about the gift. Perhaps they should ask him to share their meal. She would leave that to Amanda who it seemed, knew where to find him.

"What does one do with grouse?" asked Dawn, high on her recent success with the bread.

"Stick around here," said Jilly, "and I'll show you."

The weather was worsening by the hour and they still had not got the power back on. Despite the mysterious gift of grouse they were running short of staples. Tonight they would eat, as before, like kings but the days that followed would be less flush. Jilly was growing daily more pessimistic. In addition to her health concerns she was worrying about poor Derek. She dreaded to think what he must have thought when she simply failed to return. First, of course, he would have checked with the Pru and then, she assumed, the conference hotel. After that, if it hadn't already been done, he would have alerted the Keswick police. She knew her Derek and how punctilious he was.

Derek, however, was complicated, more than a casual acquaintance might see. He suffered from low self-esteem and was easily rattled. There was just a chance (Jilly knew him so well) that he'd take her absence as some kind of snub and would simply go to ground, assuming she'd dropped him. She sincerely hoped that wasn't the case or else she might really be up the creek. She hoped the Prudential, at least, would make efforts to find her.

Worrying, however, was not going to help. She left the others to clear up the lunch and resumed her solitary search for relevant clues. But before that the fuse box; she would try to locate it herself.

Since they'd already looked in the obvious places, she started again from the ground floor up. They had checked and found the cellar door locked but perhaps there was something down there they had overlooked. Candlelight was nice but not all the time. Jilly was getting tired of having to squint.

The hall, as always, was very dark, with the sonorous ticking of the clock to underline the emptiness of the space. The lamps had all failed through lack of power so the only illumination came from the open living room door at the top of the stairs. Candle in hand, Jilly went down, regretting now she had started at all and simply not left it for one of the men to pursue. She, after all, did most of the work. The least they might have done was find the fuse box.

There was movement. It caught Jilly's eye as she slowly descended the twisting stairs, peering into the murky darkness below her. Very slight movement but definitely there. She hoped more than anything that it wasn't a rat. She slowly moved her candle about until it rested on something pale, there by the cellar doorway. Whatever it was jerked quickly back as if avoiding the flickering light. Jilly persisted and caught it, a human face. The face of a child staring up at her, with frightened eyes and a tentative smile. A face she had seen before in the family photos.

"Hello," called Jilly and there she stood, palely picked out by the candlelight, dressed in a pretty print dress and clutching a rabbit. A white toy rabbit with pink-lined ears. Jilly, startled and shocked, dropped the candle which, of course, went out.

She could hear the blood pounding in her ears as she mounted the stairs as fast as she could and bounced through the door to the room where the others were seated.

"What?" cried Amanda, alarmed by her face, but for a moment Jilly couldn't utter a word. She stared through the kitchen archway to where the toy rabbit still sat on the Aga.

"I saw," she quavered, "a child down there. I spoke to her but the candle went out." The child had not replied nor moved, she recalled.

Richard and Angus leapt to their feet, convinced by her horrified expression. Richard grabbed the torch and, as one, they pounded off down the stairs.

"Come and sit by the fire," said Amanda. "You look as if you've seen a ghost."

There was nothing there, they convinced her of that, except for darkness which does strange things, accentuated perhaps by her overstretched nerves. They had lived too long in this strange half-light with tempers that were starting to fray and nothing beyond the windows but endless mist. Tomorrow, they promised, they would open that door and flush out whatever was hiding down there. They would search the tower and find the elusive fuse box. Meanwhile they had the evening and night to get through.

CHAPTER
TWENTY-EIGHT

During the night a storm blew up and the wind howled over the battlements. By morning the snow was ankle deep and drifting against the door. Angus was worrying about his car, where he had left it and how it would fare. Rather than being stolen, perhaps, the police might have towed it away. Things in the tower were declining fast. The shelves in the larder were finally bare and Jilly despondently tried to make soup from the sad remains of the grouse. The carrots went in, the onions too, and the wilting celery, way past its prime. She could do with some stock but, alas, there was none in the freezer.

"If you feel like stretching your legs," she said, "you could search for vegetables growing wild." Mushrooms, perhaps, provided they knew they weren't the poisonous kind.

But everyone preferred to remain by the fire except for Mark and Dawn, who were both still upstairs. Grey depression descended on all like a mantle.

"I think it's Sunday," Amanda said. It must be November by now and news of the redundancies would be public tomorrow. She glanced at Jilly, engrossed in her soup, unaware that her time was almost up. She hadn't the heart to break the news which could only heighten Jilly's sense of desolation.

Jilly had not seemed herself for days though, since she only rarely complained, it was not easy to get behind her constantly smiling façade. She must be an inspiration at work; what fools the Prudential were to be letting her go. With her pleasant manner and easy charm she was quite a tonic to have around. She was always good-humoured; her presence here kept them from falling out. A natural life-force was what she was which was why they were always watching her cook. She was one day going to make a wonderful mother.

Which was not, however, what Jilly thought. Her hopes of that happy event had all drained away. The occasional twinges she had felt lately seemed to be growing worse, though she still was sufficiently even-keeled to know it need not be more than imagination. Once an idea like that took root, it wasn't easy to shake it off. She prayed it was psychosomatic yet still feared the worst. She was glad now that Derek didn't know; it was bad enough that they were apart without him also sharing her horrible fear. Every day she hoped that the local police finally would track them down. Her ear was constantly cocked for the welcome sound of a helicopter.

The sky, however, could not be seen because of the steadily falling snow. As a child she would have been thrilled by it but all it did now was add to her feeling of doom. Supposing, on top of everything else, they were to be snowbound until the spring. The owners would not return. They'd remain undetected. She kept on thinking about that child, lurking down there in the twilight zone. She knew she had not imagined her, yet could not explain her presence there. It was like the photographs on their phones. Nothing made sense any more.

"Do you need a hand?" Amanda was there, sniffing the contents of the pot, hungry already which seemed an endemic condition. How were they ever going to survive, six of them stuck on this snowbound crag? Jilly was suddenly overcome and broke into frenzied weeping.

"Hush now, it can't be as bad as that." Amanda was useless at offering support but the two men heard and came hurrying through to check what the problem was. It shocked them when Jilly wasn't herself for she was the one in the group who kept them all going.

It was almost noon. How the time flew by, which was odd considering it should stand still, especially in these circumstances, stuck, as they were, in limbo. Richard produced the vodka and mixed Bloody Marys. He stood at the window watching the snow till inspiration struck. The woodshed was packed with all kinds of tools. Perhaps they could build a toboggan. It ought not be that hard to figure it out.

She didn't know what had come over her, said Jilly, embarrassed and wiping her eyes. It was silly, really; they were warm and snug with a solid roof over their heads. Solid indeed and the walls so thick they could barely hear the strong winds outside though the driving snow was now practically horizontal. If it weren't for the fact of the food's running out, they could count themselves lucky to be here at all. People paid fortunes to holiday in these conditions.

Mark and Dawn had now both appeared and joined the small huddle around the fire. Richard handed them Bloody Marys and told them his bright idea.

"A toboggan? You fool. Are you out of your mind?" Mark howled with mirth at the very idea, though both Amanda and Angus were taking it seriously. Richard had mentioned the Cresta Run where he'd several times raced in his younger days. He was not suggesting they went headfirst but they could perhaps construct something solid which would take at least one of them down to the valley to summon a rescue party.

"Count me out."

"You don't need to come." Both Amanda and Angus were on the case, prepared to give it a go. Anything had to be better than this, imprisoned away from civilisation with rapidly dwindling rations. They had to get out of here fast before winter set in.

"First we have to design the sledge." Which would not be easy without any plans, but Angus had cut his teeth in the fashion business. Everyone laughed but he stuck to his guns. It was mainly a matter of aerodynamics, he said.

"And after that you can make me a dress," sniffed Dawn disdainfully, yawning.

That, thought Amanda, is not the way to try to hang on to your man.

★ ★ ★

The snow continued. The fire burnt low. Jilly, ashamed of her earlier tears, was giving the kitchen a thorough working over. Mark and Dawn had dozed off by the fire but Amanda and Angus, made of sterner stuff, had kitted themselves out in weatherproof clothes and were heading off for the woodshed. Richard had already gone on ahead. There was something he needed to deal with first, he had muttered.

The path to the woodshed was frozen hard, made more treacherous by the snow. The wind whistling through the pine trees sounded quite eerie. Light-headed because of the vodka they'd drunk, they clung together; Amanda was very aware of Angus's closeness. Poor Jilly, she thought as they wove their way. There was something going on in her life worse than anything she would admit, possibly worse than the fact that she would soon be jobless.

Richard was waiting when they arrived, pale, she noticed, with mud on his sleeve, but the woodshed was warm inside and looked very inviting.

"Hey," said Amanda, looking round. "This is really great. I like it a lot. Why have you kept it from us all this time?"

Richard grinned but shuffled his feet, something which Angus picked up on at once. He knew what he was covering up so didn't ask questions.

"We're here to work," he said. "So let's get started."

He liked the idea of designing a sledge. At least it gave them a goal of sorts. The rest were just waiting for what fate dictated.

Richard showed them where everything was.

174

"Where are the rodents?" Amanda asked, but knew from his silence that he did not want to discuss it. What sissies men were, though she liked the fact that they could have a softer side. She thought of Max then shuttered her mind. This was not time to be dredging him up. More important right now was the need to survive.

At five they decided to call it a day so rubbed their hands with an oil-soaked cloth and shrugged back into their weatherproof clothes for the short walk back to the pele tower. All three were feeling quite pleased with themselves; in one afternoon they'd accomplished a lot. They felt they might be close to an imminent breakthrough. They were tired, however, and longed for a bath, a stint by the fire and a bracing drink.

Bugger, Richard thought, though did not say, we are virtually out of booze.

"Look," said Amanda. There in the porch was a pile of wooden crates.

Angus strolled over to take a look. "It looks like groceries," he said.

CHAPTER
TWENTY-NINE

Three crates of food and four cases of wine. Enough to sustain them at least for another few weeks. Angus went rapidly through it all but could not find an explanatory note or any other clue as to where it came from. There was no list of contents nor grocery bill. Not even a telephone number that could be checked.

"Weirder and weirder," Amanda said though the men were simply relieved they were not going to starve. Most probably it was their absentee host's regular monthly order. In which case she wondered why it had not been cancelled.

They thumped and shouted till Jilly came down though she didn't explain why she'd locked the front door. She'd been acting oddly since her experience yesterday afternoon.

"Surprise!" said Richard. "Santa has been." He stood back to show her the boxes of food.

Jilly just stared, as though in a trance; words appeared to have failed her.

"Help us carry it in," said Amanda, then yelled up to Dawn when Jilly just turned away. Whatever the source, to hell with it. She would not look a gift horse in the mouth. The food had arrived when they needed it; they could figure out how some other time after they'd sorted it and put it away.

It was only much later, when she stepped outside with Angus in tow to take a look round, that Amanda was struck by the fact that there were no footprints. Nor any other physical signs of how this munificence had arrived. Perhaps after all it really had been Santa.

She looked at the sky. It was snowing still though not quite enough to have covered fresh tracks. She remembered the photos they'd taken; her mind shied away. Whatever was going on in this place, the sooner they left it the safer she'd feel. There was stuff going on way beyond their comprehension.

Jilly was acting normal again, unpacking the boxes and making lists then putting everything away in its appropriate relevant place. There was milk and orange juice, even cream; fresh meat and vegetables, herbs as well and four mixed cases of truly excellent wine. Vodka, too, and a brand new bottle of cognac.

"I think I will cook you beef stew," Jilly said. Infused with a bottle of burgundy as a treat.

Nobody argued. She was the cook, self-appointed but naturally skilled. With her in charge of the kitchen they'd eaten well. And now she had Dawn as her willing slave; one good thing, at least, to have come out of this. As a group they were satisfactorily starting to bond.

Amanda considered the bright white light that had led them all here through the gathering storm yet appeared not to have any source that they had yet found. The power was off with the fuses blown; they were having to live by candlelight yet Dawn, for one, had had first-hand experience of something she would not disclose. Something had shaken her to the core so that Angus had feared for her sanity, and she had not yet entirely recovered. There was also the child that Jilly had glimpsed, albeit by flickering candlelight. The atmosphere here in this ancient place was now creating illusions. Either that or they drank too much. The sooner they left, the healthier for all it would be.

Meanwhile the food smelt wonderful; she was hungry.

So here they all were on another dark night, the wind still lashing the battlements while hailstones rattled against the fortified windows. They had none of them ever known weather like this. Any hope they might have of a rapid escape grew steadily more remote. Jilly, having prepared the stew and left it to cook on a very low heat, sat upstairs in the room they shared and poured out her heart to Amanda.

Derek, her bloke, was a wonderful guy. They had now been together for seven years and had agreed they would tie the knot in time for her thirtieth birthday in the summer. Her face was bright as she talked about it. They had seen a house that they really liked, with a garden and space for a nursery when the time came.

There Jilly's voice faltered, alerting Amanda, though she held her tongue and waited for her to go on.

"Derek sounds great," was all she said, shoving aside any thoughts about Max. What she'd not yet found for herself was a man she knew she could truly rely on. She

178

stretched out full length on the lower bunk while Jilly, dangling her feet, perched above clutching a giant panda to her chest as though it were Derek. There was something cosy about this room, with the little girl's toys, that encouraged them both to pour out their innermost secrets.

Derek was truly the salt of the earth, a driving instructor with prospects, said Jilly. The firm he worked for would soon expand and promote him to area manager. At which point, at last, they could set the date which had been such a long time coming.

"It's the way we were both brought up," she explained. "Which is why I value my job so much. You have to earn it first before you can spend it. Derek's earnings combined with mine should cover a reasonable mortgage now."

Amanda stiffened but made no sign. She kept her eyes closed and gritted her teeth. She dreaded hearing the next confession so tried to head Jilly off.

"Tell me," she said, "about that child. Do you believe she was really there?" Or was it your hormones acting up, she felt very tempted to add.

For almost a minute Jilly paused, and when she replied she sounded faintly cross. "Are you suggesting," she said, "that I made it up?"

"Of course not," said Amanda, contrite. "But you must admit that it does seem odd. Why would she be in the house on her own without the family with her?"

More to the point, where was she now? How had she managed to disappear? Amanda thought of the photographs on their phones. But Jilly, she sensed, was now upset so she swiftly and tactfully changed the subject. "Something downstairs smells really good," she said. "Shall we go and check?"

Angus was busy, designing his sledge, with Richard overseeing the sketch. A keen tobogganist in his youth, the lawyer knew more or less what would be required. They needed two runners of matching length with four cross-pieces approximately half the size.

"You also need a curve at the front in order to make it move smoothly downhill. As well as a niche to protect your feet," said Richard.

Amanda, joining them, was impressed. "How did you know how to do that?" she asked.

"Well, it's hardly rocket science," laughed Angus, who had started his working life as a trainee draughtsman.

Dawn, in the kitchen, gritted her teeth. That bitch was on to her man again. Then Mark wandered in, looking for ice, and instantly Dawn melted. All her dreams were now centred on him. Angus, in any case far too old, could do as he bloody well liked. She no longer cared.

Over a truly memorable meal (Jilly once more had excelled herself) their principal topic of conversation was the mystery of the food. Who had sent it and how had it come without their seeing or hearing the delivery man who might, now they came to think of it, have ferried them all back to safety? No one had even knocked on the door, demanding a signature on receipt. And, as Amanda had pointed out, there was not so much as a mark in the snow. Yet all those boxes and cases of wine must have been seriously heavy. And since there wasn't a road up here or even a track for a vehicle, it wasn't apparent how it had been transported.

"Perhaps," said Mark, "it came by mule. Or even huskies." You never knew. "Or pigeon post," said Amanda. Perhaps even penguins.

Since no one had other suggestions to make, they concluded the owners were coming home soon. Imminently, considering the size of the order.

Jilly flapped, as she always did, but at least if they did come, they would have transport. Amanda thought of the car in the tarn and shuddered.

CHAPTER
THIRTY

Amanda secretly envied Jilly, despite what she knew about her professional doom. Jilly was one of the world's great people who deserved a shot at a happy marriage since that was the one thing she really desired, it seemed more than anything else. She had found the right man seven years ago and was now simply waiting to tie the knot. Good luck to her; may all her dreams be fulfilled.

Jilly seemed always in a good mood despite whatever it was that often kept her awake at night. There was sadness in her clear blue eyes which faded if anyone looked at her hard. Whatever it was that was troubling her, she preferred to keep to herself. She slaved away on behalf of them all, cooking, cleaning and planning meals. Now she was teaching young Dawn to cook, which added even more to her saintly status.

She did not deserve redundancy. There was nothing, however, Amanda could do. The matter was out of her hands so she kept her mouth shut. In any case, her mind was preoccupied with her own searing worry.

She had left at three in a state of rage, determined that, finally, this was the end, not knowing or even caring if

Max were alive. Since then her anger had slightly cooled and the parlous state in which she now was had helped revive the passionate feelings she'd had. They had been together, on and off, for years but, unlike Jilly, had no fixed plans. Working together was all the involvement they needed, or so she had thought.

The anger she'd felt on that fateful night had precipitated the final row, when she had dashed her drink in his face and caused him to lose his balance. Whether or not he'd survived the fall (he must have, surely; it wasn't much of a drop) Amanda had not hung around to find out, though, looking back now, she realised that she had been callous. She had paused at home just long enough to change her clothes and grab her bag, then headed on to the motorway and the five-hour drive to the Lakes.

She wondered why Max had not followed her. He knew where the conference was being held, was, after all, her immediate boss. Either he was still as mad as hell or — heaven forbid — he'd been injured. That was the explanation Amanda most feared. The fact that they could not access news from here accentuated her frenzied state. She had behaved badly, did not deny that, but could not think now what else she might have done. Max had played that particular game once too often. This time she really had wanted out. The truth of it was he was totally wrecking her life.

Yet she could not entirely give up on him. He was, after all, the love of her life, without whom her whole existence seemed meaningless. She had sworn she could never live with him but doing without him was far, far worse. Her head was spinning with fear and desperation.

There was no way Jilly would understand. They had entirely opposing morals as well as lifestyles that did not remotely mesh. Amanda had constantly played the field whereas Jilly had eyes for only one man. Amanda respected her for that since her own life was such a mess. Of them all, the only one out of the five with whom she felt genuine rapport was Angus, with whom she was starting to strike up a friendship. He was wise and worldly and more her type than any of the rest of them. She felt confident that, in extremis, he'd know what to do.

And this was extremis, she told herself. It was time to risk her all and do something drastic.

Angus and Richard were still hard at work. Having finished the blueprint for the sledge, they had taken it out to the woodshed to source the wood. There were plenty of pine trees around the place. The skill would come in finding the one they could cut into sections to form effective runners. The wood would have to be straight and strong, with sufficient give when it hit the slopes not to splinter on impact and harm its riders.

"How many will it carry at once?" Amanda was desperate to leave there fast and Mark had agreed to relinquish his place due to his current infirmity; he didn't fancy hurtling downhill without the use of both hands. Secretly, he was holding back until the weather had calmed enough for him to attempt the dangerous climb back to where they had landed the plane. But that was something only Richard knew.

Richard was the athletic one who regularly skied and had once been a Cresta champion. An all-round sportsman, he kept himself fit with cricket and squash and occasionally golf. He had offered to take the sledge on its first test run.

"But how many passengers will it take?" Amanda needed the exact truth.

"Once we've established it passes all tests," said Angus, who knew about health and safety, "as many as can stay on without being thrown off."

How long is a piece of string, in fact. Amanda, along with the others, would just have to wait.

Angus was pleased with his achievement. It was years since he'd done any manual work and, with Richard's help, he had built the sledge in less than an afternoon. The trickiest part had been finding a tree that was young and supple but straight as well, from which they could fashion two runners that matched exactly. It had taken time but they had found the right one. They'd carried it triumphantly into the shed then spent a contented afternoon cutting and planing it to their precise dimensions. Both men enjoyed the activity which gave them a purpose and helped fill in their time. It also helped to combat their rising frustration.

The finished sledge was a work of art, and first thing next morning they tried it out with Amanda, on the sidelines, cheering them on. Angus had carefully varnished it (there was loads of stuff in that useful shed) and attached a rope with which to pull it along. The sun was out and the snow was suitably crisp. Their spirits were high.

They suggested Richard should try it first. He, they joked, was expendable and also the one with impressive sports credentials.

"Oughtn't he have a helmet?" Jilly worried.

It was not, he explained, the Cresta Run, nor would he be travelling headfirst. He was quite athletic enough to leap clear if he should lose control. He stepped aboard and positioned himself then Angus gave him a mighty shove and off he shot, unbelievably fast, straight over the brow of the hill. All of them gasped when he disappeared, the three indoors having come out to watch, and raced to the edge of the precipice, fearing disaster. Richard, however, was safe and well, having collided with a tree that had stopped him taking off into space and hurtling to disaster. He had thrown himself sideways just in time and was rolling around, unhurt and covered with snow.

"The steering's a little skew-whiff," he said.

"Then back to the drawing board it goes," declared Angus.

Eventually it was Amanda's turn. They bundled her up and she took her seat. Angus held firmly on to the sledge till she found her balance then off she went. She rocketed rapidly down the slope, screaming with joy in the frosty air, until she hit a bump and flew into a snowdrift. She was laughing so hard when Angus arrived that tears were streaming down her cheeks. He gently brushed them away with his hands then kissed her. For a very long moment they stared entranced, then Amanda turned and trudged back up the slope, leaving Angus trailing behind with the sledge.

Nothing was said. They just went on, taking turns for the giddy ride and laughing fit to bust whenever they tumbled. Eventually Richard had had enough. His hands were blue and his nose was red. "I fear this is getting us nowhere," he said. "I vote we take a rain check!"

Amanda gave Angus a sidelong glance. Something had happened between them today.

"I think," he said, "you are probably right and this is only the prototype. I will build you something a lot more robust if you're serious about it getting you down to the valley."

"Thanks," said Amanda, linking arms with him. "But, on considered reflection, I'd sooner walk."

CHAPTER
THIRTY-ONE

It was hard to believe how long they had been there. Thirteen days at the latest count and the weirdest thing was time seemed to be standing still, if not moving backwards. At first it had seemed to leap along and each time Amanda heard the clock strike she'd remembered vividly that they were stuck in a prison. She had been transported from normal life by a force over which she had no control and was now not able to contact the outside world. For the first few days it had been pure hell not knowing if anyone knew where they were, if people were actively searching for them or even if they had been missed. She remembered how she had agonised about her future and even her job. How could head office function, she'd thought, without her at the helm?

She had also agonised over Max, whether or not he'd survived that fall and if the police were hot on her trail with a warrant for her arrest. The scare had come when the food ran low and they'd had no way of replacing it or alerting the outside world. The situation had resolved itself with the arrival of fresh supplies from an unknown source, since when the atmosphere in the house had improved. The fear was still there, although less acute, and time itself had altered its pace. Somehow the urgency was gone; they were learning to live with their fate.

The balance of power had also changed. No one was fighting to take control, by which Amanda acknowledged she meant herself. Now she was content to be part of a team. Jilly continued to cook and clean, aided now by a willing Dawn, whose scowling discontent had changed into cheerful acquiescence. Jilly seemed to have accepted her lot, was resigned to whatever was troubling her and no longer cried in her sleep. Things had become more peaceful.

Amanda herself, though, found herself plunged into the vortex of a new storm. She could not get Angus McArthur out of her mind.

She could scarcely believe he had kissed her like that, as cool as anything, saying nothing. Since then she had not been alone with him though wasn't sure whether that was by design. Angus continued to act the same, a man more than comfortable in his own skin whom, now that he had relaxed, she found very attractive. She liked it that he was so much older and owned his own very successful business. Not did she mind his non-chauvinistic assumption of control; he was used to it, having had far more life experience than the rest of them. He had grown up in the Glasgow slums and left school at the tender age of fifteen, since when he had battled his way through life without help.

The only fault she could find with him was his odd aberration in choosing Dawn, a gawky misfit with not a lot happening upstairs. She was half his age, with a sulky pout and a charmless whine that got on all their nerves, though she did wear his high street range with flair because of her endemic thinness. That, Amanda could see, was a point in her favour. He seemed disenchanted with her, though, and barely registered she was there. It was just as well she now had poor Mark to flirt with.

Dawn knew nothing of the kiss but followed Mark around like a little stray dog. To her he epitomised film-star glamour with his tan, his teeth and his little boy habit of constantly tossing back his thick floppy hair. He seemed to have stepped off the celluloid screen. She could not get enough of his starry glamour.

The others could see, though, that Mark was not well from the bloodless pallor beneath the tan and the fact that he appeared to be losing weight. He also spent too much time asleep, even dropping off during conversations, which Dawn found sweet but which secretly worried the others. He was kind to her when he was awake and treated her as a gentleman should, unlike Angus who these days mainly ignored her.

Dawn had gone for Angus because he was boss, which had turned her on in a major way. She had come from nowhere and he was the ultimate prize. She had used her scrawny female wiles to claw her way out of the typing pool and into a job in the chairmans outer office. There she had worked sorting paperclips, doing the filing and making tea for two dreary years during which he barely acknowledged her presence there. Then at last Dawn came into her own by flaunting her bum in his latest sizzling fashions. Even then it had still been an uphill climb.

The other executives noticed her first and one of them took advantage of her but they all liked the way she looked in their shoddy clothes. She was just the right shape to show the lines off, as skinny as a prepubertal child with legs like a colt's and almost nothing on top. So they wheeled her into a product meeting and asked her to model the latest designs, which was how she finally caught the boss's attention. What he saw in her nobody could explain, except that he'd reached that tricky age which articles in the redtops dub menopausal. Profits were soaring, the pressure reduced. His kids were finally off his hands and Molly was very involved in her charity work. Dawn had an unformed brazen charm and knew how to put herself about. A couple of afterhours sessions had done the trick.

Lately, though, he had cooled right off and even moved into a separate room. Something had suddenly changed though Dawn didn't know what. She had truly believed he was hers at last, and only a few hours' drive from leaving his wife.

Mark, though, was far more glamorous, single and closer to her own age, and even Dawn did not really believe she could catch him. She would do what she could, though, while they were here. No one was going anywhere in this weather.

It was warmer now that the sun was out so they moved outside for a snowball fight, then started building a snowman near the front door. Jilly contributed two black olives and a carrot for eyes and nose and Amanda pinched a banana to make its mouth. By the end of the day it was six foot tall and wearing their absentee host's straw hat plus sunglasses because the olives were small and gave it a mean look. Dawn borrowed Mark's rather dashing silk scarf, which added to its slightly roue appearance.

"Meet our host," Amanda announced. "Jack Frost."

Then, just as the sun began its descent, her eye was caught by a sudden flash. She swung around quickly to see where it might have come from. With luck a vehicle; sudden hope arose. She raced to the edge of the steep slope, squinting against the glare from the sinking sun. She could not see anything, no footprints or tracks, nor hear any kind of mechanical sound, yet something must have produced that sudden flash.

Then, just as she turned away, she saw it: cautious movement against the snow. At the edge of her vision that flash again and then a spiderlike scurry into the trees.

"Quick!" she yelled. "There's someone there."

Angus and Richard were at her side.

"Down there. Between those trees," she said. Watching them through binoculars, hence the flash.

Richard shouted and waved his arms, jumping up and down in the snow. Other than Lucian, this was the first sign of life they had yet detected. He shouted again. There was no reply and now the sun was beginning to dive, a burning orb in a darkening sky, on

192

the edge of being extinguished. They waited five minutes but nothing moved.

"I think you were mistaken," said Angus. And kissed Amanda again.

CHAPTER
THIRTY-TWO

"I swear to you," Amanda said. "There was somebody down there. I saw them move." One thing she did know, that scuttling shape had been neither a deer nor anything else four-footed.

Angus held her against his chest, gently wiping the tears from her eyes. For a woman who liked to pretend to be tough, she had a very soft centre. "Whatever it was, we will find out soon." Sooner, perhaps, than Amanda knew. Another lost traveller, perhaps, seduced by the bright white light from the pele tower.

Seeing Amanda was still upset, he hugged her to him against the cold. Only recently had he begun to realise how much he liked her. To start with she'd played a haughty role, condescending and self-absorbed, certain she knew the answer whatever the question. Now, though, she'd lost that confidence, accepted they were in the same leaky boat and that, for once, there were no obvious answers. And he had started to find her a lot more human.

He was also rather turned on by her. She was feisty and brave yet stylish too. He deeply regretted his fling with Dawn which had happened when he had time on his hands and a puerile need to prove to himself he could pull. For almost the first time in his life he had given in to a purely carnal desire. Now Dawn had transferred her allegiance to Mark who for age and prospects was a far better bet, though Angus very much doubted she stood the slightest hope of capturing such a prize. Mark was a typical City chancer, way beyond the league of a girl of her class.

That night they discussed Amanda's claim that someone had seemed to be watching them. The giveaway sign had been that brief glint of glass. Whoever it was had moved away the moment they realised they had been seen. Richard backed her story; had also glimpsed somebody out there. And, despite the fact he had waved and shouted, whoever it was had failed to respond but had instead made a very rapid retreat. If it was someone looking for them, they would have been up here by now.

"But why," Jilly asked, "would they just move on? Knowing that people were lost on the fells." Word, by now, must have got around; there had to be people out there, actively searching. The police must know and the newspapers too, which would mean the rest of the media. Whatever was happening in the world, their story would have been covered.

"So with luck," said Angus on a positive note, "pretty soon the cavalry should arrive."

"I hope," said Jilly, "they won't all expect a meal."

They had all turned in though only Mark could sleep. The rest had an ear psychologically cocked in case there should be a disturbance outside or a sudden thump on the door. Even the owners arriving home could now only be a relief.

Mark, however, still slept like the dead; Richard lay listening to his ragged breathing. He would not be in this current mess had he not been beguiled by his friend's lethal charm, which had been his undoing since their paths first crossed at prep school. Mark was a bounder but none the less fun, with the brightest cockiest view of the world. It was there to be taken advantage of was the basic principle by which he lived. He was witty, charming and universally liked, but had rarely done an honest day's work. He had used his cunning throughout his life and never failed to come out on top, which was how he had managed to sucker his friend into joining him in this scam. Richard was regretting it now, but he'd left it too late to withdraw with honour. The Reykjavik jaunt was their final chance to escape indictment for serious fraud. This was a make or break moment in both their careers.

As he listened to his friend's rattling breath he wished he had someone in whom to confide. It was lonely being stuck here with a dying companion. Mark was okay, having passed that point where the future threatened in any way. He had taken a risk that had not paid off and left it to his best friend to bail him out. Best friend but lawyer too; there lay the rub.

It had seemed straightforward six months ago with the markets booming on every side and silver-tongued Mark making millions hand over fist. Iceland had been the latest hot tip which he'd shared with only the chosen few.

196

"Give me your money, lads," he had said, "and I promise to more than quadruple it."

They had simply shaken on it, no questions asked.

You did not question a man like Mark. It would be a slur on his family name. The Sinclairs had been around before Magna Carta.

So now here they were, caught in this net with the Inland Revenue closing in and the City falling to pieces all around them. While that slim briefcase containing the loot was stuck up there on the frozen crag in the borrowed Lear jet the weather had made them abandon. Small wonder, Richard wryly observed, he was finding it hard to drop off.

Amanda, too, was still wide awake, preoccupied with thoughts of Max which were not easier now she was falling for Angus. She liked his down-to-earth Scottishness and the fact he had taken her at her word. It was sufficient for him that she'd said what she'd said. Somebody skulking close to the tower with a camera or binoculars, a lens picked up by the rays of the dying sun. Jilly was right. If it was the police or anyone from the rescue services, by now they'd be circling overhead or hammering on the door. But hours had passed since she'd seen that glint and, so far, no one had come.

Amanda knew she could not trust Max, who had let her down any number of times; one reason why she was not too disturbed by thinking he might have been injured. He had many times pulled such a stunt before, from lack of caring or else just as a joke, but this time he must have known how upset she had been. She had not intended that he should fall, had simply chucked her drink in his face, a not unreasonable reaction to his continuing infidelity. He had stepped sharply back then appeared to trip and she, by reflex, had left at once. Only a row could have followed. If Max had survived.

No one knew she'd been there that night, not even whoever it was on the phone. They kept their relationship under wraps for reasons of diplomacy because they were business colleagues. Office romances were frowned upon, especially as Max was not formally free, and Amanda did not want to risk her promotion by being seen to be dallying with her boss. An official arrangement might alter that though she still suspected he'd probably force her to leave.

But that did not explain where Max was now or why he had failed to follow her here. It was not in his nature to let things rest, which was why she was certain the flash she had seen had been his. Somewhere out there on the fells was the man she loved yet could not get on with.

CHAPTER
THIRTY-THREE

The steerage on the sledge had been fixed but the mist had rolled back, even thicker than before. All of them huddled inside the tower; even Angus seemed to have lost his earlier incentive. Perhaps it was because they had food, which had blunted their hunter gatherer instincts. Like cavemen equipped with a wok, they were losing their edge.

Jilly's appointment was now well past. She would have to return to the end of the queue unless she was judged to be a priority case. The recurring twinge was not getting worse; she could go whole days without noticing it, had even convinced herself it could be indigestion. With luck, if she took no notice, it might go away.

Angus still fretted about the car, not his lost Daimler but the one in the tarn. He now had bad dreams about passengers trapped inside it. He still didn't know, though, what they could do until they had access to outside help. Perhaps by now someone else would have called the police. Even now, in early November, people still walked on the fells.

Richard was thinking about the plane and wondering how to get out of this place, regularly scanning the sky in the hope that the weather might suddenly clear. He could no longer rely on Mark but wondered if Angus might be coerced as an honorary member of the team and also, perhaps, co-pilot. The decision was a delicate one. He would have to explain about Reykjavik and underline the urgency of the mission. He trusted Angus instinctively because he had worked his way up from scratch and was, apparently, staying afloat even in the current recession. Richard felt he was likely not to ask too many questions. Mark, he suspected, might even offer to cut him in on the deal. Richard, however, was not empowered to make that decision alone. It would have to wait.

Mark had taken a turn for the worse and was now rambling incoherently. Dawn was crouched on the floor by his bed but Jilly had taken over. She was in his room with her sleeves rolled up and a bowl of hot water at her side.

"It seems the wound is infected," she said. "He needs to get to a hospital fast." Amanda was right; she would have made a great nurse.

"Is he going to die?" asked Dawn in her little girl voice.

Jilly said nothing. She did not know but could see how shaken up Dawn was. She tried to calm her down, then took Richard aside. "We have to do something fast," she said, "or I can't be certain he will pull through."

Richard came up to check, having shaken Dawn off.

Mark looked really bad, his face chalk white and his breathing uneven and laboured. But stuck up here without even a phone, Richard didn't know what they could do. Except risk their lives again in another abortive rescue mission. Mark was his best friend in the world. He couldn't just let him die.

"I'm game if you are." Angus was fit now that he had the right outdoor gear. He was also dying to get away and try to do something productive.

They looked for Amanda but she wasn't there.

"Damn," said Angus. "Just when we really need her."

Amanda was off on her own private jaunt, convinced now it must have been Max she had glimpsed. The Keswick police would have come out in force and made their presence felt. Someone alone with binoculars had to be him. And whether he came as friend or foe made little difference as long as he was still alive. Although he fell from the second floor, the balcony of the flat beneath could well, she had decided, have broken his fall. If he were dead, she felt certain the news would have reached her. They had been so close for so many years, she would know subliminally were he to leave this world. The least he would do, she was sure, was continue to haunt her.

He was on her trail, she thought, her belief endorsed by the flash of the previous day. If anything held him back, it would just be the weather. She would go to meet him quite fearlessly to let him know she still felt the same. Her terrible anger was gone. In her heart she still loved him.

She had left the others around Mark's bed, slipped down and silently laced her boots, then stepped outside into a blanket of mist. She was not afraid, had done this before. If she followed the path that led down the hill she ought to reach the plateau where she had seen Max. The fact that a night had passed did not deflect her determination. Somewhere out there in the mist she knew he was waiting.

The feelings she'd started to have for Angus were nothing when compared to this. She liked him a lot; he had filled a gap and, in other circumstances, perhaps. But Max was her man; they still had unfinished business. She felt she'd been given a second chance and that this time round it would all work out. They needed to talk and investigate their emotions.

Amanda hummed as she strode along, more optimistic than she had been since that terrible night of the fight. He had followed her here so he must still care. This time she'd open her heart to him and let him know the extent of her deepest feelings. Max and Amanda. They were a team. And had been all the years they had worked together.

After a while the sun broke through and opened up vistas through the mist. She saw sweeping plains and occasional trees, here and there even sheep. She reached the edge of the first steep slope and paused to draw breath and work out where she was. Somewhere down there must be the tarn and the elusive farm. She raked the landscape for signs of life. If this was Sunday, and she thought it was, there should be other walkers out who could show her the fastest route to where her car was. Amanda smiled as she trotted along. Some day, she hoped, they would laugh at all this, the two lost weeks up on Scafell Pike which she now determined never to see again. First she would send up a rescue team, then locate Max and then have a long soak. There were bridges to mend but Amanda was feeling much better.

Back at the tower they were building a fire on the sloping lawn where the snowman stood, using Richard's supply of logs and some of the cardboard boxes. The mist was thinning, and soon the sun broke through. In the woodshed they had unearthed an old can of petrol. With luck the blaze would attract the attention of any passing aircraft. This was the best chance Mark now had. Though they kept the conversation light, they all instinctively knew his days might be numbered.

Mark himself appeared unperturbed. He wanted to know where Amanda was.

She had just popped out for some air, Jilly said, bathing his forehead with tepid water to keep the fever in check. Dawn, now petrified, crouched and stared, occasionally whimpering in her throat.

"Go downstairs and help with the fire," Jilly told her.

Alone with her, Mark opened his eyes and stared her levelly in the face. His gaze was clear and his smile was sweet. He was definitely compos mentis. He squeezed her hand. She caressed his cheek, reflecting how gorgeous he had once been. Small wonder Dawn had been so completely bowled over.

"I'm dying," said Mark in his normal tone. "But please don't worry, it comes to us all. It's not nearly as bad as you think. As one day you'll find out."

Someone behind her suddenly moved and Jilly cried out with a sharp start of shock.

"I am sorry to startle you," Lucian said. "I came as soon as I could."

Gently manoeuvring Jilly aside, he moved up close to the bed and took Mark's hand.

CHAPTER
THIRTY-FOUR

A cloud passed briefly before the sun, casting its shadow across the fells, and Amanda instinctively paused to establish her bearings. To the best of her knowledge, she had stuck to the path and carefully negotiated the scree. She could see the glint of water which must be the tarn. There was no sign of life but she didn't care; her resolution was as strong as ever. Somewhere nearby was Max, she was certain of it. She shaded her eyes and looked around. The water was still, as before, without even a ripple. She fleetingly wondered about the car, whether or not it had yet been found, but this was no time for irrelevant thought. She was on a mission.

She reached the path that bordered the lake and stood for a while in the crisp clear air. There were no signs at all of other walkers. It might be Sunday but no one appeared to be out. Which did seem strange, even at this time of year.

She was not quite certain which way to walk so took the path they had followed before in the direction, Richard had said, of the farm. The least she might do was find it now and beg a lift to the valley floor. Also get help for poor Mark, who was rapidly failing. She pulled out her phone for a routine check but, as before, it was dead.

She suddenly halted in her tracks, her eyes caught by movement across the tarn. On the level ground was a small stand of trees and, just for a second, she fancied she saw someone there. She stood quite still and held her breath, concentrating on the clump of pines. That glint again; she sensed she was being watched. Nothing moved except a curlew that skittered across the tarn with a raucous cry. She watched it drop like a falling stone almost as low as the water's surface, then right itself and shoot upwards into the sky. What amazing freedom; she watched it fly, wishing she were that agile. Then she jumped as she sensed further movement among the trees.

Something was there, she could see it now, a darker shape that was standing so still that at first she believed it to be an illusion of shadow. But then it moved and her heart gave a jolt. She was not mistaken: there was something there which, from its size and stance, could only be human. Someone was standing there watching her. Of that she suddenly had no doubt. It moved and she caught the glint of glass in the sunlight.

She started to walk as fast as she could and, across the water, the figure moved too, now quite clearly a man advancing towards her. It had to be Max. She shouted and waved, all of a sudden convulsed with joy. He had survived and, furthermore, had come to find her which meant that he must still love her. She waved again and shouted his name but all he did was continue to walk in the same direction as her on the lakeside path.

Lucian was calm and very controlled. He placed both hands upon Mark's chest and, after only a minute or two, Mark's breathing returned to normal.

"Mark?" whispered Jilly, electrified, unable to trust what she saw with her eyes, and slowly Mark raised his lids and smiled at her sweetly.

"Jilly," he said, extending one hand, and the skin no longer felt clammy to touch. He curled his fingers round hers and gave them a squeeze. Jilly started to sob.

"Don't," said Mark and stroked her hair. "I had a truly amazing dream and suddenly I am awake and feel much better."

He looked it too. The pallor had gone and his eyes had regained their healthy shine. Stupefied, Jilly turned to Lucian, who was quietly leaving the room.

"I can't believe it. What did you do?"

Lucian smiled and inclined his head. "Let him rest," he said, "and he'll soon be better."

Jilly, unable to leave it at that, followed Lucian out of the room and down the stairs to the kitchen where Dawn was waiting. "I can't believe what you did," she said. "A moment ago I thought he had died."

"It's the mountain air," said Lucian. "It can work wonders."

"Wait," said Jilly. "Please don't go. We've been hoping to see you for several days but whenever we need you, we never know where to look."

Lucian smiled. "I'm around," he said. "If you need me enough, you can always find me."

"We have to get out of this horrible place." Dawn, at last, had recovered her voice and, though she was shaken, her spirit was fast returning. "The first thing we need is a phone," she said. "The one here appears to have been cut off and none of us can get signals on our mobiles."

Lucian shrugged. "I don't know about that. I am not conversant with technology but perhaps you will find it is all for the best and will give you time for reflection."

"Give me a break," Dawn snarled at him, heartily sick of his endless evasions. "All we need is a number to call to get us back to our real lives."

"Sorry," said Lucian. "I don't understand. Things don't get much realer than life up here. Talk to Mark when he's up to it and I'm sure you'll find he agrees."

He stopped at the door with his hand on the knob. "As you, of them all, I should think will understand."

She was moving fast but they weren't getting closer which meant the distance was further than had first appeared. Amanda kept quickening her pace and Max (if it was Max) fell into step, slowing whenever she needed to pause for breath. She shouted again but he did not respond though the fact he was moving to meet her encouraged her greatly. How odd that they should have met up at the tarn, almost as if he had known her plans. Or perhaps he was still on the upward climb and here by coincidence. Nothing surprised her any more. At least he had clearly survived the fall and must be in excellent form to embark on this trek. She squinted again against the sun but all she could see was his general shape. He was wearing black spandex as far as she could make out.

Dear old Max. He was not all bad. Amanda could not now envisage her life without him. He could be uncaring and also abrupt but had other aspects that turned her on. He was sharp, astute and occasionally witty and, between the sheets, second to none. Because of her own competitive spirit, she liked a man who would rough her about and Max rarely let her down in that department. Her pulses quickened and so did her pace and, gratifyingly, his did too. They had been apart for too long which should make their reunion all the sweeter.

Where, she wondered, could they go now? Back to the lake, if he had a car; back to her own car to pick up her stuff before returning to London. It must be all right or he'd not be here. She anticipated their making up and a visceral shiver shot right through to her core. The first thing she'd do, though, was use his phone to alert the authorities to Mark's plight. He would have to be air-lifted from the tower without further delay.

The others would want to be out of there too, though were not quite so desperate now they had food. With luck she would never go back again to that terrifying old pele tower. She wondered if they'd remain in touch, doubted it somehow, though she definitely thought she would try to keep contact with Angus. Since they both lived in London that should not prove hard and she felt they had areas still to explore. In another life they might even have made it together.

They were almost there; she could now see his face though his eyes were eclipsed by his sporty shades. Her heart was beating fast in her chest, not only through the exertion. But now the weather was changing fast and the sun had vanished behind more clouds. The mist was rising and closing in over the water. Damn this weather. Her hands were cold; she had left so fast she'd forgotten her gloves. She rubbed them hard to restore the circulation.

Almost there, twenty yards or so, but Max had now vanished from her sight, nor could she even make out the towering shape of Scafell Pike. There was no one around, not a single sound except her footsteps and laboured breathing.

"Max," she called, slightly desperate now.

To be met by an utter and devastating silence.

CHAPTER
THIRTY-FIVE

How she got back she would never know. It took her hours on her hands and knees through mist so dense she could barely see her hand in front of her face. The scree was the worst, lacerating her palms and making her curse she'd forgotten her gloves. Frequently she was obliged to stop and try to control her weeping. She had shouted for Max and cursed and screamed but heard nothing more. He had disappeared. When she reached the place where she'd seen him first, nothing remained except the thicket of trees. Trees and an ever worsening mist which made her fear she would never get back to the only place she knew of where there was shelter. In the end it was Lucian again who found her, distraught and almost out of her mind. She clung to him as he helped her back to her feet and led her home.

Home, he called it. She might have spat but her fighting spirit was almost spent. She was tired and frozen and half demented with grief and a terrible anger. What had she done to deserve this fate, constantly banging her head against bricks? She had always worked hard and passed her exams; won a scholarship, got a good degree and been selected as a trainee by the highly prestigious Prudential. For most of her life Amanda walked tall, proud of her job and also her looks. She had fought major wars on behalf of her sex and been instrumental in smashing through the glass ceiling.

Now, however, she felt like a wreck, having lost her lover as well as her way, and after many cold hours in the dark, during which she had prayed she would not survive, found herself back where she'd started from, in a mediaeval tower at the top of a mountain.

The others were pleased — well, of course they were — and came running out with their arms spread wide, which should have made her feel loved but instead made her cry. Mark was improving; the news was good. Out of nowhere it seemed he had turned a corner and now was rapidly making up for lost time. Jilly was throwing together a meal to celebrate Amanda's return. For more than one reason, today had been extra stressful.

"What happened?" asked Angus, eyes filled with concern, taking Amanda aside to find out. She saw from that look that his feelings were more than just friendly.

She wasn't ready to cope with that. Her emotions were now all over the place, the more so because she had no idea what Max had been after or where he had gone. He seemed to have melted into the mist but might still materialise on their doorstep.

"I'm sorry," she said, pushing Angus away. "But I'm still too shattered to talk about it yet."

★ ★ ★

"What happened?" Richard was keen to know, having been outside with the bonfire when Lucian arrived. He had seen the back of him, walking away, though Lucian had not even stopped for a chat. Richard noticed that he was lightly dressed and strolling rather than hurrying off. He might even, he thought on later reflection, have been wearing some kind of a swirling cape and carrying in his hand a silvertopped cane.

Jilly was still at a loss to explain exactly what had occurred that day except that Lucian, it seemed, had revivified Mark.

"Precisely what do you mean by that?" Revivify: an archaic word, but Jilly was no kind of scholar so where had it come from?

"I'm not quite sure." She was confused, still unable to understand what precisely had happened. Mark, she could almost swear, had been dying until Lucian came along and . . . revivified . . . him.

"Is it resurrected you mean?"

"Yes," said Jilly, "I suppose it is." And don't ask any more questions, she warned, as she could not explain it either. All Lucian had done was touch Mark with both hands and Mark's laboured breathing had instantly changed. One moment he seemed like a dying man, the next he was smiling and stroking her hair. "Ask Mark," she said. "He was there." And would confirm it.

Mark, though still weak, was propped up in bed with Dawn devotedly feeding him soup. The familiar laughter flared in his eyes when his old mucker, Richard, walked in.

213

Richard punched his fist, choking back tears. "How are you feeling now?" he asked.

Surprisingly well, which Mark demonstrated by emptying the bowl and asking for more. At this rate, he said, he'd be up very soon and ready to take the adventure to the next stage.

"What did he do?"

"I can't really say." Though Mark did recall, as he drifted away, being gently drawn towards a very bright light.

Amanda came by to pay her respects, a shadow of her usual self. A day on her own on the fells in the mist seemed to have greatly reduced her. Her nose was red and she snuffled a bit, due to emotion and the bitter cold.

"Take care of yourself. We need you," said Mark, who only that morning was on his way out. Now he was back to his charming self with a gleam of wickedness in his eye. Soon he'd be up there with the best of them, dancing.

Dawn hung round him, his number one fan, having shed all trace of her arrogance. She said very little but looked quite cute though only had eyes for his lordship. Richard, amused yet also impressed, bit back the urge to make tasteless remarks. As a lasting couple they would never gel but right now it was rather sweet.

"We need to get this show on the road," said Richard as soon as he'd cleared the room.

"Ready when you are," said Mark, whose arm had stopped hurting.

"Since we don't know the state of the markets right now, it's hard to assess how much time we still have."

Mark laughed. "Fast learner," he said. "Top marks. I vote that we go as soon as we can, depending on the weather."

The weather indeed. It would be no joke, even on the mildest of nights. The thought of doing that climb in reverse made both of these stalwarts shudder. Though not complain; they'd been bred to take whatever was thrown at them head on. Stiff upper lip and all that guff, though they'd never admit that, not even to each other.

"What do we do if we can't take off?"

"We'll cross that bridge when we have to," was Mark's reply.

That night it snowed superabundantly. The heavens just opened and down it came like baskets of feathers tipped from a giant's hen coop. Amanda and Jilly watched it through the narrow slit window, designed for defence, caught in the light of the lantern that glowed in the porch. This was the light that had led them here, that had drawn them unwaveringly up to these heights, a beacon steadily glowing through undulant mist.

Not only them but the flying boys too, whose plane had ditched on a frozen crag and who'd slithered down here, risking life and limb, to try their luck at the pele tower. Also the motorists, Angus and Dawn, having somehow missed the right motorway turn and found themselves creeping round the back-waters of Keswick. If only Dawn had had her way and insisted that Angus keep pressing on, their paths would never have crossed at this fateful juncture.

Amanda stood there, watching the snow and wondering what had happened to Max, if it had really been him at the tarn and not just a malignant illusion. If it had been Max then where was he now? Would he not have followed her up to the tower where, sooner or later, at least in this snow, he would surely have made himself known? Or had he, perhaps, had a car parked nearby and driven back to the conference hotel to which he had already tracked her down, though for what purpose she was now not entirely sure.

She could not settle, just fidgeted there feeling the need of some sort of action. She could not let matters rest until she knew what had happened to Max.

"What's the matter?" asked Jilly. "Can't you sleep?"

"Don't mind me," Amanda said, sliding into her jeans in the dark and pulling on two pairs of socks she had pinched from a drawer. "I'm just popping out for a minute or two, to check if there are any footprints."

CHAPTER
THIRTY-SIX

The snow had drifted at least two feet deep, so it came swirling in when Richard unbolted the door next day to pick up more logs from the porch.

"Wow!" he shouted. "Take a look at this. Talk about winter wonderland, this is fantastic."

The sun, for the first time in days, was bright and the landscape resembled an alpine scene. The sky was mostly blue though a flutter of flakes still fell. Their snowman, slightly the worse for wear due to proximity to the dead fire, had lost its nose and the hat which had blown into a nearby bush. Richard rescued it and replaced them both, tweaking Mark's scarf for a jauntier air. Then, pleased with his achievement, he shouted again.

"Wake up, Jilly," said Amanda, herself again after a drug-induced sleep. A single look at that pristine snow was enough to get her blood racing. Today would be the day, she was sure, when they'd finally get away from this place. At which moment, from the distance, she heard an engine.

"A helicopter, I think it must be," she said, pressing her face to the narrow pane. And, indeed, there it was, way off in the sky, a hovering black beetle of a thing with POLICE painted boldly on its side.

"Hallelujah! They've finally seen us," she shouted in relief.

She dressed at speed before racing downstairs without even dragging a comb through her hair. Richard and Angus were out there already, gazing enraptured up at the hovering aircraft.

"They've arrived at last! We're safe!" she said. She swung Angus round in a spontaneous hug. Angus reciprocated in spades, relieved she was so much more cheerful.

The helicopter hung in the air, its noisy engine scattering the birds while the three of them leapt up and down and waved to ensure that they had been seen.

"Come and get us!" screamed Amanda. If she'd had a hat, she'd have thrown it in the air.

She rushed upstairs and made Jilly get up. "We ought to sort out the bedding," she said. They couldn't just leave without doing their bit to make the place shipshape again. The freezer, once more, was fairly well stocked, as were the wine rack and liquor chest. She only wished there was time to launder the sheets.

The sound of the engine was fading now.

"The bastards are moving off," Richard said.

"Probably just to summon reserves," said Angus, less easily rattled. Since they were six, they were going to need extra transport. News of their plight must indeed have hit the headlines.

Even Mark was now out of bed, moving slowly but with steely resolve. He wanted to shower and shave before facing his public.

"How do you feel?"

"Not too bad," he said. His formerly livid scar was already fading.

Dawn appeared, having slept through it all, surprised at so much activity. They had all skipped breakfast and Jilly was plumping up cushions.

Amanda anxiously scanned the horizon. For once there was hardly a cloud in the sky and the snow had finally stopped.

"Don't worry," said Angus, "they'll soon be back."

But Amanda's mind, once again, was on Max. He had to be out there somewhere, she thought, and now that the weather was not so bad she was pretty sure he'd put in another appearance. While she was waiting, she helped tidy up. No doubt the police would alert the owners. They ought to leave them a note of thanks for having, inadvertently, saved their lives.

"Later," she said, "we can send them a case of champagne."

When, after two hours, the police were not back, Jilly decided they ought to have lunch. They had no idea how long it might take for them to be finally rescued.

"Are you quite sure they'll be able to land?" she asked Mark, the expert, who reassured her.

"Helicopters can land on a sixpence," he said, "which is why they're used for traffic control." No doubt they'd be sending a larger one to accommodate them all.

With luck they would also spot Angus's car. He couldn't wait to get back on the road and was hoping Amanda might give Dawn a lift. The guys, he now knew, had their own alternative plans.

"Do you think you'll be able to climb?" Richard asked.

"No problem," said Mark, with that luminous grin. His recovery was miraculous; he could move his arm freely again.

"Maybe the cops can drop us off," said Richard, who hated the thought of that climb. Once had been quite enough for him and this time it would be in reverse after a week of snow, now frozen solid. They had barely survived the downward climb. He shut his mind to the dangers of getting back up there.

Mark, though, appeared to be resolute despite the fact he had nearly died. This expedition was strictly illegal; he wouldn't take any more chances. Of which Richard, his lawyer, was all too well aware and should not need reminding.

Jilly had made chicken noodle soup to sustain them until they reached the hotel. She stood outside and studied the sky, still clear and blue though with gathering clouds.

"You are certain they will come back?" she said. It still seemed too good to be true.

"Absolutely," Angus replied. He was expert at leading teams and raising morale. Secretly, though, even he had qualms. It was several hours since the helicopter had paid them a flying visit. It was probably paper-work holding them up. He would feel more confident once he could hear that engine approaching again.

Mark thought it might want to land on the roof so perhaps they should start making plans for that now. They all trooped up to the top of the tower and opened the battlements door. They were buffeted by a mighty wind which almost threw Jilly back down the stairs.

"Careful!" yelled Angus. "Hold on tight. We don't want to risk any accidents now." Mark had been right: there was plenty of room to land.

"Ought we to sweep it?" Amanda asked, scared the snow might drive the police away.

Mark explained that helicopters were very versatile. They could, though, he said, write a sign in the snow to indicate the best place to land. With his toe he wrote the word HELP in six foot letters. That, he said, ought to do the job. Then he led them all back downstairs to wait in the warm.

It was almost dark when they heard the noise and knew the helicopter was back. It hovered above them with flashing lights, still making that terrible racket.

"I wonder if they can see our sign." Jilly was still in a state of nerves.

"Perhaps not now," said Angus. "But it shouldn't matter." The important thing was that they had returned. He suggested they all go back on the roof, ready for instant takeoff when the thing landed. None of them had any luggage, which was just as well.

They stood in a row on the battlements while the helicopter hovered above, giving no sign it intended to land, perhaps awaiting instructions.

"Look," shouted Richard, pointing up. They seemed to be opening up a hatch from which they were now unrolling what looked like a ladder.

"Cripes," said Jilly. "I'm not climbing that."

"It's better than being left here," said Mark, who was reconsidering whether or not he wanted a lift to the top.

Amanda stared. They were climbing out and the helicopter was swooping low, apparently unaware of them all on the roof. "Hello," she screamed, waving frantically, but nobody took any notice. Two men in jumpsuits proclaiming POLICE were poised on the ladder to leap to the ground, apparently at the front porch next to the wilting snowman.

"We must go down." Angus wrestled the door which the wind had blown shut and now would not budge. Even assisted by Richard and Mark, he could not get it to open.

"Bugger," he said, then yelled at the top of his voice.

The policemen were trying the main front door. It didn't open, so they scribbled a note. They stood for a while by the snowman, deeply conferring.

Angus frantically rattled the door while Richard was leaping around on the roof, making urgent signs to the helicopter, still hovering above them.

222

"I can't believe they can't see us," wailed Jilly, her hopes of survival diminishing fast as the uniformed men climbed back up the ladder and the helicopter rose in the air and, in seconds, was out of sight.

"Bloody hell," said Mark. "They stole my scarf."

CHAPTER
THIRTY-SEVEN

"Why didn't they see us?"

"I really don't know."

At supper that night they were all subdued, having tried the battlements door again and this time found it unstuck and easy to open. Angus was through it in a flash and they'd followed him down the twisting stairs, all of them shouting to the police not to leave. As always, the front door opened smoothly though, only seconds before, they had watched the policemen try it and apparently find it locked. The note through the door simply gave the date and approximate time they had made the call. There was no instruction to get in touch; it was merely a routine check.

It didn't make sense; having come all this way, the least they might have done was try to gain entrance. Now all six stood outside in the snow, staring into the empty sky where threatening storm clouds were once again starting to gather.

"I find it hard to believe," Richard said. "That they'd come and look and then just go away."

"They took my scarf," grumbled Mark. "It was Hugo Boss."

"I think," said Angus, "they came because of the snowman."

Amanda said, after a startled pause: "You mean they never knew we were here?"

Angus nodded. "It looks like that," he said.

"But the helicopter . . ." squawked Jilly.

". . . was checking things out."

They sat in silence, utterly stunned, while Jilly served chicken, cooked to a turn, with a garnish of bacon and perfectly roasted potatoes. The fact that they still had food was their one consolation.

"You mean we haven't been missed?" spluttered Richard, his lawyer's brain working overtime.

"So it would appear," said Angus, equally in the dark.

"But that's lunatic." Amanda was angry. She held out her wine glass for Mark to refill. What, in heaven's name, could be going on? And where was Max? He had nothing to do with any of this and should, by now, have appeared. Why should he bother to come at all unless he wanted to patch things up and possibly let her know he was okay? A burden was lifted, and she mentally slumped. For the past two weeks she had carried around an almost insurmountable weight of guilt. Now it would seem she was off the hook but what, in that case, had happened to him? She could only suppose he had lost his way in the mist.

Angus was raging about the police, who seemed to have come on a false alarm. Someone had spotted the snowman and sent them to check. The least they might have done was enquire but it seemed they had only tried the front door, then left without knowing if anyone was at home. The fact that there were people on the roof, jumping, shouting and waving their arms, had mysteriously appeared to escape their notice. All they had left was that futile note, though if they had cared they'd have stuck around. It seemed they were not aware that the owners weren't there. Unless they were routinely checking things out. Either way, their visit seemed totally futile.

Mark, meanwhile, now the cops had been, was even more anxious to get away. Verging on the desperate, in fact. What little time he had was running out fast.

He needed to get to Reykjavik and deposit the money before he was caught. Asset stripping had now become illegal. He'd have been there and back in a couple of days if they'd not been obliged to abandon the plane. He had to get back to it now very fast and hoped that weather conditions would let him take off. A very long shot but still worth a try, provided Richard would come with him.

"If possible, we should leave tonight."

"You must be out of your mind. In the dark?" Richard had nerves of steel but this was plain crazy.

"Look," said Mark. "They now know where we are. Or soon will." They had stolen his scarf.

"You're suggesting we scale that cliff in the dark, a few hours after a heavy storm with temperatures well below zero?" Richard spoke calmly. "Only days after you almost died from injuries caused on the downhill climb? We would need at least crampons and a rope as

226

well as a flashlight and possibly flares." Not to mention the kind of luck that Mark too easily took for granted.

"We don't have a choice," insisted Mark, who would sooner die than lose face at work. He had battled with far greater odds before and survived.

"Well, we're not going anywhere tonight. You can put that idea right out of your head." Richard was mainly passive by nature but when he laid down the law he would not budge.

He led Mark back to a seat by the fire and fetched the bottle to top up his glass. They would sort this out in the morning when they were sober.

Lucian might well hold the key to it all. He seemed to turn up when they needed him and Mark would never forget how much he owed him. There was nobody else he would trust with his foolhardy plan for risking his neck. The others, like Richard, were likely to try to stop him. So, once they had eaten, Mark slipped away, saying he needed an early night. He had been through a lot in the past few days and had squandered his strength when he really should have conserved it. Richard agreed. He was sick of the whole affair.

Instead of going to bed, however, Mark crept up the stairs without making a sound in search of the ever elusive Lucian Demort. Something compelled him towards the man, an inner force that sucked him in as compulsively as a moth is drawn to a flame. He could not exactly nail what it was, some power emitting from Lucian's brain that acted like a magnetic force on Mark in his weakened state. Since the incident of the healing hands when he had felt his life ebbing away, he had been in some sort of thrall to the dynamic stranger.

Right now he needed him on his side for something for which he had limited time. Downstairs he could hear the grandfather clock striking midnight.

Lucian was there when Mark opened the door, seated in front of a glowing fire, comfortably settled in a wing chair, a heavy book on his knee. He wore pince-nez and a velvet cap that matched his elegant monogrammed slippers, and looked like someone not quite of this world possessing some mystic wisdom.

"Mark," he said, unsurprised. "Come in. I was expecting you."

It seemed he had all the time in the world as he closed the book and riddled the fire, then reached across to an ornate box and offered Mark a cigar.

"No thanks," said Mark. It was not his thing. He had many vices but not that one. He folded his hands above his head and tipped himself back in his chair. "I need to get up to my plane," he said. "As soon as it can be arranged. Tonight. For which I will need an expert guide who really knows the terrain."

Lucian flashed him a vulpine smile. "Not that easily done," he said. "Where exactly did you land? Remind me."

"High on a crag on Scafell Pike. The mist rolled in and we had no choice. I guess we were lucky to land at all in such weather."

Lucian studied him long and hard, weighing up something in his mind. "And where is it you are headed next?" he asked, as if he'd forgotten.

Mark pointed north. "Up there," he said. "There's something I urgently need to deliver."

"How urgent?"

"Very. I'm practically two weeks late."

Lucian lapsed into silence again, gazing thoughtfully into the fire. Nothing seemed to faze him. He barely flickered.

"Ideally you need a team of dogs. Though not even they could reach that crag. Certainly not at night in this freezing weather."

"I will take my chances," said Mark, "with a human guide."

The pair locked eyes for a loaded second. "Do you think you are fit enough to climb?"

Mark felt the breath in his chest seize up for a horrifying split second. But he trusted this man. "I will do what it takes," he said, "if we leave tonight."

Lucian silently stared at the fire, drawing long and hard on his fine cigar.

"All right," he said. "Just wait while I change my shoes."

CHAPTER
THIRTY-EIGHT

Richard came down for his breakfast tight-lipped, having woken to find Mark was not in his bunk. He had not thought to check the previous night when he'd stumbled upstairs in the early hours and fallen into an instant booze-driven coma. Mark must have been gone several hours by then which Richard preferred to keep to himself. The last thing he needed was fluttering in the hen coop.

The wind had dropped and the mist had cleared; the mountain peak was gilded in brilliant sunshine. If it weren't for the biting cold outside, it looked like a perfect day for a hike. Richard lured Angus outside and sounded him out.

"Do you feel like a serious climb?" he asked.

Angus readily jumped at the chance. He found the atmosphere of the tower increasingly claustrophobic. "When do you plan to set out?" he asked.

"As soon as we can," whispered Richard.

Not a word to the women, though, whom he had fobbed off with a concocted story. Mark was under the weather again and spending the day in bed.

"I think that's the least he could do," said Amanda crisply.

"Where do you think he went?" Angus asked.

Richard pointed at Scafell Pike. "Up there," he said. "There is something he needs from the plane."

"And you are going to attempt to stop him?"

"I'll certainly do my damnedest," said Richard. If Mark, in his fragile state, took off he'd be doomed.

Richard had brought a rough diagram of the route they had taken down from the top which had been in mist and biting cold, through narrow passes and over rocks. There must be an easier path they could follow in daylight.

"Mark must be crazy," said Angus, impressed.

"What else did you expect? He's a City trader."

Dawn, disconsolate, drifted around, bored with nothing to do with her time. Without Mark there it felt like the sun was obscured. Yesterday they had been ready to leave, only to have their hopes cruelly dashed. It was incomprehensible that they had not been rescued.

Jilly had thought the police might come back.

"I doubt it," said Amanda.

Amanda and Jilly were up in their room and Angus and Richard had gone for a walk. With Mark hors de combat, Dawn was left with nothing to do but wander. She thought about going to talk to Mark but he might not be in a sociable mood. Sleeping it off was what Richard had said; all three men had certainly had a skinful. She stood at the window and stared at the view but nothing would drag her out there today. The breakfast dishes were cleared and put away; she had time on her hands.

She drifted upstairs where the others were and could hear them laughing behind a closed door. They worked for the same mammoth company so shared insider gossip. Dawn felt very much out of it, though knew if she knocked they would welcome her in. But their conversation would then go flat and make her feel she was intruding. Whatever it was they were laughing about would be something entirely above her head. They both had managerial jobs; Dawn was very aware of her own limitations.

Angus now slept in the playroom alone. She opened the door and wandered inside then started, as a reflex, to go through his pockets. His suits were expensive and beautifully cut, all bespoke from Savile Row. She thought it odd that he did not produce them himself. She had mentioned this and he'd been amused. She had no idea about taste, he'd said. What was good enough for the high street hordes he would not be seen dead in himself. His wife and daughter bought all their clothes in Bond Street or even Paris. It was double standards of the very worst kind but Angus did not see it that way. He had worked for it so he'd spend it. End of subject. His shirts were hand-tailored from Jermyn Street and he had an array of expensive cufflinks though had brought a single pair for this dirty weekend. They were still in the cuffs of the shirt he had worn; she pressed it against her face and sniffed his cologne. Angus was all the things she desired in a husband who'd love her the rest of her life. Had she read Jane Austen, she would see him as her Mr Knightley.

Although he came from working-class roots, he owned his business and was very well off; his picture often appeared in the press with celebrities from the fashion world, like Kate Moss. His share price was quoted; he advertised with double page spreads in the glossy mags. He represented all Dawn had ever wished for. Her girlfriends said he was far too old but she knew that they really envied her. But now it seemed he was sliding out of her reach.

Because he was off on a mountain hike, he had left his wallet behind on a shelf. She emptied its contents and checked through them one by one. He carried three hundred pounds in cash plus five prestigious gold credit cards as well as the one from his very exclusive club. There was also a snap of his boring wife wearing a ludicrous Ascot hat. On the two occasions she'd met her Dawn had thought her slightly pretentious.

Bored, she put it all carefully back and replaced the wallet on the shelf. Then she climbed on the rocking horse for a solitary ride. The only good thing about this trip was the night in the fabulous five star hotel when she'd driven Angus to unsurpassed heights of passion. Then he had said he would leave his wife, but now he appeared to have changed his mind. Since being here, he had not so much as touched her. In any case, Dawn would sooner have Mark who was smarter, savvier and nearer her age. Also Mark was unmarried, a definite plus. Before they parted she intended to slip him her number.

She rocked away for a little while more then climbed off the horse and looked at the other toys. Which was when she discovered the cute little monkey with cymbals.

They climbed for an hour without speaking a word, conserving what energy they had left. Angus rejoiced in the crisp mountain air and the sense of stretching himself to the utmost limit. Richard was younger and fitter by far but Angus kept up surprisingly well. They stopped when they reached the serious part and roped themselves together.

"Have you climbed before?"

"Not for many years." Not since he'd left the forces, in fact, but instinct showed Angus where he should place his hands. It was still very cold but the sun was bright and he liked the feel of it on his face. Every fifteen minutes or so, Richard suggested they rest.

"How much further?"

"Five hundred feet." The crag they were after was just out of sight and no other climbers appeared to be out, not on this side of the mountain. Mark might have taken a different route or even turned back because of his arm; he shouldn't be climbing at all in his condition. Richard strained his ears but could not hear a sound. The one he most feared was the roar of the Lear jet's engine.

"How do you feel? Are you game to go on?"

Angus nodded, proud of getting this far.

Ahead of them was a grassy knoll where Richard suggested they take a break. If they'd brought a flag, this was where he'd have planted it.

They both sat down and unroped themselves and Richard produced his hip flask. It felt good to be sitting on level ground for a while.

"Look over there. There's a stone," Richard said and crawled across on his hands and knees to examine the moss-covered rock, which appeared to be some sort of monument. He scraped away at the granite face on which faint lettering now appeared. It looked very ancient; perhaps it was some kind of shrine. There was an inscription, Latin he thought though much of it had been eroded away, surmounted by a grinning skull and crossbones.

Angus crawled over to look at it too, not trusting himself to stand in this wind.

"My God," he said. "I wasn't expecting that."

Richard produced his Swiss army knife and scraped away with a little more force, revealing another word, about six inches high, above what looked like a date. "It can't be a gravestone up here," he said. "It's so far off the beaten track that very few people could reach it except serious climbers."

He went on scraping while Angus watched as slowly the letters revealed themselves.

"Good heavens!" said Richard. The word on the stone was *Demort*.

CHAPTER
THIRTY-NINE

Dawn was laughing when they came down, clapping her hands to the cymbal sound, dancing round the room like a thing demented.

"Goodness," said Jilly. "We heard you upstairs and thought perhaps you had lost your mind."

"No," said Dawn with a radiant smile. "Just found myself a playmate."

The monkey was cute with a cheerful grin and glittering eyes in its dark brown fur and it banged the brass cymbals for all it was worth, making a sound like a tambourine. And, as it banged, it very slowly rotated.

"It belongs to the children," Dawn explained. "I found it upstairs on the playroom shelf." She was like a child herself; it seemed to have raised her spirits.

Jilly laughed. "It's enchanting," she said. It brought the family back to life. Until she remembered the rabbit stuffed down the drain.

"I've been up there riding the rocking horse," said Dawn. "I needed some exercise."

"You're daft," said Jilly, then was brushed aside by Amanda who snatched the eight-inch toy and, whooping with joy, proceeded to rip it apart.

"Hang on a second," said Dawn, appalled, clawing at Amanda to get it back.

"Batteries," said Amanda, intent on her plunder.

It should have occurred to them before: replacement batteries for the transistor radio. All the time they'd been going mad, entirely cut off from the outside world, this monkey had been laughing behind their backs.

"Where are the men?"

"Not yet back from their walk."

"And Mark?"

"As far as I know, asleep." Perhaps they should wake him now and tell him the news. It was almost lunchtime.

Dawn was delighted to have an excuse. "I'll go straight up and wake him," she said.

"Be careful," said Jilly. "Remember he's still very fragile."

Amanda was tuning the radio in, frantically seeking a weather report, also keen to catch the mid-morning headlines. Their deprivation had been complete; they had been cut off from the world now for two whole weeks. At the start she had been worrying about Max; now, at least, she knew he was safe. Except that she didn't know where he was, which was baffling.

"I wonder where the others have gone." They had slipped away at the crack of dawn, muttering something about a walk, though now it seemed they'd equipped themselves with crampons and a rope. Typically male. Amanda laughed. Big swinging dicks they were known as at work. They just couldn't let the testosterone settle but constantly had to show off.

The weather, she heard, was cold and dry though Arctic storms were threatening. If only those bloody policemen had not left them stranded. Still, now that she'd got the radio to work, the least she could do was find the fuse box and sort out the lights. Then, if someone would only fix the TV, she could almost face spending the winter here. The longer she was away from work, the more remote it became. She felt an instant pang of guilt about Jilly.

Dawn suddenly came rushing in. Mark was not in his room, she said, and furthermore only one of the bunks had been slept in. She had checked: the bathroom was empty too, his flying jacket was gone from its hook and his boots had disappeared from the downstairs cloakroom.

Amanda and Jilly exchanged a look. They remembered that last night he'd seemed quite keyed up and had slipped off to bed very early, which wasn't his style. Something was brewing; they didn't know what but now Angus and Richard had gone too.

"You don't suppose they've abandoned us," wailed Dawn.

"They wouldn't do that," Amanda said, though there was no reason why they should not. It was purely by chance they were here at all, three separate couples sheltering from the weather. The men would be able to move much faster if they dumped the women and did their own thing. Mark had said something about the plane. Perhaps they had all done a runner.

"Hang on a sec," interrupted Jilly, who had managed to find the BBC news. "He mentioned London. I'm not quite sure . . ." But then the transistor went dead.

Angus stared at the word *Demort*. He'd heard it before, only recently, though he'd been out of circulation a couple of weeks. Then he suddenly got it.

"Lucian," he said. "It's his family name, I remember now. He told Amanda and it rather goes with his looks." Distinctly foreign, perhaps with a touch of the Gallic.

"So how come," said Richard, "it is stuck up here? Unless it's some kind of boundary stone?"

"Which might explain his assertiveness. He probably owns the mountain." Which wasn't all that far-fetched, now he thought of it. They were fairly close to the border here; the pele towers had been designed to repel marauders.

"But the French?" said Richard, not getting it yet.

"You are talking to a proud Scot," said Angus. "I may not know much about history but I do know our most famous queen grew up in France."

Mary Stuart. Both of them laughed then leaned back comfortably in the sun. Richard offered Angus another swig from his hip flask.

"Don't go leading me astray." Angus laughed. "I am quite as high, as it is, as I care to be."

They stared up into the deep blue sky at the frozen crag they were aiming for. Now that the history lesson was done, they ought to get going again. They replaced

239

their crampons as well as the rope and Richard prepared to lead the way.

"I sincerely hope," muttered Angus, "that this will be worth it."

"Bloody hell!" Amanda ranted. Just when she'd thought they were finally fixed they had managed to lose the wavelength for Radio Four. Jilly was full of apologies, but try as she might, all she got now was static. Amanda wrenched the radio out of her hand and took it outside and continued to fiddle. Jilly, who knew not to argue, shrugged and went back to fixing lunch.

It seemed it would just be the three of them, since all the men had now disappeared. She considered making a quiche then abandoned the thought. They would come back some time and quiche would not do. Soup would be better: they were bound to be cold and Jilly was a naturally nurturing person. She would use up the remnants of the chicken and throw in a handful of this and that and hope it would do them all until tonight.

As she gathered her ingredients, she thought about Derek, and realised she was thinking of him less and less. Also, she no longer worried about the pain to which she had gradually become accustomed. It was probably nothing and would keep until she was home and could get to a doctor. She was less concerned now about long-term plans. Survival was the main thing.

She chucked some chillies into the soup to warm them all up and improve their flagging morale. Dawn was in a tizz about Mark, even more so since he had disappeared, but had felt the same about Angus when they first met her. In fact she had bragged that they, too, had marriage plans. Already, however, her target had changed. It seemed now that Mark was the chosen one. Closer to her in age, perhaps, but still way out of her class.

Soft-hearted Jilly was rarely unkind but felt Dawn was punching above her weight. Restored to reality she would bet that neither of the gentlemen would come through. Especially now that they seemed to have disappeared.

The one that puzzled her most was Amanda, highly placed in the executive chain, who'd been sent to the convention to rally the troops. Jilly had been both impressed and inspired by the sheer virtuosity of her speech. Onwards and upwards had been her message to all Prudential employees. And when Amanda had singled her out for a Sunday hill-walk on Scafell Pike, Jilly felt all her Christmases had come at once.

Now, though, Amanda was growing more fraught as well as obsessed with catching the news from London. For no obvious reason that Jilly knew, unless it concerned the mysterious Max whose name Amanda repeatedly said in her sleep.

CHAPTER
FORTY

The main essential they lacked was power. Transistor batteries were not enough. They could not continue to live like this, like cavemen devoid of contact with the real world. While they waited for the men to return, they decided to hunt the fuse box down. They'd eliminated the obvious places so it wasn't likely to be too hard. They made a list of places to look, most of which they had already checked out. Not the kitchen, which they knew well and which, since both freezer and fridge still worked, must be on a separate circuit.

The living room did not bother them. It had the fire and the candlelight which all of them had agreed they rather preferred. Along the dark corridor past their rooms were gaslights they only occasionally lit; a hand-held candle, they'd found, was as effective. There weren't any fuse boxes on this floor. Angus had checked when the power first went off and, as far as Amanda could recall, Lucian's amazing library was illuminated by oil lamps and candlelight.

The floor above, where Dawn had got lost, was in perpetual shadow due to the narrowness of the arrowslit windows. The iron sconce on the spiral stairs threw only a limited circle of light. It would seem that this floor was seldom used except, perhaps, for the room at the end where Dawn had reported seeing the bright white light. No sign of that now in the afternoon and she still had not expanded on her experience. It wasn't something she cared to discuss, perhaps because she was still not sure what had happened. Up here it was also quite exceptionally cold.

"It gives me the heebie-jeebies," whispered Jilly.

"Hang on a mo," Amanda said, shining the torch she had brought upstairs over the walls. There was no sign of anything like a fuse box. Up here had not yet been renovated, which might explain the temperature drop: the windows were unglazed and the floor was simply stone flags without even a rug.

Something moved at the very far end by the door that led out to the battlements. For an instant Amanda thought she saw someone there. The torch revealed only emptiness, but then it seemed Jilly sensed movement too.

"Over there," she said urgently, tugging Amanda's sleeve.

"Please let's get out of here," muttered Dawn, who could not forget that alarming night. The longer they stayed here, the realer it became.

"There," said Jilly. "Quick, move the torch." The beam caught a small pale oval resembling a face.

The child again, she was sure of it, though nothing showed in the dark except the face.

"Is there anyone there?" asked Amanda to absolute silence.

★ ★ ★

Back downstairs by the friendly fire they shook so much they could barely speak. It was growing dark but still the men were not back.

"What's keeping them?" Dawn was scared and shrill. It was clear she was reaching cracking point. Amanda and Jilly were equally thrown but trying to get a grip. It had been a face, both could swear to that, though whose they were still not prepared to guess. Jilly remembered the child with the rabbit and shuddered. If they let fantasy intervene, they might all end up in the madhouse. Meanwhile they still had a problem they needed to fix.

Below them was the great empty hall, tunnel-vaulted and windowless, which had once accommodated the herd but was now some kind of waiting room dominated by the grandfather clock. On the far side, facing the spiral stairs, was a second massive iron-studded door which, they had always assumed, must lead to the cellar. They tried it again as they had before. It was locked.

Jilly was curious. Why should that be? What could possibly be down there that they needed to keep it locked? The first Mrs Rochester, maybe, or even Bluebeard's slaughtered brides. Jilly had always been an ardent reader.

"Wine," said Amanda authoritatively. "From the vintages we have sampled here I would guess they have serious money invested in that."

"Perhaps he does it professionally. Imports wine." An obvious use for a tower like this with its solid walls and

244

presumably spacious cellar. Which could also account for the cases left in the porch.

They were getting nowhere, still had no light which might mean having to force the cellar door lock. Another job they would leave for the men's return.

They had reached a ledge and could not progress. The rockface before them was steep and sheer and as glassily cold as a skating rink tipped on its side. They both peered up at the towering peak that mocked them with its very remoteness. It seemed to be sending a message — *try if you dare.*

Angus spoke first. "I don't know about you but I, for one, feel like packing it in." Nothing was worth a risk like that, especially not Mark whom he hardly knew. He had had enough exercise for one day. Yet he still deferred to Richard, his climbing companion.

Richard considered the situation. The only way up there was vertical and he could not see many places the crampons would fit. "We ought to have brought an ice axe," he said, though it was too late now.

The sun at that moment rode high in the sky but would very soon fall behind the peak when the temperature was likely to plummet. It was cold enough as it was in the sun, without that it would be unbearable. They needed face masks and several more layers of clothing. Angus was not prepared to gamble. He had a sizeable business to run as well as a family to support and would not risk his life for a madcap banker set on a hopeless mission.

"What is it he is so keen to find?" He knew Mark was aiming to reach the plane but there had to be easier ways, like a helicopter.

"There are papers he needs and he plans to take off. Crazy, I know, but that's what he's like. He didn't get where he is without taking chances."

"He must be a bloody lunatic," Angus growled.

Richard agreed but remained concerned about the safety of his childhood friend, who was in no physical shape to be climbing mountains. He raised his voice to shout then stopped, knowing he would never be heard. Also, in conditions like this, he risked setting off an avalanche.

"I'm sorry I dragged you along," he said, "but I figured it worth a try." He'd been bailing Mark out of similar scrapes since prep school.

They slowly began retracing their steps, hugging themselves because of the cold, and this time Angus took over the lead without comment. The scenery was spectacular and they tried to keep up a reasonable pace, aware that the light would soon fade and they might lose their bearings.

"Where were you hoping to go in that plane?" It had to be very important. Both Richard and Mark had significant jobs as well as a first-class education. It must be something reasonably big for either to take such a massive risk. Since Angus's life was in danger, too, he felt he was entitled to some explanation.

Richard considered. He understood that but was ethically bound not to say too much. But Angus was a businessman too, so he decided to trust him.

"We were on our way to Iceland," he said. "For the purpose of buying a bank."

CHAPTER
FORTY-ONE

Amanda was frantic. "Where have you been? We'd have called the police if we'd had a phone."

"And what have you done with Mark?" shrieked Dawn. "Last night his bunk was not slept in." Like she would know, but they didn't go into that.

"God," Richard said, "we assumed he'd be back. Are you sure he didn't sneak in without you knowing?"

"No," said Dawn. "Check, if you like. You must have known he was gone when you slipped away."

Richard felt dreadful. He had truly expected Mark to be safely back by now, slumped in front of the fire, a drink in his hand. Now he wondered what had happened to him. He could not have reached that summit alone. To make doubly sure, he went up and checked but found their room was empty. And Mark's flying jacket was gone, as well as his boots.

The crazy fool; had he really believed he was fit enough to get up to that crag without proper climbing equipment or help when he'd just been so seriously ill? He must have some kind of death wish. Richard no longer knew what to do. To hell with friendship. He was not going back to risk his own neck by looking for him in the dark.

He signalled to Angus he wanted to talk without the others, in particular Dawn, overhearing and throwing a wobbly.

"What happens now?"

"I have no idea." Angus was equally at a loss. They could hardly abandon Mark to his fate, but he had no idea where they ought to look next and this mountain was not ideal for amateur rambling.

"What should we tell them?"

"Only the truth." Like it or not, they were all in this mess together.

"Is he mad enough to try to take off?"

"Anything's possible, knowing him." Mark was in it so deep, he might well take that risk. In his present crazy state there were no guarantees.

"We can't just leave him out there to freeze."

They all agreed but had no ideas. It was madness to even consider a rescue attempt. Where was Lucian now he was needed? He might know what to do. Another bonfire might act as a beacon that Mark might conceivably see. Angus went out and stared at the top of the tower, now shrouded in darkness. The snowman had more or less melted away, thanks mainly to the afternoon sun. Angus retrieved the owner's straw hat and returned it to the cloakroom.

"We need more logs." There were some in the shed in addition to those still stacked in the porch. The men went out to assemble the fire while the women were sent to find paper to get it going. They had burnt most of the boxes before, and the same applied to the petrol they'd found in the woodshed. There wasn't a lot in the tower they could use without intruding more than they had, but Jilly unearthed, from the side of the couch, a newspaper containing an unfinished crossword. She did recall Angus working on it but reckoned he'd hardly miss it now. In any case, it was better than tearing up books. Just to be on the safe side, though, Jilly ripped off the crossword page and put it aside.

They lit the fire then stood back to watch. It smouldered at first but eventually caught. A whoosh of flame shot up through the central funnel.

"That ought to do it," said Richard, pleased. Provided the endless mist held off there was a very strong chance that Mark would see it. Assuming, of course, he was still outside. Knowing Mark, he had probably gone to ground and was roasting his bum by some other fire, almost certainly in a pub. He reassured Dawn, who was snivelling still. "Don't worry," he said. "I have no doubt at all he'll show up."

"Now," said Amanda as they trooped back inside. "There is just one more task for you boys to do before you take the weight off your feet and we feed you. Hang on to the axe. We need you to find that fuse box."

The cellar door had been made to last as effectively as the main one. "I very much doubt we could chop it down," said Richard.

Apart from which, they were trespassing here, with no right at all to be damaging things. But they did need more than just candlelight and the torch was wholly inadequate. Its battery was already petering out and would soon expire. Primeval living was getting them down. Firelight was fine to a certain degree, mainly when they were drinking together at night. They had also adapted to candlelight provided they moved around as a group, but the strain on their eyes was starting to give them headaches.

They had hoped not to have to remain here so long. It was over two weeks since they first arrived and there still was no sign at all of impending rescue. They needed light; electricity too, if only to charge up their useless phones and perhaps even get the television to work. They were city folks, every one of them, with no desire whatsoever to be in these parts. Not one of the six of them was here by choice.

But the cellar door. "It's a shame," Angus said, "that we don't possess a loaded gun or else we could shoot off the lock without much trouble."

And find what? They had no idea, though with luck the fuse box would be there, along with whatever it was the owner kept hidden.

"Bodies," said Richard with a sepulchral laugh.

It was late. They had eaten and were ready for bed. There was no sign of Mark though the bonfire still blazed and the mist held off, though the top of the tower still lurked in enveloping darkness. Richard and Angus took it in turns to patrol the perimeters of the grounds and throw more wood on the bonfire to keep it alight. After a while they doubled the watch and, without discussion, went out as a pair. There was something about this eerie place that made even men of their stamina want not to be out there alone.

CHAPTER
FORTY-TWO

Few of them got any sleep that night, especially Richard, who was filled with dread. Mark had been his closest friend as long as he could remember. He could not believe he had left him there, alone on that mountainside in the dark, making a crazy attempt to reach the plane they'd been forced to abandon. He knew in the end he'd have gone with him, but Mark had left without letting him know. Why he had done that he could not imagine, unless he had been bent on a suicide mission. If he didn't succeed in making this work, Mark's City career would be pulverised and all his vaulting ambition would go up the spout. At thirty-four he was too old to get back on the horse and ride again, but still too young to abandon the fight entirely.

Or so Mark would think. Richard knew him too well, had encountered such craziness in him before. One of the reasons for Mark's success was his persistent refusal to face defeat. He was one of the City's best-known Young Turks with a reputation he jealously guarded. Too much depended on that one briefcase for his pride to allow him to give up now. Wiser men might have thrown in the towel but not Mark.

★ ★ ★

He was up before dawn with a splitting head and renewed determination to rescue his friend. The mist had returned, obscuring the peak where Richard imagined Mark might be marooned, always assuming he had even survived. He boiled the kettle on the Aga, relieved that they still had some source of heat, and made himself coffee while quietly thinking things through. One thing he did know, he would not quit without discovering the certain fate of his friend.

The police, it would seem, were entirely inept and Lucian had vanished into thin air as far as Richard could fathom. As Amanda had frequently pointed out, he was never around when they needed him, yet had a knack of just turning up if ever they tried to leave. He reflected upon that ancient stone with the mossy inscription that bore Lucian's name. Should they meet again, he would ask its meaning.

There were too many unanswered questions for now. The absentee owners, the half-eaten meal, the phone and TV that did not work, the little dead dog's pathetic head. Not to mention the ghost of the child Jilly claimed to have seen. And Lucian himself, who came and went yet never appeared to be dressed for outdoors and simply materialised by the library fire. Whose family name was inscribed on a stone close to the peak of the mountain.

The mist remained. It wreathed outside, entirely eclipsing the rugged crag where Richard feared Mark might have come to grief. What they needed now was that blasted helicopter.

Richard twiddled the radio knobs and got first crackling then a local voice, saying the weather had not improved and advising against all unnecessary travel.

"Can you find the BBC news?" asked Amanda, appearing without a sound. "Here, let me try. I managed it yesterday."

Richard started. If things weren't so fraught he might well have had a fight on his hands. Who did the woman think she was, Mussolini? As it was, though, he meekly handed it over and wandered off to refill his coffee cup.

Amanda twisted the plastic dial, frowning and pushing the hair back from her eyes. Covertly Richard studied her. As strong women went, she wasn't too bad. He knew the type; they were hell in the office but often surprisingly good in bed. They seemed to work off their aggression between the sheets. Angus appeared to fancy her too; he had seen the occasional glance pass between them. Back in London he might look her up. She lived in Chiswick, he'd heard her say, which was not too far from his Notting Hill pad. Provided she played her cards right.

"Damn," said Amanda, who'd had no success, switching the bloody thing off.

"Right," she said later, once she was dressed (she was sick to death of the same dirty clothes). "What are we going to do today, apart from tracking down Mark?"

They still had no news of his whereabouts and the mist was closing in again, denser with every minute.

"We could take a longer walk," Jilly said, though dreading even the thought of it. "In the daylight we might find an easier path to the summit."

"I don't think that's likely," Richard said, having studied the map with considerable care. "We would do better to alert the emergency services."

"How?" asked Amanda.

"I don't know," he said. "I just feel so useless stuck here in this tower." But the bonfire they'd lit the previous night had failed to attract attention. "Of course," he added, "we still have that cellar to tackle."

They had all agreed not to do any damage and hoped their burglary skills might just do the trick. The door was solid but the lock was old. Perhaps with patience and olive oil they might, by sleight of hand, be able to crack it.

It was worth a try. What else could they do while the mist hung low and obscured the view and even the bonfire had not proved effective?

"A coat hanger makes a great burgling tool," said Angus, warming to this pursuit. "Or, even better, a plastic detergent bottle."

"What do you do with that?" asked Jilly.

"Find me one and I'll show you," he said. He had once learnt a handy trick from the police.

"You seem to be expert at picking locks."

"I had a wasted youth," admitted Angus.

It took two hours but they came up trumps. The rusty lock eventually gave, revealing a flight of steep steps leading down to the cellar. It smelt damp and musty and rarely used and Angus swung his dying beam around it in an arc before venturing in. Amanda was right: it was full of wine in customised racks running wall to wall. In the darkness he could not read the labels but the place felt very authentic. Cautiously he descended the steps while the others stood and watched him from the doorway.

Amanda told him to keep an eye out for the fuse box.

"Yes ma'am," he said, ignoring her but looking instead at the rows of racks and the great oak barrels, stored on their sides and piled on wooden trestles under the rafters. He breathed in the delicate yeasty smell and admired the cobwebs denoting great age. He would bet there were some amazing vintages here that perhaps they might sample.

He shone his torch up and over the walls but could see no fuse box nor even a light. The age-old drippings of candle wax revealed that this part of the house was untouched, adding to the original rustic charm.

"Shall we come down?" Amanda asked, hesitating because of the gloom and also slightly spooked by the wavering torch beam.

"Don't bother," said Angus. "There's not much here." He swung the beam round in another wide are and noticed the running damp on the walls that probably meant an underground stream, hence the sharp temperature drop. An ideal place to keep wine and perhaps also make it.

The women now chose to withdraw upstairs where the fire was lit and the room still bright. They would just have to live by candlelight till they were rescued.

Which was not, in fact, too great an ordeal, as the flickering firelight enhanced the brass and brought out the muted colours of the stonework.

"May we please go now and look for Mark." Richard was itching to get away, but needed Angus to help him search because of the treacherous weather.

"Hang on," said Angus, drawn to a chest, ornately carved out of cedar wood, a pair to the one upstairs where the liquor was stored. It stood on its own, away from the wine, and something about it cried out to him. Why, he wondered, would it be down here instead of upstairs with its twin?

He gently fingered the ornate carving, identical to the other one. It was probably empty and kept down here as a spare. He lifted the lid. He'd been wrong; it was used as a linen chest and contained starched and well-laundered sheets with something, carefully wrapped, laid neatly upon them.

At first it looked like a china doll; he took a step forward and lowered his beam, then was hit in the throat by an odour so foul his stomach churned and he almost puked. He dropped the torch with a clatter. Its light went out.

"Angus," called Richard from the stairs. "Is anything wrong? Are you all right?"

"No," said Angus, dropping the lid. "I am not."

CHAPTER
FORTY-THREE

"You can't just leave it. We have to go back." They were gathered around in the sitting room while Angus sipped brandy prescribed by Jilly for shock. He was slightly embarrassed.

"I am not setting foot in that cellar again." Even the memory still made him retch. Angus was not an emotional man but this was beyond comprehension.

"Was it the dog?" Richard asked him, sotto voce.

"What dog?" asked Amanda, whose hearing was good.

"Worse," said Angus despondently. "A child, I'm pretty certain."

As one, they all swivelled to look at the family snaps.

"Shit," said Angus. "We don't deserve this." And neither did that poor creature entombed in the cellar.

Richard felt bound now to fill in the girls on his gruesome discovery in the shed.

"Why didn't you tell us before?" asked Amanda.

"I wanted to spare your feelings."

"For goodness' sake!" She was quite annoyed at the chauvinist way he'd assumed control. Who did they think they were dealing with: silly women? Dawn was stricken but she was wet; Amanda and Jilly could well hold their own and this latest discovery called for definitive action. They might be marooned in this weird old tower that was now revealing its grisly secrets but either they got out fast or else they took a proactive stand.

"I'd prefer to sleep rough on the fells," declared Jilly, "than spend another night in this place. In fact, I think we should leave without further delay."

They all agreed. They must do it now and this time make a concerted attempt to reach safety. So they piled on their clothes, taking anything warm they had managed to annex from the tower, and Richard, as a precaution, topped up his hip flask.

"Should I bring food?" Jilly wanted to know, a nurturer even in times of great stress.

"No," chorused Angus and Richard. The thought was abhorrent.

"We need to leave a note for Mark."

Absolutely. In case he came back.

"What will you say?" Amanda asked.

"That we've gone to summon help."

In single file they stepped into the mist and Richard led them down the familiar track.

"This is where we run into Lucian," said Jilly.

Not today, though. The mist was too thick for any sane person to wander abroad. Richard had Jilly's compass and acted as leader. They still had never located the farm that was tantalisingly marked on the map.

"Let's aim for the tarn again," he said, "and perhaps this time we will find it."

It was where Amanda had last seen Max, so her heart beat faster in her chest though the odds against his being there were colossal. Still, any action was better than none and they could not possibly have stayed where they were once Angus had uncovered that thing in the cellar.

"Was it a child?" That was what he had said.

Angus nodded. He was almost sure. At a guess, the little girl in the photographs. In the very dim light she'd looked small and compact, almost a waxwork except for the blood which had covered the whole of her front like a stiff red bib. Against his will, the details came crowding back. As with the dog, the throat had been slit. Whoever had done it must have used a very sharp knife.

"How did it happen?" Amanda asked. "Is it possible that they never left?" The revelation hit them all like a steam hammer. But the evidence they had stumbled on insisted they face the appalling truth. The family had left a half-eaten meal as well as their half-packed bags.

So where were the others? Around, she supposed, then remembered the sunken car in the tarn and the horror on Jilly's face on confronting that child. The nightmare was suddenly closing in. It was definitely time they left.

The lower they got, the clearer it was and now and again the sun broke through. Soon they saw the familiar glint of water. This time they really must get to the farm, call the police and raise the alarm. A terrible crime, or crimes, had occurred in the pele tower. But what could be Lucian's role in it all? Was he a villain or on their side? Could they rely on his helping them, was the main question.

They spoke very little; all were too stunned and the men had bad images to suppress. Both were traumatised by what they had seen. Jilly was thinking: those beautiful kids, the pink-eared rabbit and now the dog. Amanda was wondering where the parents could be. Domestic violence, it is well known, very often stays close to the home.

They mounted a ridge and there it was, the silent tarn with its deep dark waters spread out beneath them as if welcoming them back. The sun was quite warm so they took a break and sat in a row to admire the view. Despite the horrors they had encountered, from here it was truly astounding.

"What would you guess has happened to Mark?" Dawn asked in a small, scared voice.

"I really don't want to think about it," said Richard.

Amanda's eyes were skidding about as she combed the horizon for any sign of Max. At the water's edge, almost out of sight, something far in the distance moved, catching her acute peripheral vision. Matchstick figures were milling about, doing something with ropes and a truck, and she watched for several seconds before the penny eventually dropped. There were people there; they could seek their help, perhaps even hitch a lift in their truck. She'd been out of circulation so long her reflexes had grown rusty.

The submerged car, the one they had seen. They appeared to be dragging it out of the lake.

"Quickly," she cried. "Before they move on, we have got to get down there."

Right. In one fluid movement they rose and hurried along to the place way ahead where, they now realised, lay their sole hope of salvation. Richard shouted but nobody turned; they were too intent on raising the car. Jilly took off her scarf and frantically waved it. From here they could see no easy way down, no obvious path to the water's edge. They would have to slither and hope for the best, through the very loose scree.

"I'm game if you are." There wasn't a choice. The only thing that mattered was that they reach safety. Richard went first with them all close behind. "If you feel yourself starting to slip," he directed. "Curl into a ball and then simply roll."

It seemed much further than they had thought. The matchstick men with their Dinky Toy cars and truck were still just distant dots as they hurried towards them. The vehicles had been joined by an ambulance now into which they appeared to be shifting something from the salvaged car.

"It doesn't look good." They stopped to watch and Jilly tried waving her scarf again but the group by the water were grimly involved and unaware of their presence.

They were closing the doors of the ambulance now. "We had best get our skates on," said Richard, "or else we won't make it."

They didn't. To their blank disbelief, all they could do was stand and stare as first the ambulance left the scene, then the truck, and both police cars. It was like a repeat of the other night; despite their shouting and Jilly's scarf, and the fact they were halfway down the slope, they failed to attract attention.

"Bastards!" screamed Richard as the cars drove off, leaving the five of them stranded there on the hillside. He shook his fist but none of them even looked up.

Jilly broke into hysterical tears. "I can't believe it," she cried in grief. She slumped to the ground and buried her head in her hands. "They didn't even see us," she sobbed. "Either that or they just didn't care."

Angus tenderly stroked her hair. "They saw we're not natives of these parts and therefore couldn't be bothered to come to our aid." He'd be kicking ass in a major way the minute he got to a phone that worked. Whoever ran the police in these parts would find themselves out of a job.

"What now?" asked Amanda.

"We go on." Richard was resolute. They must raise the alarm. And at least the mist was clearing a bit so that visibility was better. The fells all around them were silent and still, with no sign of movement except for the birds. Under other circumstances, it would be idyllic.

Angus helped Jilly to her feet and dried her eyes with his handkerchief. "We will laugh about this some day," he said. "I promise."

Which was when Amanda saw it again, the solitary figure across the lake, exactly where it had stood before and, it would seem, still watching. Again she sensed the glint of a lens, and when she jumped up and down and waved the figure began its progression again as if moving forward to meet her.

"Max, my darling," she cried with relief. In her heart she had always known he would show up.

CHAPTER
FORTY-FOUR

The rabbit still sat in its place on the Aga, a mischievous glint in its boot button eyes as if ironically waiting to welcome them home. Just the sight of it made Jilly cry because of the ghastly connotations. Twice, in the dark, she'd encountered the child whose favourite toy this was, and now they had found her remains, though not yet the dog's. There was evil here in this ancient pile as well as stuff that could not be explained: invisible presences messing with their heads.

They had not found the farm. They had screamed and shouted but failed for a second time to attract the attention of the police. That had been almost the creepiest part, the fact that their voices had not been heard. The helicopter had not even bothered to return.

Creepier still, though, was what they had found when they'd wandered dejectedly back through the mist. Even though they had not yet found the fuse box, the power appeared to be on again and the light at the top of the tower shone like a beacon. Not one of them was prepared to explore. There were things about this tower they'd prefer not to know. They just huddled together downstairs by the fire knowing that Mark, if he did come back, at least should be able to find his way by

266

that brilliant beckoning light. They had no need any more for another bonfire.

Nor did they have any appetite. They would sooner just drink and discuss in low voices what might have happened to Mark. Richard now was blaming himself for having allowed him to slip away. If he'd only checked when he went to bed he might have been able to head Mark off and stop him attempting that suicidal climb.

Amanda was quietly obsessing again, wondering what could have happened to Max. If he'd spotted her at the edge of the tarn — which he had; she no longer doubted that — then why had he not yet made it up to the pele tower? The light was on full; he could not have got lost. The others had seen him and vouched for that. Yet he seemed to have disappeared again into the mist.

"Tell me about him," Jilly said, aware that Amanda was not quite herself. She wanted to be of help if she could yet was equally anxious not to appear intrusive. If Amanda wanted to talk to her, though, she would offer a sympathetic ear. A trouble shared was a trouble halved, it was said.

Amanda was still inclined to hold back. Distantly Max was Jilly's boss too and she did not want gossip leaking out in the office. Then she remembered how things stood, that Jilly would shortly be out of a job and therefore in no position to spill the beans. More than that, though, she needed to talk, so she briefly sketched out the situation, carefully omitting to mention his name. They had been an item for a number of years but had had a spat just before she left and hadn't been able to sort things out because the phones weren't working. They needed to talk to make things up but kept on missing each other.

Jilly totally empathised. She was worrying too, in a different way, about Derek.

"He obviously knows where to look for you." She had seen Max too from across the tarn and been aware of Amanda's agitation. A tall man, dressed in black climbing gear with those stylish dark glasses you saw in the ads. Very impressive though not at all her own type. But she sympathised; she knew the pain of misunderstandings and going to sleep on a row.

"I am sure he'll find you. He must know we're here." He had also been seen on the lower slopes and this was the only habitable dwelling for miles. "And he has the number of the conference hotel?"

He had, indeed. It had been his show. It was Max who had chosen the Lakes this year in order to soften the blow of impending cutbacks. He was the one with the bright ideas, Amanda the ninny who carried them out. He would emerge from this squeaky clean whereas she would be seen as the axe man. But that hardly mattered as long as her darling was safe, which she now knew he was.

Impulsively she gave Jilly a hug. "Thanks," she said. "I know you're right. I feel much better now just talking it through."

Jilly beamed. Just like that, she thought. Would that her own deepest fear was so easily sorted.

Meanwhile Angus, still horribly shaken, was quietly and painfully spewing up his guts in the children's bathroom.

Dawn was waiting when he emerged, gaunt and ashen and greasy-skinned, looking older even than his true age. Instinctively she recoiled in disgust. He smelt of vomit and cigarettes, reminding her of her grandpa, now long dead.

"What's got into you?" she asked, uncaring.

Angus looked at her with cynical eyes, seeing her as she really was, a flirt whose only interest in him had been money. She had caught him at a vulnerable stage but had never meant much to him, had never really been anything more than a fling. He should not have let things get this far but knew that she now had her eye on Mark. With luck, she would now move on. Assuming, of course, that Mark returned, but this was not the best time to think about that.

But she'd asked him a question. He thought for a while.

"I have had the misfortune," he told her coldly, "to witness the perpetration of absolute evil."

Angus returned to the living room and looked around for something to do. Without a television that worked the evenings here passed very slowly. Then he found it where Jilly had put it, the crossword he'd started but never completed, waiting for him, neatly folded by her, tucked underneath a lamp. Idly he ran his eye over it. A third of the answers still remained blank but an obvious clue stood out so he groped for his pen. It should, at least, take his mind off that grotesque doll in the old carved chest. Whenever he closed his eyes he saw the sad little face with its half-severed neck, the eyes still bulging with terror. He settled down on the sofa to finish the puzzle.

Jilly, watching him, sympathised. She had glimpsed his expression after leaving the cellar. She had never seen anyone change so much or look as shaken as he had then. He had not described in detail what he had seen and Jilly had not dared ask. Angus had his own demons to face. She admired him for keeping the full horror to himself.

Which set her thinking of Derek again. It was over two weeks since they'd last been in touch when she'd sent him a postcard of Scafell Pike, announcing that she was off for a hike with a manager from head office. She imagined his pride on reading that and how he would show it around in the pub. "Our Jilly's getting above herself," she could just imagine him saying with that twinkling smile that she loved so much and he'd probably stand them an extra round and they'd all clink glasses to Jilly, his soon to be wife. But that just started her fretting again about what he had thought when she didn't come home. He'd have called the hotel but they wouldn't have known where she was, which would have alarmed him further.

She wondered if he had come looking for her, as Amanda's boyfriend apparently had. But where would he even begin to search, since she hadn't known where she was going?

Dawn was wailing that Mark was lost and claiming he was the love of her life. No one was seriously listening, though; they were sick of her histrionics.

Angus had filled in the last few clues and was crumpling the paper to chuck it away when his eye was caught by an item on the back page that was headed STILL MISSING.

It is exactly one year ago today [Angus checked the date. The end of October, the day they had first arrived] *that a Keswick family went missing from Scafell Pike. John and Margaret Richardson and their two young children, Peter (9) and Amy (7), together with the family dog, disappeared from their house on the fells. Nothing has ever been heard of them since. It is almost as if they vanished into thin air.*

"What are you staring at?" Richard asked, having come to top up Angus's glass. Silently Angus handed him the paper.

Richard read it, then read it again. "Where on earth did you find this?" he asked.

"It was lying here on the table," said Angus. "On the night we first arrived."

CHAPTER
FORTY-FIVE

It did not make sense, none that they could see. The newspaper cutting was very concise and stated that the family had been missing now for a year. Yet a fire had been burning when they arrived, there was food on the table and steam on the mirror. The bread had still been fresh and the wine at its best.

"Where did you find it? The paper, I mean?"

"Here, on the dining table," said Angus. At the time he had simply assumed someone else had brought it. They hadn't, though; two had come by plane, scrambling down over treacherous rocks, while Jilly and Amanda had simply been out for an afternoon stroll. If anyone else had been in the place, there wasn't a clue as to who it was except possibly Lucian who came and went as he pleased.

It didn't add up, which was nothing new. They were all here and safe apart from Mark who they still very much hoped might turn up soon. And now that the power was on again, things were more or less back to normal. It occurred to Amanda, if the lights now worked then why not also the television? All it would take was a very sharp knife, electrical tape and a cable splice. She was irritated with herself for not thinking of that before. Richard went out to the woodshed again and came back triumphant with secateurs and a handy roll of black insulating tape.

Result. Amanda felt justified. "Who wants to do the honours?" she asked. They left her to it. If this worked, perhaps she would also tackle the landline. Though she knew that would be more tricky.

So once they had eaten they dragged the TV from its silent corner and into the kitchen where Amanda did the surgical bit with the rest of them observing. They held their breath when she switched it on and screamed in delight when the screen lit up.

"Blast," said Jilly. "We've missed *Coronation Street*."

They fiddled around with the aerial and moved the set back to where it had been which produced, to their huge relief, a perfect picture. The next news report was not until ten so, by mutual agreement, they all settled down to watch *Taggart*.

"I still don't understand," Richard said, "why anyone would have cut the cable." But then there were numerous other imponderables here. He cringed whenever he thought of the dog and wondered why it had been chopped up. He also remembered Angus's face when he stumbled up from the cellar. Now they'd discovered the family had supposedly been missing for over a year. But food had arrived without explanation and the power seemed to switch itself on and off, while the doors on occasion were locked and at other times not. It was all too much for his mind to absorb. He settled back with the others to watch the cop show.

Dawn was still obsessed with Mark and wondering if she would see him again. She lay curled like a foetus in front of the fire, absent-mindedly sucking her thumb, still very much a child though she tried very hard to cover it up. She had no idea what had happened to her but it had scared her half to death, that beckoning light and the voices too, plus the sharp temperature drop. Yet something about the experience stayed in her mind and enticed her. One of these days, when she had the strength, she might even go back and explore the third floor. There were questions, loads of them, still demanding answers.

She considered that Angus had let her down, having tossed her aside like a broken toy. He had feted her at that poncey hotel and even mentioned the word divorce, only to lose all interest as soon as they got here. She thought of that endless trudge through the mist once they'd dumped the car and were lost on the fells. She had only survived because she was young, and hardy enough to withstand the abysmal conditions. She had taken off her designer shoes and walked for most of the way barefoot. She wondered now how she'd ever made that almost impossible climb. But the bright white light had been beckoning to them and they had managed to reach this place. And now the bastard was chatting up Amanda. Well, if that's what he wanted, good luck to him. Amanda was pushing forty, at least, and would soon be losing her looks.

274

Amanda herself was preoccupied, not with Angus, though she liked him a lot, but with Max, who she felt must be still out there, lost. It ran through her consciousness endlessly, that instant he'd caused her to lose her rag by mocking her for getting annoyed when he'd taken the private phone call. He was endlessly playing sadistic games, winding her up till her temper snapped, then wooing her back with bouts of tempestuous sex. They had known each other too long for that: it cheapened and also degraded her. The very least she deserved was his respect.

She had blindly lashed out when he laughed at her after sidling back into his place by the rail. The South Bank that night was all lit up by some pageantry on the river. There were fireworks, too, which had muffled the sound Max made when she flung her drink in his face and he'd stumbled and then toppled backwards over the railing. She had been so mad she had not hung around, just grabbed her car keys and headed off, seething with indignation and rage, aware that she had an early start in the morning.

She realised now that she should have stayed, at least to check that he was all right, but she'd had one drink too many which always proved fatal. If she'd stayed the police might have breathalysed her and she had that long drive up to Keswick next day, also a fairly momentous task to perform. A lot had depended on how she did when dishing it out to the luckless drones who were due to lose their jobs on that doomed weekend.

She was sure she'd have heard if he wasn't all right. After all, she had been at the conference from Friday to Sunday and he was the one who had set the whole thing up. She had guessed that all he was doing was punishing her. At least she now knew he'd survived and was hot on the trail.

When *Taggart* ended Dawn went to bed. The news was next but she couldn't care less. She was tired of the stuffy bunch she was stuck with, older than her and almost as boring as Angus.

Richard offered them all a drink while Jilly, who just couldn't help herself, set about laying the breakfast table for the morning. She would one day make someone a wonderful wife, thought Amanda, her tongue firmly in her cheek. Well, horses for courses was all she could add to that.

The news came on and Jilly returned. They were all of them keen to know if they'd hit the headlines. But two weeks had passed since they disappeared so other things may now have taken their place. It was all doom and gloom about the recession and how many people were losing their jobs. Amanda sucked in her breath for fear they should mention the imminent cutbacks at the Prudential.

"Wait for the local news," said Angus, who could not believe he had not been missed. Perhaps they were planning to do a Cumbria special.

But they hadn't finished with London yet. Jilly was on her way up the stairs when she heard Amanda's scream and went racing back.

"It's Max!" she was shouting, and there he was. His photograph on the screen. There could be no doubt.

CHAPTER
FORTY-SIX

The police were asking, the bulletin said, for witnesses to a suspected crime that had recently taken place on London's South Bank. A man, whose name they did not disclose, had been critically injured in a fall in the early hours of the morning two weeks before. He had either fallen or been pushed. No one so far had come forward with information.

Amanda, aghast and clutching her mouth, was making audible choking sounds. Angus requested that she shut up so he could catch what the newsman was saying. They had taken the victim to hospital where he had died in intensive care. They were notifying the next of kin and looking for anyone who might have seen him on the night in question.

Though Angus was listening, Jilly was not. She was more concerned with Amanda's distress. She stroked her hand and tried to calm her down.

"It may look like him but it can't be your Max. That guy is dead but Max is alive. Safe and well and waiting for you on the other side of the tarn. All of us saw him." A man dressed in black, athletic and fit with those fashionably trendy Armani shades. Who had, it now seemed, been trailing Amanda for days.

Angus and Richard, having now cottoned on, out of respect had switched off the set. As soon as Amanda had gone to bed they would try to catch it on Sky. Deprivation and solitude were slowly taking their toll of them all. Amanda, it seemed, was now starting to have delusions. It's the toughest ones that crack first, Angus thought, having never subscribed to the popular theory that women make better executives than men. They might be efficient at getting things done but they buckle under pressure.

"It was Max, I know it," Amanda wailed. The imposing stance, the superior air, the haircut. For years his image had dominated her dreams. Yet what Jilly had said was undoubtedly true: they had seen him up here only hours ago. However unlikely, the dead man must be an impostor.

Back upstairs, tucked into their bunks, there was no way Amanda and Jilly could sleep. Correct or not, the news report had been disconcertingly unnerving. Too much had happened in too short a time for anyone to make sense of it, though both of them agreed about certain things. First the power had totally failed and then, without warning, come on again. Doors that had once been locked now easily opened and vice versa. Stranger still, the police had come and, instead of investigating the tower, had concentrated on the melting snowman. Those in the tower had done what they could to attract their attention by making a noise and even writing a prominent sign on the roof. Yet the helicopter had circled but not even landed.

And then there were the more gruesome things: the dog, the dead child, the submerged car from which they had seen bodies being removed. Things were happening in this place way beyond their comprehension. And now it appeared that the family had been missing more than a year.

"You don't suppose we have all gone mad?"

"A kind of epidemic, you mean?" It would be a comfort to think it was that easy.

Next morning, on arriving downstairs, they found Angus and Richard already dressed for a mountain walk, with all their gear assembled except for their boots. Even Dawn was up, which showed just how desperate times had become. Amanda, getting a grip on herself, assumed her natural leadership role. If they didn't leave now they ran the risk of the mist's rolling in and preventing it. This time, whatever it took, they would reach that valley. No more messing with compasses: they would follow their noses instinctively and, by pure determination, come through. They would walk downhill for as long as it took until they had safely reached civilisation. They would stiffen their spines and encourage each other until whatever evil it was in the tower had loosened its grip.

They were all agreed. Amanda was right. They were healthy, well fed, and equipped with walking boots. Even Dawn now came up to scratch after Jilly had managed to kit her out in a mix of the children's clothes and those of their mother.

What about Mark? Should they not wait for him?

"No," said Richard. He would know where they'd gone. Their own safety mattered most now. Mark would understand.

"Should we take food?" Jilly wanted to know. Richard had already topped up his flask.

"Take nothing," instructed Amanda, assuming command.

They left at nine when the sun was well up and the mist so thin they could see the sky. Richard led and they walked in line, holding hands wherever they could and breaking occasionally into snatches of song. Amanda remembered her days as a Guide; even the choruses they had sung. She found it helped keep her mind off Max and added a spring to her step. Her car would be waiting at Seathwaite Farm and she felt much better when she thought of that. She would drive Jilly back to the conference hotel, and perhaps take Dawn too since she wasn't too big, then send back some sort of transport to pick up the others.

The very first thing Jilly planned to do, before she even removed her boots, was telephone Derek to let him know she was safe and on her way home. After that she would call the clinic to fix up another appointment soon. She had made up her mind: it was time to face up to the truth. She had the rest of her life to consider: her wedding, the mortgage and if she should stay in her job. She liked the work and always had but marriage would mean a big change in her life. Her energies would be family-based from now on. Derek wanted a little girl first but Jilly hoped it might be a son. One of each, close enough in age for them to play together. Positive thinking; that was the thing. She put all her worries on hold.

Just before noon they reached the tarn. Amanda was keeping an eye out for Max. Jilly was right; there must have been some mistake. But now dark clouds began rolling in as they always did when they reached this point and the mist came down like a sinister woollen blanket.

"All hold hands," commanded Amanda, "and follow Richard. He knows the way." Her heart was working overtime; she was determined they'd make it.

They walked for at least another four hours, occasionally stopping to catch their breath and consult with each other about which direction to take. Because of the mist they could not see the peak nor even the lights from the valley below though soon, they presumed, they would reach the bridge, beyond which it should be plain sailing. At one point they came to a rocky ledge requiring the use of both hands and feet where the scree was loose and hard to negotiate. At another point they were obliged to backtrack when they reached the edge of a gully.

Dawn was whining and Jilly was tired, though canny enough not to let it show. They were in this together and nothing must now defeat them. Finally, after what seemed endless hours, they glimpsed a dim light through the swirling mist. At last. They had made it. They quickened their pace and Jilly began to warble again till the ground rose suddenly upwards. They froze with shock.

Here it was again, the familiar path that led up the slope that they knew so well. It couldn't be happening again and yet it was.

And that was when they finally understood that they were doomed.

CHAPTER
FORTY-SEVEN

Mark was seated in front of the fire, calm and relaxed with a glass in his hand and Lucian standing beside him, beaming with pleasure. Mark looked much better. His pallor was gone and the arm seemed as good as new. He was wearing a clean pressed shirt and immaculate jeans.

"Hi," he said with his lazy grin. "We were starting to worry. What took you so long?"

"Come and sit by the fire," Lucian said, "and warm up."

The room was cosy; the lights were all on. Lucian was playing the genial host. It was six o'clock, the cocktail hour. Downstairs they heard it chime.

"Mark," said Richard, gripping his hand and surreptitiously rubbing his eyes. "Where in God's name did you get to? I have been out of my mind with worry."

"Me too," whispered Dawn in that little girl voice, only this time she wasn't just putting it on. She crept across and crouched on the floor at Mark's feet. Without any makeup, her hair sleeked straight back, she looked scarcely more than fourteen.

Jilly was gobsmacked, Amanda severe. "Where did you get to for three whole nights?" No one, surely, could survive that long out on the fells in this weather. Yet Mark had, so perhaps Max had too; all Amanda could do now was hope and pray.

"I am sorry if I caused you concern, but I urgently needed to get to the plane. And Lucian here was sporting enough to offer himself as my guide."

Lucian? It hardly seemed his sort of thing, though they kept their amazement to themselves. He was not an obvious choice for such a potentially dangerous mission.

"The least thing you might have done," Angus said, "was let us know first or else leave a note." He resented the fact he had risked his life for what turned out to be such a lightweight escapade.

"Sorry," said Mark. "I can see that now. Selfish of me; I won't do it again. It was all rather spur of the moment. Please forgive me." He looked down at Dawn, who was gazing at him with her customary rapt adoration.

"She might forgive you but I never will." Richard was genuinely cross and hurt. It was typical Mark behaviour to act without thinking.

They were all, however, relieved he was back. Lucian opened champagne and they raised their glasses.

"Well," said Richard, a bit more relaxed. "Did you get what you wanted? I hope it turns out to be worth it." He still could hardly believe in his friend's survival.

Mark hesitated, then gave his sweet smile. "I did," he said, "apart from one minor hiccup."

Lucian left them to it and went upstairs. He seemed never to want to share their meals which was just as well because he was still an outsider.

"I shall be upstairs," he said, "if anyone needs me."

On impulse Amanda followed him out. There were questions that needed answers right now. "What precisely is going on?" she demanded.

She saw he wore his monogrammed slippers and wondered when he'd had time to change; also where in the house he kept his things. Perhaps he had a room of his own. He was always so dapper and well turned out, in no way an obvious action man. Though he clearly must know the mountain well, having lived on it most of his life.

"What do you want to know?" he asked with a smile.

"To start with why you are so often here and who exactly you are," she said. Which was long overdue. It was time they got to the truth.

Lucian fell silent as if in deep thought. He steepled his fingers and pondered a while. "Soon, I promise," he said, "you will have all the answers."

Soon would do although now would be better. She was tired of his endless prevarication. She also disliked his slight condescension which he made no attempt to disguise. "We need to know what the setup is here. Who are the owners and where are they now? Why did they suddenly disappear, apparently in a hurry?" The dog, the child and the car in the tarn Amanda would keep for later.

286

Lucian smiled. "But the service is good. I am not aware there have been complaints. And if you really wanted to leave, you could."

"No," said Amanda. "That's just not true. Whenever we try you keep herding us back."

"Mark got away."

"But you brought him back."

"I assure you, only with his consent. He would still be lost on that mountainside if he hadn't had me to protect him."

Amanda was growing still more confused. His arguments made logical sense and yet she felt something was fundamentally wrong. Conversations with Lucian went round in circles.

"Look," he told her, acting sincere. "Go and eat then come back and we'll talk."

"Where will you be?"

"Upstairs," he said. "And do me a favour. Try not to bring the others."

Of course they wanted to know where she'd been. Jilly was serving venison stew and Richard opening bottles, his appointed role.

"Having a word with Lucian," she said. "Is there anything I have missed?"

"No," said Mark, whose eyes seemed unusually bright. He looked even healthier than before and his film-star smile was fully restored. It was easier now to understand why Dawn had developed her crush.

"Mark was telling us about his climb," said Angus, "and how he reached the peak whereas Richard and I were stumped by that daunting ice sheet. It seems that Lucian knew the way and they reached the plane without needing climbing equipment." It didn't add up; he still hadn't figured it out.

"So how come you didn't take off?" Richard asked. He'd been sitting there listening all this time, seemingly as unconvinced as Angus.

Mark looked him straight in the eye, long and hard.

"I've told you already," he said. "There was a slight hitch."

The food was delicious. Seconds were served and they polished off more than one bottle of wine. They were all becoming accustomed to lavish living. They cleared the table and dealt with the dishes. Amanda had not forgotten her date. Nor Lucian's request that she come upstairs on her own. She had every intention of pinning him down; perhaps he would finally open up and provide her with answers to the crucial questions.

But then she remembered the TV now worked. It was practically nine, almost time for the news. She could not possibly leave the room without first checking the headlines. She switched on the set and they all gathered round, as keen as she was to know what was going on. They had been too long out of touch with the world as it was.

They were quite unprepared for what happened next. The opening shot was of Scafell Pike with a grim-faced reporter, heavily muffled, shouting into his microphone through a blizzard. "Here," he was saying, "was where they located the wreckage of the plane."

A police helicopter had spotted it first then alerted the rest of the rescue teams who, even though unable to land, had checked the identity of both fliers. They had taken off from Canary Wharf two Sundays before, just the two of them, thought to be City traders heading for Iceland. Nobody spoke as the pictures appeared — quite unmistakably Richard and Mark — taken aboard a racing yacht in some luxurious location. Both were laughing into the wind, clearly having the time of their lives, without a thought for the millions they had ripped off.

Amanda switched off the TV set. There was total silence throughout the room. All eyes were focused on Richard and Mark who just sat there, faintly embarrassed. If they had crashed two Sundays ago (Amanda rapidly did the maths) it had been the night they had first arrived at the pele tower. She remembered the weather, the snow on their clothes and Mark with his mutilated arm. She also remembered the grandfather clock striking midnight.

Mark eventually broke the silence, which nobody else seemed prepared to do.

"Sorry," he said. "I'm afraid we just didn't make it."

CHAPTER
FORTY-EIGHT

For a moment she thought he might be asleep, he sat so still in his great wing chair, a massive leather-bound tome on his knee, a glass of port at his elbow. After a moment he beckoned her over to sit. Amanda complied. She was shaking so much she could scarcely speak; her teeth were chattering from delayed shock and she drew in great gulps of air, on the edge of hysteria. Lucian, unmoving, continued to sit gazing peacefully into the fire, with all the time in the world at her disposal.

Finally Amanda spoke. "Please help me to understand," she begged. She could not believe what she'd just been told, was trying against all rational thought to absorb what Mark had said. Lucian stayed silent for a while, letting her voice her confusion aloud, his expression unreadable in the flickering firelight. In order for her to grasp the truth she needed to figure it out for herself. There was no hurry, for here time moved in a totally other direction. What mattered was that she understood where she was now in the universe. She could have as long as it took to comprehend it.

Dazed and confused she stared at him, her face quite bloodless with fear and shock. Slowly the pieces were starting to slot together.

"We all arrived here that very first night within a couple of hours of each other. Jilly and I were lost on the fells and saw the faint glimmer of a distant light that turned out to be the pele tower drawing us to it."

They were new acquaintances, working colleagues thrown together by random chance, their sole link being that both worked for the Prudential. It was she who had first sought Jilly out, liking her style and the way she'd performed when she'd done her stint on the platform. Both, it turned out, were weekend ramblers who hoped to fit in some hiking here so, since they had Sunday off, they had teamed up.

The weather was great when they first set out but then the mist began to close in so that soon they found they had strayed from the designated path. Jilly had brought a compass which had seemed, at the time, slightly over the top but the terrain grew quickly more rugged than they had expected. They were not concerned, were enjoying themselves and very rapidly starting to bond. The walk was a tough one but nothing they could not handle. It was neither too cold nor too strenuous, at least for the first few miles.

But after a while they'd reached treacherous scree, loose stones that shifted underfoot. Jilly, the more experienced hiker, warned Amanda to watch her step.

"Be very careful," she'd said. "It is easy to fall."

So up they had slogged, in a sudden brisk wind which caused them to put their jackets back on, and all of a sudden had found themselves on the edge of a steep ravine. She remembered they had debated then as to whether or not they should go on, but neither had wanted to be the first to quit.

Lucian was watching Amanda closely but still he had not uttered a word. She, remembering, suddenly faltered then stopped.

"I lost my footing." She looked at him. "And grabbed at Jilly as I started to fall." She recalled telling Jilly that she would have made an excellent Girl Guide.

"So," said Lucian, speaking at last. "Tell me what happened next."

The weather conditions had grown much worse. The temperature dropped and the mist rolled in. They tried to turn back but had lost their orientation. At that point it had become very scary. They'd been losing heart when they saw the light and followed it, like a guiding star, over ground so steep she had not believed they would make it.

"Which was how we came to be here," she said. "And safe."

The rest he knew. The door was not locked and a fire burned cheerily in the grate, with food and a bottle of wine waiting on the table.

"It seemed like heaven," Amanda said; then, catching the gleam in Lucian's eye, stopped as understanding overwhelmed her.

Lucian poured her a glass of port and watched as she sorted things out in her head. It was essential she find her own way to the truth. She sat for a while considering it as slowly things started to fall into place. Things that had never occurred to her until now.

Richard and Mark had then arrived, by coincidence it seemed at the time. It was just gone midnight; she remembered the downstairs clock striking. She suddenly buried her head in her hands. It was obvious now though had not been then. Her face when she looked up was white with horror.

By the time they banged on the door both Richard and Mark had been dead.

Even after thirty-eight years, with a degree in philosophy, Amanda's mind was in no way attuned to accept such an alien truth. Her eyes grew large as she stared at him, her brain refusing to play the game. They had seemed such regular guys, so *alive*: handsome, laughing and cracking jokes. City boys, she'd picked up on that, obliged to interrupt their flight because of the sudden bad weather. They seemed to have considered it no big deal. The weather would clear, they would take off again. Mark had injured his arm in some way but Jilly had managed to fix it.

"I always assumed, if I saw a ghost, I would know it," Amanda whispered.

Lucian said nothing. It was not yet the time. She needed to figure it out on her own before he could face her with the ultimate truth.

After a while she spoke again, this time with wonder in her voice. "Does that mean they can never leave here? That they're stuck in this place for ever?"

She was starting to grasp it.

Lucian stood up. "I think that is more than enough for one night. Once you are ready, but not until then, we will continue our chat."

She was on her way slowly down the stairs, still grossly perturbed by all she had learnt, and paused halfway to peer through the arrow-slit window. It was brilliant moonlight, the mist had gone and the slopes surrounding the tower looked dipped in silver. A still dark figure stood motionless just beneath her.

She assumed at first it was Angus or Mark, stepping outside for a cigarette or a lungful of bracing night air. But Angus and Mark were both still inside — she could hear their laughter in the living room — and Richard was far too athletic to be a smoker. She peered again. The still dark figure was tall and spare, dressed head to foot in black climbing gear and, even at this hour, wearing his fancy shades.

Amanda's heart leapt into her throat. Max, she thought. He had come at last and, for whatever reason, was waiting outside. Perhaps he had knocked and they just had not heard. These solid walls were impermeable. She practically flew down the last flight, frantically fumbling with the bolts as she opened the heavy door. She stepped out into the brilliant night and opened her arms to greet her love but nothing stirred. There was nobody there, not even footprints across the frost-rimed grass.

"Max!" she shouted, searching for him, but her voice echoed into sheer emptiness. Which was when she knew for certain that he had gone.

Amanda heard voices a distance away and paused to listen in case it was Max. She stood in the shadows by the great door and prayed that she had been wrong. And then she saw lights coming over the ridge, advancing slowly towards where she stood and definitely voices, several men she would guess. Fell-walkers lost in the mist, she assumed, even though up here it was clear and bright. She could see them now as they struggled along, three of them weighed down with heavy backpacks.

She remained where she was without making a sound. They were here at last but had come too late. She knew there was nothing now they could do for her. The moonlight illuminated the tower though tonight, for once, the light was not on.

"Look," one shouted. "Some kind of house. Perhaps they'll be able to set us on the right track."

"I could do with a drink and a nice sit down." The older man clearly had walked far enough. "They might even give us a bed for the night if we're lucky."

She was still in the shadows. They walked straight past but instead of knocking just stood and stared.

"It's a ruin," said one as he flashed his lamp and picked out the crumbling battlements. "A pele tower put up to defend us against the Scots."

"They certainly knew how to build in those days. It must have been here for centuries. I bet those old stones could tell us a good few stories."

They did not linger, it was late and cold; just paused for a while to catch their breath. Amanda watched until they moved on then silently slipped back inside.

CHAPTER
FORTY-NINE

She had started to fear for her sanity. Pure reason precluded the possibility that things she had been presented with could be so. Either she had finally lost it or else she was trapped in a derelict tower at the top of an inaccessible peak, in endless mist, with a handful of living dead. It occurred to Amanda, as a last resort, that it could be a drug-induced fantasy brought on by something she'd eaten, like magic mushrooms. Or else perhaps her brain was diseased. She would prefer almost any explanation but the truth.

She stood in the cavernous downstairs hall, listening to merriment from above. Alive or not, her house-mates shared a capacity for enjoyment. Silently she manoeuvred the stairs, avoiding the half-open living room door, seeking only the sanctuary of her bedroom where she could think. Jilly was there already, asleep, a smile of contentment on her face, dreaming, no doubt, of the wedding that would not take place.

Amanda dropped her clothes on the floor, the same grubby garments she had worn for two weeks. She did not bother to brush her teeth; it now seemed entirely futile. She stood at the window and stared at the moon, hanging huge and white over Scafell Pike. Somewhere up there, on a frozen crag, was scattered the wreckage of a plane together with two shattered bodies.

And now this latest. The time had come for that further talk with Lucian.

Again the library door was locked but Amanda refused to be foiled by that. She would talk to him again, whatever it took. She needed to know all the answers. Slowly the dots were joining up but one or two spaces remained to be filled. Starting with the riddle of Max and where he had disappeared to.

The third floor was the obvious place since the rest of the tower they already knew. Lucian must have his private quarters somewhere. Up there, where the battlements were and Dawn had had her unearthly experience, was where Amanda decided she would look first. Enough of this holding back on things. There were secrets here that must be revealed. Amanda gritted her teeth and advanced up the stairs.

The temperature dropped quite dramatically and the only light came from the sconce on the stairs. Beyond that the long dark corridor stretched, soulless and uninviting. Methodically she opened each door, swiftly assessing the contents inside. No room was furnished except for occasional pieces. All that remained were just odds and ends, the detritus of an earlier time when perhaps the ancient tower had been lived in full time. Occasional furniture, heavily draped; a shelf of books, a boxful of toys. The sad reminders of life that was no longer lived here.

So where did the elegant Lucian reside with his timeless clothes and fastidious tastes? There was only one door remaining she had not yet tried. The one at the end, by the battlements, where Dawn had experienced her Damascene moment. Against her better judgement, Amanda advanced.

The door opened easily to the touch. Amanda, having knocked, still hesitated. What she saw now took her breath away, not only because of the biting cold. She had expected a scholarly den with books and papers and, maybe, a fire, but what she was confronted with was a ruin. An empty space with unfinished walls and a gaping hole in the roof through which a snowstorm was now drifting. A sharp breeze slammed the door with a bang, leaving her staring up at the sky through the shattered rafters beneath the gaping stonework. The room was quite empty and smelled of neglect from the rotting floorboards and cobwebby beams. Amanda took one step forward and stopped, fearing the floor beneath her was unsafe. If this were the source of Dawn's white light she had been either drunk or hallucinating. This room had been out of use for years, as evidenced by its state of advanced decay.

Amanda withdrew and closed the door, shaken by what she had found inside. Whatever she'd guessed about Lucian's life had been wrong. She suddenly sensed she was not alone. Beneath the light at the top of the stairs a solitary figure was standing, silent and still.

"Good morning," said Lucian, fastening his cuffs, as well groomed as he habitually was, dapper today in tweeds and those soft suede shoes.

"You weren't in the library," Amanda said, guilty at having been found up here, ashamed in case he thought that she had been snooping.

"I am on my way now. Come with me," he said, leading the way down the twisting stairs. "You will find it more comfortable there in the warmth by the fire."

Following him, Amanda got the full picture.

The room was warm but he threw on more logs. The library was tranquil as well as remote. Despite herself, Amanda began to feel better.

"Things are beginning to slot into place."

"I thought they might after a good night's sleep."

"We are all in this situation together," she said.

He did not disagree so she knew she was right.

Mark and Richard. She understood now and was coming to terms, too, with Angus and Dawn. They had lost their way on the motorway and taken a lesser road in the mist. So how had they managed to get up here in their evening clothes and her silly shoes? Till now it had made no sense; now she understood.

"Do they know yet?" Amanda asked.

Lucian said no. "Mark and Richard, yes, though, so far, not the others."

"And Jilly?"

"She is not quite there but well on the way."

Amanda paused. She feared the truth but could not stop now; that was not her way.

300

"Max?" she asked and then bit her lip, reluctant to hear the answer.

"Max is different," Lucian said. "You gave him a shove, he fell over the rail. There are serious issues to be resolved before you'll be able to see him again. Assuming you want to now you are here. You do still have free will."

They sat in silence a very long time while Amanda endeavoured to take it all in. For some strange reason, with Lucian she felt safe. At last she summoned the strength to speak, fearful of what the answer might be yet, at the same time, ready to face the truth.

"And me?" she asked. "Where do I fit in?" She knew the answer before he spoke. "Was it when I slipped on the scree?" And Jilly had failed to catch her.

Lucian nodded.

"Thank you," she said. She leant across and he took her hand.

His fingers were icy cold yet reassuring.

CHAPTER
FIFTY

All of a sudden the weather improved. The mist receded, the sun shone bright and Scafell Pike had rarely looked more inviting. Jilly was clearing the breakfast dishes, assisted by Dawn, her devoted slave, who seemed reconciled to not being Mark's chosen one. Having mastered the basic essentials of bread, she was turning her talents to home-made pasta and Jilly, with infinite patience, was supervising. They made a great team.

"You really ought to have trained as a chef. You are wasted on selling insurance," Amanda told her.

"I am only basic and strictly self-taught. But I must say I do enjoy it," said Jilly. She seemed much happier, more at ease, now she was coming to terms with the truth. The might-have-beens had all gone; there could be no future.

It's a shame, thought Amanda. She would have made a great mother.

She was still holding her breath about Max. She had a dream that their paths might yet cross though Lucian had warned her such things could take time. There were certain procedures involved, he said, but eternity is for ever.

Richard and Mark seemed happy enough, playing an improvised version of squash and settling down every night with the cards to play poker.

"I wonder what happened to all that dosh." They could use it now, for the stakes were high.

It had not been mentioned at all in the news when the mountain rescue helicopter team had winched themselves down to inspect the wreckage and sift through the scattered debris. They were more than welcome to it, said Mark. The Reykjavik bank had not survived when the whole Icelandic economy had gone under.

"It's a funny old world," he said, quoting Margaret Thatcher.

He'd accepted his fate in an indolent way and now played the role of perpetual clown. To his relief, the liquor supplies continued to replenish themselves, as did the food which arrived after dark, still with no indication of where it came from. They didn't care, were content just to cook and not have to worry about supplies. Amanda had drawn up a strict kitchen rota to prevent all the chores being dumped on Jilly and Dawn.

"Fair's fair," she said and they all agreed. They were working now as a well-meshed team and it gave this new existence an odd kind of structure.

Angus had loosened up a lot now that he knew all there was to be known. At first he had fretted about the business and whether or not it was in safe hands, but was gradually coming to terms with the situation. The kids were now grown, with lives of their own, and

Molly had her charity work. She was still a fine-looking woman who might well remarry.

Dawn seemed surprisingly unaffected, had been slightly dazed ever since she saw the white light. Most of her aggression had gone; now she was gentler and sweeter. More like Jilly, with whom she'd become very close.

Lucian was around a lot more, part of the ménage though still detached. He spent many hours in the library alone, poring over his ancient tomes and disappearing for days on end without any explanation. But he also occasionally joined them around the fire and told a few stories.

"Tell us about yourself," Richard said, "and what to deduce from that stone on the crag. The inscription has practically worn away so we couldn't make out what it says."

"We thought," said Angus, "it might be a boundary stone."

Lucian's smile was inscrutable. "Something like that," was all he would say though Amanda guessed in a flash what it really was.

"Your grave," she said. "High on Scafell Pike. Keeping an eye over all of us and other poor souls who lose their way in the mist." She knew from the way he smiled she had scored a hit.

"You are," Lucian said, "a very perceptive woman."

Later that night the mist returned, blocking out their view of the stars. It was cold and blustery too. The wind rattled the shutters. Jilly and Dawn were baking a ham and the air was infused with its sweet spicy smell. Richard had banked up a blazing fire and Mark was doing his nightly thing with martinis. Amanda and Angus were deeply engrossed in their highly competitive regular chess game, which had had the effect of drawing them closer together. Lucian, wearing his smoking jacket, was in the corner, pouring himself a cognac.

Jilly, making Madeira sauce and tasting it for consistency, suddenly stiffened like a pointer dog at a distant sound that rang immediate bells. The drone of an engine, approaching fast. She glanced at the group who were still absorbed. It had been a while; it could be she was mistaken. None of the others had picked up the sound. But then it drew closer and she was right. The sound of voices and slamming doors; the chatter of children, the barking of a dog.

And then, more alarming, the sound of a key in the lock.

All of them, except Lucian, froze. For one fleeting second time seemed to stand still as they listened to the homecoming sounds from below. Then up the stairs they came, chattering and laughing, and the door to the living room was flung wide as in they all spilled, the family finally returned.

Sun-tanned parents, vibrant and young, he in shorts and a polo shirt, she in a simple linen dress that matched her espadrilles exactly. The children were straight from the photographs, angelic-looking but demon-eyed. Richard went white when he saw the dog at their heels. The father carried a couple of bags, the mother an armful of coats and things. The little girl whooped when she saw her squeaky clean rabbit.

"Something smells nice," said the mother without much surprise.

She seemed not to notice the rest of them there, six total strangers, agape with shock, assembled around her family dining table. She dumped her armful, glad to be home, gave a great sigh and kicked off her shoes.

"What I'd kill for now," she said, "is a cup of tea. I am simply gasping."

She looked around with appreciation. It was all just the same; it felt good to be back. It was true what the old song said: there is no place like home.

Lucian placidly nodded to them from the corner table where the drinks were kept.

"Welcome home," he said. "Did you have a good trip?"

Downstairs the grandfather clock began striking midnight.

Also available in ISIS Large Print:

Dead in the Family

Charlaine Harris

If you think your family relationships are complicated, think again: you haven't seen anything like the ones in Bon Temps, Louisiana. Sookie Stackhouse is dealing with a whole host of family problems, ranging from her own kin demanding a place in her life, to her lover Eric's vampire sire. And Sookie's tracking down a distant relation of her ailing neighbour (and ex), vampire Bill Compton.

In addition to the family issues complicating her life, the Shreveport werewolf pack has asked her for a special favour. But this favour for the wolves has dire results for Sookie, who is still recovering from the trauma of her abduction during the Fairy War.

ISBN 978-0-7531-8708-1 (hb)
ISBN 978-0-7531-8709-8 (pb)

Dead to the World

Charlaine Harris

Sookie Stackhouse is a cocktail waitress in Bon Temps, Louisiana. She has only a few close friends, because not everyone appreciates Sookie's gift: she can read minds. That's not exactly every man's idea of date bait — unless they're undead; vampires and the like can be tough to read. And that's just the kind of guy Sookie's been looking for. Maybe that's why, when she comes across a naked vampire, she doesn't just drive on by. He hasn't got a clue who he is, but Sookie has: Eric looks just as scary and sexy — and dead — as ever. But now he has amnesia, he's sweet, vulnerable, and in need of Sookie's help — because whoever took his memory now wants his life. But there could be even greater danger to Sookie's heart — because this kinder, gentler Eric is proving very hard to resist.

ISBN 978-0-7531-8706-7 (hb)
ISBN 978-0-7531-8707-4 (pb)